# MORE STRANGE THAN TRUE

THE COURSE OF TRUE LOVE NEVER DID RUN SMOOTH

*Dear Betty —*
*Thanks for the*
*support. Here's hoping*
*your wishes always*
*come true.*

# C.J. SPATARO

*CJ Spataro*

Sagging
Meniscus

Set in Sabon with LaTeX.

ISBN: 978-1-952386-95-4 (paperback)
ISBN: 978-1-952386-96-1 (ebook)
Library of Congress Control Number: 2024932658

Sagging Meniscus Press
Montclair, New Jersey
saggingmeniscus.com

*For Larry—who has inspired me every day with his passion for public service and his love of books*

More strange than true: I never may believe
These antique fables, nor these fairy toys.
Lovers and madmen have such seething brains,
Such shaping fantasies, that apprehend
More than cool reason ever comprehends.
The lunatic, the lover and the poet
Are of imagination all compact:
One sees more devils than vast hell can hold,
That is, the madman: the lover, all as frantic,
Sees Helen's beauty in a brow of Egypt:
The poet's eye, in fine frenzy rolling,
Doth glance from heaven to earth, from earth to heaven;
And as imagination bodies forth
The forms of things unknown, the poet's pen
Turns them to shapes and gives to airy nothing
A local habitation and a name.
Such tricks hath strong imagination,
That if it would but apprehend some joy,
It comprehends some bringer of that joy;
Or in the night, imagining some fear,
How easy is a bush supposed a bear!

—*William Shakespeare*, A Midsummer Night's Dream, V.*1*

*Though I am old with wandering*
*Through hollow lands and hilly lands,*
*I will find out where she has gone,*
*And kiss her lips and take her hands;*
*And walk among long dappled grass,*
*And pluck till time and times are done*
*The silver apples of the moon,*
*The golden apples of the sun.*

*—William Butler Yeats, "The Song of Wandering Aengus"*

# Contents

ONE · *1*

TWO · *12*

THREE · *26*

FOUR · *42*

FIVE · *65*

SIX · *86*

SEVEN · *102*

EIGHT · *132*

NINE · *174*

TEN · *198*

ELEVEN · *221*

TWELVE · *233*

THIRTEEN · *257*

# MORE STRANGE THAN TRUE

# ONE

EWELL BLINKED hard and the room came into focus. The soft lights, the plush leather upholstery, the voices of the other patrons talking over the background music. She looked up and there was Melody Ramirez, her best friend since childhood, and Melody's boyfriend, Bobby Fellowes, owner of the fine establishment in which they now found themselves. She tried to concentrate on the conversation. The two of them yammered away, obviously trying to distract her from her own thoughts, but they might as well have been speaking Chinese. Everything since the end of her father's memorial was blurry and soft around the edges.

"The service was beautiful," Melody said.

"Thanks." Jewell looked at her friend. How often, since her father's death late last spring, had Melody been there for her—ten, twenty, a hundred times? Gratitude was an inadequate word.

Bobby wrapped his arm around Melody's shoulder and smiled at Jewell. It was no wonder that Melody was crazy about this guy. All that South Philly charm. He could be a prankster and a bit of an ass, but when he looked you in the eye and smiled, something shifted. Whatever your burden, it just felt a little lighter somehow. Jewell couldn't explain it, but right now, she was grateful for whatever that was, too.

"It was great seeing all of Dad's old friends again," Jewell said.

"Especially hearing them play," Melody said. "Remember when your dad used to sneak us into the clubs when we were kids? I felt like such a grownup."

"If Mom had been around, he wouldn't have gotten away with that."

"No, I guess not," Melody said leaning into Bobby. They were so comfortable with each other. Jewell sighed a little.

"Those cats could play," Bobby said.

Jewell laughed. "Cats. I haven't heard anyone say that in a long time."

"It's so old school. I love it," Melody said.

Jewell propped her elbow on the table and rested her chin in her hand. "Dad loved playing at that church."

"I've never been there before," Bobby said. "It was incredible."

"Those stations of the cross make you feel pretty humble." Jewell let her gaze wander over Melody's shoulder and out the smoked glass picture window at the front of the restaurant.

Melody reached across the table and squeezed Jewell's hand. "You made your dad really happy today."

"I think it made his friends feel better to get together and remember him." She blinked hard again and did her best to muster up a smile. "And me too, of course."

"Hey," Bobby said. "How about I get us something to eat."

Jewell looked down at her watch. "I kind of thought Simon would be here by now."

"I was surprised he wasn't at the service." Melody cast her eyes sideways at Bobby but said nothing.

Jewell shrugged. "Said he had a client meeting." She leaned back in her seat. "I don't know. He doesn't really like jazz."

"That's hardly the point, right?" Bobby said.

"He came to Dad's funeral, and he'd never even met him."

"Well that was big of him," Bobby said. Melody shot him another look.

"Not today, okay?" Jewell said.

"Okay," Bobby said.

Melody's face was so full of sympathy Jewell wasn't sure she could take it. She focused on the scene outside the window. Busy Center City dwellers hustling home, heads down, determined to get to their destinations. Soon the restaurant would be full. Puck's Place was Bobby's most recent venture and as popular as all his other restaurants. He'd offered to host the memorial, to shut the restaurant down, but Jewell had told him no. The Church of the Advocate had been a special place for her father, and she couldn't imagine having the service anywhere else. Her parents had been married there. Her father had done outreach community music workshops there. As a professor of jazz studies at Temple University, he'd dragged his students along, too. He wanted them to understand the history of the church that stood just blocks from the university and its place in the civil rights movement. It would have been wrong to have his memorial anywhere else.

Her father had wanted his funeral to be simple and quiet, and then, a few months later, he told Jewell she could have a memorial service if she wanted to—and not because he felt like there was any great reason to eulogize him. He'd explained that he liked the idea of knowing his friends, bandmates, and students were getting together one final time to make music. When he'd spoken to her about it, he'd laughed. "You tell Charlie he better bring his flute, because I won't be there to play the solo on *Spain*." There was still some mischief in his eyes despite the chemo. "Tell him I'm going to write it into my will, and if he fucks it up, I'll haunt him forever." Jewell had followed his instructions without variation, and Charlie begrudgingly arrived at the service with both his sax and his flute. She'd done everything her father had wanted and now she sat here with Melody and Bobby in Bobby's shiny new restaurant waiting for her boyfriend Simon who said he couldn't be bothered to take a day off. She glanced at her watch again and then checked her phone.

"Maybe he's stuck in traffic?" Melody said.

"From 15<sup>th</sup> and Market?" Jewell's voice sounded harsher than she intended.

Bobby reached across the table and patted her arm. "You need a drink."

"No, really." Jewell shook her head. "I'm sorry. I don't know what's the matter with me."

"You just spent the afternoon memorializing your father. You don't have to apologize to us."

"Simon should be here," Melody said, her eyes narrow accusations.

"Mel, please," Jewell said.

"Okay, okay." She hooked her arm through Bobby's and pulled him close. "I just think you deserve someone who treats you like a queen."

"I don't want to be anyone's queen. Simon is probably just hung up at work." Jewell glanced at her phone, but there were no messages. He wasn't that late, was he? She sent him a text:

> Are you coming?

She set her phone on the table.

Bobby waved his hand and a waiter seemed to appear from nowhere. "We need a round of drinks," he said making a circular motion around the table. "You know what we like." Jewell started to protest, but he held his finger to his lips, silencing her. "The perks of owning your own place. All I have to do is snap my fingers."

And there was that grin again. Jewell felt the tension in her shoulders ease, and she settled back into her chair. The waiter arrived and set different drinks down in front of each of them. "A Paloma for you," she said. And of course, that was exactly what Jewell wanted but hadn't known. She started to ask Bobby what his secret was when her phone buzzed and skittered across the table. She blinked hard at the text:

> its not u its me, babe.

"Is it Simon?" Melody asked.
Jewell nodded. She typed back:

> What are you talking about? Where are you? We're waiting.

> 😳 cant do this in person dont wanna c u cry

> ?? Where r u?

> not coming – in AC 🎰 lol dont h8 me 2 much

> Hate you? What's going on?

"Is everything okay?" Melody said.
Jewell shook her head. "No. He said he's in Atlantic City. I think Simon is breaking up with me." She typed:

> Are you breaking up with me?

"What?" Melody said. "I thought you said he had clients."

"That's what he told me." Jewell gulped her cocktail as more text scrolled across her phone.

Simon:

> 2 much 🐾 so little time 🐱 ♂

Jewell's chest tightened. She typed:

> What??? ARE YOU SERIOUS!

"Oh my god," she said looking back and forth between Bobby and Melody. She leaned back over her phone and typed:

> Do you even know what day this is?

His response was swift:

> shit my bad memorial right? ima dick for sure but im honest

> I can't believe this - what is wrong with you?

> i appreciate u, but cant be with you. 🐱 😿

> 💀 🍓 🏺

> guess this means u dont wanna be friends?

> let me spell it out: HELL NO!!!

> ok - 😵 🫦

"You look like you want to kill someone," Melody said.

Jewell slammed her phone down and gave it the finger. She looked up and saw a woman at the next table over scowling at her. "What?" she said.

"Hey, Jewell, go easy," Bobby said. "These people pay my mortgage."

"Sorry," she mouthed. The woman turned back around.

"Are you okay?" Melody asked leaning across the table.

"Not really." She looked down at the phone. *ima dick* stared back at her outlined in a bright blue bubble. He was a dick. And lazy. But she'd thought he'd been her boyfriend, or if not her boyfriend then at least someone to whom she'd meant more than a text message where he couldn't even be bothered to, what, spell out all the words? He'd managed to spell out pussy, she thought with an audible grunt. Typical. Today of all days. What was wrong with him? "Simon just broke up with me."

"When?" Melody leaned forward like she was hard of hearing. She did this a lot. Sometimes it annoyed Jewell, but now it just seemed funny. Or maybe Jewell didn't know what else to do except laugh, or half laugh, or whatever it was that she was doing now.

"Just now. Via text. And I quote, 'too much pussy, so little time.' Although he used the taco emoji. I don't know if that makes it better or worse."

"Are you kidding? What an asshole!" Bobby said.

"I know. Right?" She took a long gulp of her drink. She wanted to slam the empty glass on the table, but somehow it

7

was still half full. "Honestly. Is it me? Is there something wrong with me?"

"No way," Bobby said. "J.J., you're the best. That guy is a turd with a capital T."

"You deserve better, Jewell," Melody said.

Jewell's eyes filled with tears. "I do deserve better. Seriously. What the hell." Her voice was a terse whisper. And the thing that made her the maddest: *this* is what had made her cry. She'd managed to keep it together all day long. Until now.

Melody shook her head.

"I mean, what did I do?" Jewell said. "I just saw him a couple of days ago. He seemed fine. Maybe a little preoccupied, but not too preoccupied to spend the night."

Melody muttered. "*Ese cabrón, hijo de puta.*"

"You got that right," Bobby said.

"What is my problem, Mel? Why do I keep attracting such douchebags?" She took another drink of her cocktail. "I'm a good person, right? I'm not a supermodel, but I'm okay. No one's ever complained about my skills in the sack." She took a deep breath. Suddenly all the luxuriousness surrounding her made her feel sad. Sadder even than she had felt before, if that was possible. "I must be doing something wrong," she said. "Putting out a douche-magnet vibe. Who breaks up with someone on the day of their father's memorial service?"

Melody shook her head. "It's not you, J. It's them. Men are dogs. All except for my Bobby, of course." She gave Bobby a little squeeze.

"Of course." She lifted her chin in Bobby's direction. "Bobby's the best. Who doesn't love Bobby?" Jewell rubbed her eyes.

"Wait!" Melody grabbed Jewell's hand, trying to stop her. "Too late." She dug in her purse and pulled out a wet nap. "Here," she said. "You look like a raccoon."

"Thanks," Jewell said. She dabbed the area around her eyes and looked up at Melody.

"You're good," Melody said inspecting her face with intensity.

"This is what I get. He was too damned good looking." She waved the mascara smeared wet nap for emphasis. "I should have known he'd be a hound."

"There's always Alan," Melody said almost under her breath.

"Who's Alan?" Bobby said.

"My previous ex." Jewell folded her arms. Why did Melody always have to bring him up?

"Didn't he call you the other day?"

"Yes. Because he'd seen the notice about the memorial in the *Inquirer*. It was nothing."

"I just don't see why you can't forgive him. He's trying so hard to be your friend."

"He only wants to be my friend because Cynthia dumped him." Jewell pressed her lips together. "Simon was right. At least he was honest."

Melody sighed, which she also did a lot, and this time it did annoy her.

"I'm sorry Mel, but I really do not want to talk about Simon or Alan. You're right. Men are dogs." She reached for her phone and threw it into her purse. "No. You know what? They're worse than dogs. My dog is totally loyal to me. He doesn't cheat, or send me shitty text messages, or try to pretend to be my friend when all he really wants is to not feel guilty about being an asshole." She pushed her chair back and stood to leave. "I need to go home."

Melody reached for her hand and got her to sit back down. "You're right. I shouldn't have brought up Alan. I don't know why I thought that might make you feel better. He's not a bad guy, just not the guy for you."

"You are correct, friend. He is not the guy for me. I'm going to go home, open a bottle of wine, and spend some time with the only male in my life who seems to actually give a shit about how I feel."

"Hey," Bobby said.

"Present company excluded, of course."

"Listen, I had planned a great meal for us. I wanted you to try one of my new dishes. *Linguine ai funghi incantati.* You like mushrooms, don't you?"

"Sure."

Bobby smiled and nodded waving his hands like an old Italian grandmother. "Good. I mean Craig LeBan of *The Philadelphia Inquirer* says my mushroom dishes are magical."

"Who am I to argue with Craig LeBan?"

"Good. So, you'll stay. Screw that Simon."

Jewell shook her head. "That's really nice, but Oberon's been cooped up in my apartment all day. Plus, I kind of think I'm done." She paused, trying to decide if she should say what she wanted to. "I just wanted this day to be about my dad and now . . ."

Melody looked at Bobby. It was one of those *do something* looks. "Well, the kitchen has already started working on dinner. Let me go wrap something up for you. Something delicious. With mushrooms. That way, at least you won't have to worry about cooking."

She stood to go. "It's okay, Bobby, really, I—"

Bobby pointed his finger at her and lowered his hand. "Stay put," he said. She sat back down. "I'm not letting you leave here without something to eat." He gestured to the table. "You've hardly touched your drink. Relax for a minute. I'll be right back." He didn't wait for her to answer but disappeared into the kitchen.

Jewell stared at the sweating cocktail glass, which was now somehow full of bitter grapefruit juice and tequila. She lifted the glass and held it out to Melody. "Here's to Dad," she said. Melody clinked her glass.

"Don't take this Simon business to heart, okay? You'll find the right guy."

# TWO

## I.

EWELL WALKED home from Puck's Place, which was on Chestnut Street just off Independence Mall. She walked west, toward her building at $24^{th}$ and Locust, carrying a full bag of takeout. On any other day, Jewell would have enjoyed taking the long walk home to her apartment. The afternoon was brisk. That's what her father would have termed it. Brisk. The midwinter sun hung low, setting the city blocks aglow with warm amber light, but the air was crisp with the promise of spring.

She was 33, too old to be dating men who acted like they were still in college. Most of her friends were married, had children, or were thinking about children. Melody had Bobby, who despite his penchant for practical jokes loved her desperately. Anyone who spent any time with them could see they were magic. And why not? Melody was brilliant—had a PhD in cellular biology—and she was beautiful and funny. But more than that she was probably the kindest person Jewell had ever known. It was this kindness that seemed to fuel Bobby's affection. Jewell was no shrink, but suspected Bobby had been hurt deeply. Maybe all his joking and charm was a cover, but whatever the reason their relationship was rock solid. They had each other. The thought almost made her cry.

What did she have? She had her job. She'd worked hard to become a respected member of her firm and enjoyed her work as an environmental engineer, but the invitation to be a partner or run her own office hadn't come. Numbers, formulas, science were where she shined, but she suspected that some of the men in her office would be more comfortable if she was the one getting the coffee, not supervising toxic cleanups. She made a comfortable living and enjoyed her work, but her job was a place to put her hard-earned skills to use, practice her patience, and collect a paycheck.

Since her father had died, one of the few things that had brought her happiness was her dog, Oberon. In the winter, the late afternoon sun filled her living room. She and Oberon often fell asleep on the couch, both basking in the slant of light as it streamed in through her apartment windows. She should probably feel embarrassed about that, but she didn't.

She needed to get her act together. Simon hadn't been her husband and she'd been dumped before. That wasn't it. She clenched her fists. Why couldn't Simon just let today be about her dad? "Asshole," she muttered.

If only she could be more like her father. He'd managed to pick up the pieces of his life after her mother died. He'd never married again but had still found a way to be happy. "Your mother would come back and wreck me," he'd said to her more than once. "We have to make this life count."

She looked down at her watch and picked up her pace. Oberon would be in desperate need of a walk by now. She'd bring him to the dog park, let him run around a little bit. That might make them both feel better.

A few minutes later Jewell was slipping her key in the lock. She could hear Oberon pacing on the other side of the door, his nails clicking on the hardwood floor. As she pushed open the door, she bent down to greet him, dropping her purse and the takeout bag on the floor. She grabbed him by the ears and let him lick her face furiously. "How's my buddy?" she said as if she were talking to a small child. "Did you miss me? Who's my stinky-winky?" She stood and gathered up the take-out. "Just let me put this away and we'll go to the you-know-where." Oberon wagged his tail so hard the whole back half of his body shook from side to side. Jewell stowed the food in the fridge and hooked the leash to Oberon's collar. "Come on buddy," she said. "Let's go for a walk!" Oberon let out a short bark that said, "Okay!"

## 2.

After their short walk to the dog park, Jewell guided Oberon through the gate and closed it behind her. As the sun set, the temperature dropped. Oberon didn't seem to care. He strained against the leash, itching to be let loose with the other dogs. Normally, she would have tugged the leash, made him heel, but not today. She laughed as she set him free and watched him chase after a bull terrier who raced around the benches and down to the other end of the dog run. Jewell wrapped the leash around her wrist and parked herself on the far bench away from the other dog owners. From her seat she could see the river. The sun's rays slanted over the top of 30$^{th}$ Street Station, and shafts of light hit the river in golden glimmering arcs. Around her, children squealed on the playground, young mothers pushed baby strollers, hardy cyclists were coming in from their evening rides. Maybe she should get a bike, join a group.

She pulled her wool coat in around her. She'd actually liked Simon—or maybe she was only telling herself that now to confirm what a lousy judge of character she was. She was always so easily swayed by good looks and the promise of good sex. A promise rarely fulfilled. Simon had been attractive, but he hadn't been much of a conversationalist. He didn't read. Well, that wasn't true. He read comics and Yahoo sports. Because he was such a comics fan, she'd convinced him to go to a special illustrators' exhibit at the art museum. That had been fun.

Melody always teased her about being a book nerd. She read everything from Shakespeare to N. K. Jemisin. She'd inherited her father's love of jazz and his extensive vinyl collection. One of these days she'd meet a guy who liked these things too and wasn't a dick. She bit her lip and blinked into the setting sun.

Her dad would have known exactly what to say to her. She thought about how, after her mother died, her dad would sneak her and Melody in the club with him. The two of them, friends since fourth grade, would sit in the back, drinking Shirley Temples and trying not to choke on cigarette smoke. They knew all the tunes, mouthing along to "God Bless the Child" and "A Foggy Day in London Town." She knew that nothing would have made her father happier than to see her follow in his footsteps, and she tried. She took piano lessons and learned to play the saxophone, but it had been her physics class that got her out of bed in the morning. Her proudest high school moment came when she clinched the district mathlete title for Central High School.

She sighed. This was some pity-party she was throwing herself. Steady girl. Simon was not worth going off the deep end.

"Mind if I sit here?"

She looked up. Why was it, with all the benches in the park, this guy just had to sit next to her? "Oh, sure. It's a public bench, right?"

The man nodded. "Hi. My name's Steve," he said and extended his hand. "Steve Munroe."

Jewell gave him a half smile and clasped his hand. "Jewell," she said. She did not see the need to tell him her last name.

"Come here often, Jewell?"

She lowered her chin and looked at him over her glasses. "Really?"

He laughed. "Wow. I was not thinking at all."

She shoved her hands deeper into her pockets and nodded toward the dogs with her chin. "Which one of these beasts is yours?"

Steve tucked his scarf into his jacket and sat down on the opposite end of the bench. "See that Pomeranian over there that has the husky mix backed into the corner?" He pointed to the two dogs at the far side of the run. Jewell nodded. "The husky is mine. His name is White Fang."

Jewell smiled even though she didn't want to. "Jack London."

"Yes!" He turned to look at her and then back to the dogs. "But I call him chicken shit."

"That's not fair," Jewell said with an exaggerated pout. "He's beautiful."

Steve smiled. "He is beautiful, but any little thing scares him. The wind blows the wrong way, and he hides under the bed. 'Fang,' I say to him. 'It's okay. It's just a vacuum.' "

Jewell looked at Steve: Mid to late thirties probably, handsome in that slightly older male underwear model kind of way. He still had all his hair, an athletic build. He was a dog person— always a plus. And at least he'd heard of Jack London, which made him a literary genius compared to Simon, who thought Ernest Hemingway was the guy from the Cuervo Tequila commercials telling everyone to, "stay thirsty, my friends." Simon had tolerated Oberon, but never really tried to bond with him. Oberon, who was normally a very friendly dog, never really bothered with Simon, either. That should have been her first clue. Always trust the dog. A labradoodle rushed past her, and she turned her attention back to the man at the end of the bench. "Poor baby. So, was he a rescue?"

"Kind of. I got him on Petfinder. They didn't tell me that he'd been mistreated, but you never know."

Jewell felt sad for this dog suddenly. "Maybe he just wants to be part of a pack. That Pomeranian should be with the small dogs, but she's such a bully they won't let her in."

Steve nodded. "So, which one belongs to you?" he asked.

"I've got the standard poodle, over there, sniffing the bichon's butt."

"Ah, the old butt sniff."

"I'm sure it tells them a lot."

"Can you imagine sniffing someone's butt instead of shaking their hand?" Jewell looked at Steve in the waning light. "Wow," he said. "That was also a weird thing to say."

Jewell shrugged. "Not that weird. If sniffing someone's butt told me I could trust that person, I'd probably have a go. Could have saved myself a lot of trouble."

"I see your point."

For a while, they sat together on the bench and watched the dogs run around. Eventually, Oberon made his way over to her and set his head in her lap. She rubbed his ears and kissed the top of his curly head. "Steve, meet Oberon."

Steve held out his hand, palm up and Oberon sniffed him skeptically, then nuzzled his palm. "Nice to meet you, Oberon.

I'd introduce you to Fang, but he'd have a heart attack." Steve patted Oberon, scratched behind his ear. The dog looked back at Jewell as if to ask, is it okay if I enjoy this? "He's friendly," Steve said. "That's nice. Fang's a good dog, but I wonder if living in the city is the problem. I bring him here to try to help him be more comfortable around other dogs and people. I make sure to get him plenty of exercise, but I'm not sure if I'm not making it worse."

Jewell shook her head. "I thought huskies were super adaptable, but just wanted to run all the time." She took a squishy ball from her pocket, showed it to Oberon and then threw it across the park. Oberon took off after the ball, loping easily. "Maybe Fang needs a doggie shrink."

"Do they have such things?"

"I know a guy who's a certified dog whisperer. He helped me train Oberon." Jewell dug around in her purse for a pen and a slip of paper. All she could find was a business card, and she wasn't ready to give her contact information to a guy she'd talked to for five minutes on a dog park bench. "Do you have a card or something?" she asked. "I can give you his email. The guy's a genius."

Steve reached into his jacket and pulled out his wallet. He handed Jewell two cards. "You can keep one," he said. She nodded and wrote the trainer's name and email on the back of the other card and handed it back to him. She slipped his card into her pocket without looking at it.

"Oberon. That's Shakespeare, right? A Midsummer Night's Dream?"

She nodded.

"What are the chances—two dogs with literary names?"

"Does seem like an unusual coincidence," she said.

"You're not a writer, are you?" He leaned forward, and Jewell couldn't tell what kind of answer he was hoping for. She shook her head. "Afraid not," she said. "Strictly a reader."

He exhaled audibly. "Me too. I dated a writer once," he paused. "I'll leave it at that."

She laughed. "So, what do you do besides terrify your dog with a vacuum?"

He had his hands deep in his pockets and his collar turned up. Jewell liked the cut of his jacket. "I'm an assistant curator at the Philadelphia Museum of Art."

"Really? You didn't have anything to do with the illustration exhibition, did you?"

He smiled and seemed to relax a little more. "Yes, actually. That was mine. Or at least partially mine."

"I saw that exhibit with a—" She paused. "With a friend of mine. I thought it was wonderful."

"Thanks," he said. "What about you? What do you do?"

"I'm an engineer. Work for a consulting firm. I specialize in wastewater treatment and groundwater contamination."

"Sounds very technical."

She turned to him smiling. "Is that code for boring?"

"Not at all." He raised his hands to his chest, in what seemed to Jewell a genuine gesture of sincerity. "More like code for way over my head."

"Sometimes it is boring," she said. "But mostly it is very technical." She looked down at her watch. "Wow. I did not realize how late it was."

"I hope it wasn't anything I said."

Jewell stood and gathered up Oberon's leash. "Actually, it's been very nice talking to you. It's just that today may have been the longest day of my life." She looked down at him with his close-cropped hair and his square chin, like some kind of hipster

Clark Kent. Looks were always so misleading. "If I knew you better, I'd bore you with the details."

"Fair enough," he said. He seemed to be sizing her up too, but Jewell was afraid that Simon had permanently broken her instincts.

"Oberon, come!" she called. The dog snatched up the ball and sprinted across the dog run, stopping and sitting immediately at her feet.

"Impressive," Steve said.

"I wish I could say it was my outstanding patience and skill, but poodles are very smart." She rubbed under the dog's chin and attached his leash. "Huskies are smart, too. You should call that guy. I'll bet that Fang was mistreated as a puppy and you'll just need to re-socialize him or something."

"It's nice that you've given Oberon his dignity. No goofy haircut."

Jewell laughed. "That fancy show cut actually serves a specific purpose. Most people don't know that poodles, especially the standard size, were bred as sport dogs. Breeders left those fluffy patches to protect their joints when the dogs were retrieving birds from cold water."

She could feel Steve's gaze appraise her before he spoke. "You seem to know a lot about dogs."

She shook her head. "Not really. I'm home alone a lot on Saturday nights watching Nat Geo Wild with you know who." She pointed to Oberon. "He thinks Dr. Pol is incredible!" She laughed at her own corny joke, too tired to be embarrassed.

"That surprises me." He stood up, took a step closer to her. She could feel Oberon tense next to her and then relax.

"What?"

"That you're home alone on a Saturday night."

Maybe it was the way she sensed that Oberon had accepted this seemingly kind stranger, but before she could really think better of it, she'd started blurting out an invitation for coffee.

"Oh, hey," Steve said taking a step back. "Wow, that did kind of sound like a come on." He shook his head. "I'm sorry. You seem super great. And your dog, he's the best. But—"

What had she been thinking?

Steve held out his hand, palm up, as if to explain. "God. I'm an ass. I'm seeing someone right now. And I kind of just don't want to be that guy. Although you make it tempting. Not that I—"

"Stop," Jewell said. "It's me. I seem to only date that guy." She held out her hand and Steve shook it. "It was nice talking to you Steve." She scratched Oberon's head. "Time to go."

"Listen I didn't mean to—"

"It's okay. We had this thing today for my dad, who died a few months ago, and then I got . . ." she started to tell him about Simon but changed her mind. "It's just been a super shitty day. It was nice talking to you, though, and I've got your card. I'm sure I'll see you and Fang around here again."

"I'm sorry about your dad," he said. "And I am going to call that guy."

"Well." She tapped her thigh and Oberon stood at her side. "Good luck."

"It was nice to meet you, Jewell," Steve said as she walked away.

She turned and looked over her shoulder. "You, too," she said.

# 3·

Once she and Oberon got back to her apartment, she kicked off her boots and tossed her coat over the back of the sofa. Oberon waited patiently for her to unhook the leash. Once he was free, he headed into the kitchen for a drink of water. Jewell followed him in, moving from cupboard to counter, opening a small can of wet food and filling his bowl with dry, then topping off his water. "Now for me," she said. "Thank you, Bobby." She pulled the boxed-up food from the fridge and reheated it in the microwave. The aromas of sharp cheese and earthy mushrooms filled the kitchen. She was hungry. Starving in fact. Bobby had clearly outdone himself and that was something, given his standing as a chef. Along with the pasta, he'd packed her some beautiful bruschetta, the tomatoes and basil glistened. He'd also included an arugula salad dressed with a peppery vinaigrette. She placed the food on a tray, along with a large glass of oaky cabernet, and carried it out to the living room where she allowed herself to sink into the couch.

Oberon climbed up next to her, sniffing her plate before settling on the cushions next to her. He looked up at her expectantly, the shallow rim of the whites of his eyes making his glance seem mournful. "This is mine, pal," she said. "You had your dinner." He licked his chops in return. "Okay," she said feeding him a cheesy mushroom. "This is no good," she said, "feeding you people food." She took a big twirl of the pasta and washed it down with an equally big gulp of wine. "Feeding myself this crazy fattening food." She laughed. "What the hell— who cares?" She raised her glass. "Here's to you, Dad!" Then she waved her glass toward Oberon. "And here's to you, Oberon. To fidelity." She set the glass down and picked up the remote, flicking through the channels before deciding on an episode of *The*

*Incredible Dr. Pol* that she'd already seen. Why make a liar out of herself? She let her hand rest in Oberon's soft curly-haired ears. The dog set his head on her thigh and let out a small sigh.

"We're quite an exciting pair, aren't we?"

He shifted his eyes up toward her face but didn't move his head from underneath the tender stroke of her fingers. "That guy Steve seemed nice, didn't he? So nice he didn't want to cheat on his girlfriend." Oberon moved his head closer to her lap, so that the top of his head was pressed against her ribs. "Think there might be another one of those out there for me? Probably not." Oberon puffed an exhale out through his nose as if he might be trying to disagree with her, but knew it was pointless. She bent over and kissed the top of his head, gave his ears an extra rub. "You, my buddy boy, you possess all the qualities of the perfect mate. If only I could find a man like you. What a match we'd be. We like to do the same things, like the same kinds of food. We already sleep in the same bed." As she stroked his fur, she could feel him relax against her completely. Would she ever feel such contentment? Probably not. She took another slug of wine. "Oh, to be fair Titania! I could be her! Without all the arguing and donkey-headed shenanigans, of course. No love-in-idleness necessary!" She leaned in close, grabbed Oberon by his jowls, lifted his head, and looked him in the eyes. "Shenanigans is a funny word, isn't it?" He seemed to blink at her, and she let his head drop back into her lap.

"What did Shakespeare say?" She paused, wanting to get it right. "Ay me! For aught that I could ever read, could ever hear by tale or history. The course of true love never did run smooth." She raised her glass again. "What fools these mortals be!" Then she took another twirl of pasta and followed it with a piece of that beautiful bruschetta. She sighed, savoring each magnificent bite. It was like she'd never tasted food before. She alternated

bites of pasta and salad and bruschetta until she was so full, she
thought she might cry from happiness. For once. She let her head
sink back against the couch. "Titania," she murmured. "Titania,
Titania . . ." Then, as if from very far away, Jewell thought she
heard the tinkling of tiny bells. She sat up and cocked her head,
frozen for a moment, listening, thinking perhaps it was the television. But no, Dr. Pol was shoulder deep inside a cow, like he
was on most episodes. Oberon sat up, too. All the way up, like
he'd also heard something. He barked, twice, at the bookcase
behind the sofa and wagged his tail. Jewell patted his head and
convinced him to lie back down.

She examined her apartment. There were stacks of books
on the table in the front bay window. Books that she'd read,
books that she'd meant to read, books that she meant to give
away. She stared up at the Wally Wood print hanging on her
wall. A gift from Simon. The only nice thing he'd ever given her,
in fact. A token from their trip to the illustrators' exhibit. It was
an expensive print of an old *Galaxy Magazine* cover from the
60s: a hunky spaceman and a bodacious space babe, of course.
She liked it, but now it would always remind her not just of
Simon, but also of this random guy Steve, who had curated the
exhibit. —*too much pussy, so little time.* Who says something
like that? Maybe he'd been drunk when he'd sent it. Maybe it'd
been a joke. What a shitty awful joke.

She shook her head and drank the rest of her wine. Her apartment was full of stuff. Stuff from Alan and Simon and finally
stuff from her father. The weight of it all pressed at her, but
she couldn't manage to bring herself to do anything about it.
She needed to hire a cleaning service. The place was cluttered
with more than just books. Knick-knacks, mementos, clothes,
papers, notebooks, shoes, dog toys, her father's vinyl collection.
She'd inherited all her father's things, most of which were in stor-

TWO

age or had been sold at an estate sale, but what she'd brought
back to her apartment she'd had a hard time finding a home
for. Each photo, record, and book had its own set of memories
attached. Sometimes she found comfort in these memories, and
other times, when she looked at it too long, it was as if someone
had sucked all the air out of the room.

She patted Oberon's belly, the quiet tinkling bells she thought
she'd heard forgotten. "You know, sometimes it's better to just
call it a day and go to bed. Come on pal, let's see what tomorrow
brings, okay?" She rose. Oberon followed her into the bedroom,
where he waited for her to change into her pajamas and slide into
bed before he hopped up next to her. Normally, he slept at the
foot of the bed, but for some reason, and Jewell didn't care, he
curled up next to her with his head on what used to be Simon's
pillow. She rolled onto her side, resting her wrist on the dog's
shoulder. "If only there was someone for me who loved me the
way you do," she whispered. "That's what I wish." She closed
her eyes and from somewhere inside an upswelling of emotion
almost overcame her. Words spilled out that she didn't realize
she knew. "O, how ripe in show / Thy lips, those kissing cherries,
tempting grow . . ." she murmured. "That pure congealèd white,
high Taurus' snow / Fanned with the eastern wind, turns to a
crow / When thou hold'st up thy hand. O, let me kiss / This
prince, this seal of bliss!" She hated herself for it, but she let
tears dribble down her face as she fell asleep. She was glad that
her father wasn't around to see her feeling so pathetic.

# THREE

INSIDE THE GREAT HALL of the royal palace, Titania rose from her golden throne and rushed to the window. She pushed back the heavy silken drapes and gazed over the gauzy horizon of the Realm searching for the source of the sound. But the urgent tinkling bells weren't coming from the dewy teal leaves that rustled in the enchanted glade, nor was it coming from the charmed brook that ran through the valley. No one in the Realm would ever ring a bell. Not for her. They knew better.

"What is it?" Ondine asked. "Oh!" she said.

"You hear it, too." Panic swelled in Titania's chest. She turned to face her sisters and the other faeries gathered in the great hall. "Summoning bells. Who would dare?"

"Yes," Iolanthe said. "Who indeed?"

"We all hear them," Ondine said. She put her hands to her ears. "They're ringing very loudly and they're ringing for you, Titania."

"Come," Titania said reaching out to Iolanthe and Ondine. The other faeries, who had gathered in the chamber, chattered and clutched each other as they backed away. No one liked to be summoned, but to summon the Queen—that would take some formidable magic—and no small amount of courage. "Please,

26

come with me," Titania said to her sisters. "There's strong intention behind this summoning—too much for me to resist." Ondine and Iolanthe held on to each other but did not step forward.

"What if we can't do what's requested?" Ondine said. "What
if we can't get back?"

"Please," Titania said. "You know I hate the human world,
but you two. Oh, how you love your humans!"

Iolanthe pulled Ondine toward their sister. "Now is not the
time to be afraid, sister. The three of us together can counter-act
any spell." Titania had started to shimmer against her will, her
body phasing in and out of the light, but she was still corporeal
enough for them to grasp on to. Titania fought the summons as
long as she could, but the call was too strong, sucking all three
of them through the thin membrane that separated the world of
faeries from the world of humans.

Shimmering through the veil felt as if their bodies were being pushed through a fine kaleidoscopic sieve, disassembled and
then reassembled not quite in an instant, but nearly so. Where
would they be reassembled? What was behind this desperate
summoning, and who had invoked Titania's name?

They faded into existence, stumbling and groping for balance, inside a human woman's dwelling, just behind her divan.
When they saw the canine, and heard him bark twice in greet-
ing, they knew he could see them. Reflexively each of them
pressed themselves against the bookcase. The beast looked harmless enough, friendly even, but with animals one never knew.

A woman sat with her back to them staring at a strange flat
box covered with moving pictures. "What kind of magic is that?"
Titania whispered to Iolanthe.

"I have no idea," Iolanthe said. She moved toward it, but
Titania held her back.

"Until we know why we've been summoned, it's best we stay concealed."

It was unclear to Titania and her sisters whether the woman could see them. Usually, faeries were invisible to humans, even humans who summoned them, but not always. They could make themselves be seen, if they chose, but it required some effort, and most chose not to expend the energy unless there was a compelling reason. Titania never failed to be irritated at how faeries were frequently depicted in both ancient tales and contemporary cartoons. Faeries were not tiny bug-like creatures with wings and magic wands. They were equal in size to humans and did not have wings. What did distinguish them was their pearlescent skin, which came in a variety of shades, like humans. Faeries also had delicately pointed ears, eyes that changed color with their mood, and their natural hair color corresponded to the base element of their power. Titania's base element was fire, but she could draw on all the elements, which was why she was queen. This also made her very powerful.

Titania took a step toward the dog and lowered her hand, commanding him to lie down, which he did. The woman sat on her couch, stroking the beast and staring at the magic box. Occasionally, she took a bite of food from a plate on the table next to her.

"It seems clear she does not have the sight," Iolanthe said. "The animal, however, is clever."

"Why has she summoned you, sister?" Ondine asked.

"Your suppose is as good as mine," Titania said. "So often it's the play, that awful, awful play. I cannot express my regret deeply enough at having revealed myself to that human William Shakespeare. And that Robin!" She clenched her fists at her side and a vermillion glow filled the room.

Ondine placed her hand on Titania's arm. "Go gentle, sister." Her touch sent a cooling shiver over Titania's skin.

Iolanthe cast a glance at her sister Ondine. "We know this is why the human world vexes you so—but usually there's no intention associated with the play, no wish strong enough to pull you through the veil. They are just actors saying lines. Master Shakespeare did not cast a spell over you."

Titania turned on her sister sharply. "No, but Robin did, and this feels like it has the power of a spell." She looked about the drab and colorless abode cluttered with books and trinkets and the platter of food the woman ate from. She was repulsed by the clutter, but whatever it was the woman was eating had filled the room with an intoxicating aroma. She stepped toward the plate of food and, out of view of anyone, plucked up one mushroom and then another and popped them into her mouth. The morsel exploded on her palate with such pleasurable force that she had to suppress a moan of delight. "Perhaps there is other magic at play," Titania said licking her lips.

"What do you mean?" Iolanthe said.

"The food," Titania said. "I believe it may have been enchanted."

"That's not possible. By whom?" Ondine said. "Aren't all the faeries in the Realm?"

Titania turned on her sisters. "How should I know where all the faeries are?"

"Sister," Iolanthe said. "What makes you think the food has been enchanted? You didn't eat any of it, did you?"

"Of course not," Titania said. "Do you think I'd be so stupid?"

"It does smell wonderful," Ondine said.

Iolanthe shook her head. "There is nothing magical here, save us. Only a sad woman and her dog."

"Whatever is going on, it was strong enough to pull all three of us through," Ondine said. "It's been a long time since I've felt desire that fervent." Her eyes misted over, and she blinked.

"Dear Ondine," Titania said. "Please do not think on Palemon. He didn't deserve you." She squeezed her hand.

"We can't all be strong like you, sister," Iolanthe said. "Although we were able to resist this woman's dinner."

"I told you, I did not eat any of it."

"Of course, my queen." Iolanthe curtsied.

"Sarcasm does not become you." Titania frowned. "If only you knew how much I envied you both. You've known the soaring joys and devastating sorrows of true passion, while I've never known true love. Only Master Shakespeare and that damned play." She gestured to the woman sitting on the couch in front of them. "Who is this woman? What does she want from me? Surely the dog did not summon me. He cannot call through the veil, nor cast a spell. He's incapable of desire that strong."

"Listen," Ondine said. "She speaks."

"You know, sometimes it's better to just call it a day and go to bed," the woman said to her dog. "Come on pal, let's see what tomorrow brings, okay?" She rose. The dog followed the woman into her bedroom, and the faerie sisters followed the dog.

"Look how attentive he is," Ondine said. "He's waiting for her to change into her night clothes."

"Her body isn't so bad for a woman," Iolanthe said. "She's no faerie, but her arms are slender, and her bosom is full and firm."

"What does that have to do with anything?"

"Probably nothing," Iolanthe said. "It's just human men care about these things. It's why they always want to be with us. Because we never grow old or lose our beauty."

"Until you give up everything for them," Ondine said. "And then they cast you aside because they can."

Iolanthe's eyes snapped up. "You took your revenge on Palemon, and yet you still pine for him. I will never understand you."

"Nor I you, sister."

"Enough!" Titania said. "Look, the dog comforts her. His devotion moves me." The dog had curled up next to the woman with his head on the adjacent pillow. This made the woman roll over onto her side. She rested her arm on the dog's shoulder, let her fingers tangle in his soft fur.

"If only there was someone for me who loved me the way you do," the woman murmured. "That's what I wish."

As the woman spoke, an invisible force pulled Titania to the foot of the bed. Her sisters grabbed her by the elbows and held her back so that she did not go flying on top of them. The dog lifted his head slightly as if to ask, what's the problem, faeries?

She pointed at the dog on the bed. "What is your name, beast?"

The dog did not answer but closed his eyes as the woman whispered in his ear. "O, how ripe in show / Thy lips, those kissing cherries, tempting grow / That pure congealèd white, high Taurus' snow / Fanned with the eastern wind, turns to a crow / When thou hold'st up thy hand. O, let me kiss / This *prince*, this seal of bliss!"

Titania clapped her hands together in anguish. "It *is* the play! It's always the damned play."

"But listen, sister, to her intention," Ondine said. "If only there was someone out there who loved me the way you do."

"O, let me kiss / This *prince*," Iolanthe said. "That's not the play—not exactly anyway."

"So now you have the play memorized?" Titania said.

"I have a good memory! Why must you be so disagreeable?"

"Me?"

"Sisters, please, can we not concentrate on the task at hand?" Ondine said.

"Yes, of course. It's a spell. She's cast a spell and doesn't know it." Titania retreated to the far corner of the woman's bedroom and crossed her arms. "What does she mean? She says these words to a dog! A beautiful clever creature, but a dog nonetheless."

"Look how she cradles the beast," Ondine said. "Such tender affection."

"The kind of affection that many feel for such animals, humans and faeries alike," Titania said. "But it means nothing!"

"Sister, did you not feel the weight of her loneliness? Her longing?" Iolanthe said. "Thy lips, those tempting cherries grow! You may think on Shakespeare with great dismay, but it was you who inspired him."

"Yes, yes! I will not speak about Master Shakespeare."

"Forget the play, sister," Iolanthe said. She touched Titania's arm, let it linger. She waved her other hand releasing a swirl of iridescent emerald faerie dust that spun up to the ceiling and then down, circling over the bed and settling on the dog as he slept. "See the woman. Feel her desire."

"You two can see it, but I cannot. Speak it plain to me. Does she seek love?"

"Yes!" Iolanthe said.

"And she wishes that her dog, this noble beast, to be a man."

"Maybe?" Ondine said.

Titania turned on her sister. "Maybe?"

"She clearly wishes to find a mate who loves her with the same devotion," Ondine said. "Have you ever felt such intensity of intention?"

Titania shook her head.

"And even for you, dear sister, it would be impossible to conjure a man out of thin air," Iolanthe said.

"So, we turn the dog into the man?"

"Yes. Once spoken the wish must be fulfilled. You know this better than any of us," Iolanthe said.

Titania took a deep breath. Such magic once performed could not be undone. "This could be more mischief than magic, sisters. I may not have the power to see it through."

"Do not doubt your power," Iolanthe said. "You've performed magic more complicated than this."

"You returned me to the Realm," Ondine said. "You restored me, made me whole. I was supposed to die an old woman, abandoned by my human husband, but here I stand." Ondine brushed back another tear. "You are our queen for a reason, Titania. You have the power of all the elements, and we are here to help you. This woman's desire is so strong, it called the Faerie Queen through the veil."

"Look upon the beast. Perhaps he does not want to be a man." Titania looked at the sleeping woman and her dog. It was a tranquil scene. Perhaps this was comfort enough. "This woman does not know what she asks."

"Sister, don't let your own lack of love's joy prevent you from helping another find it," Ondine said. "What happens after is up to her and the man."

Titania stepped to the end of the bed. "He won't make much of a mate. He is without testicles."

"Oh, dear," Iolanthe said. "They are important."

"Unequivocally," Ondine said. "Can you restore him? You restored me."

Titania turned to her sister. "You were not missing anything so vital. Still." She turned away and paced the length of the bedroom, lost in thought.

"Why would he be missing his testicles?" Ondine asked.

"It must have been some kind of horrendous accident," Iolanthe said with a shudder. "How tragic." The sisters fell silent, each contemplating the magic required to restore testicles. This would be a problematic series of spells and it would require all three of them.

Titania paused and looked first at Ondine and then at Iolanthe. "Clearly, we need to restore the dog," Titania said. "To do that we'll need Hessonite Garnet, Tiffany Stone, and Tangerine Aura."

"So much?" Iolanthe asked. "Seems excessive."

"Perhaps," Titania said. "But it can't hurt."

Iolanthe laughed, and sparkling bubbles floated from her mouth.

"What?" Titania asked.

"What if we restore his testicles and because we used so many stones, they reappear the size of juju melons?"

"Oh," Titania said. "That would not be good." She smiled for the first time since she'd heard the summoning bells. "Let's start with the Tangerine Aura and see how it goes." She rested her hand on Ondine's shoulder. "Did you bring the stones with you?"

"They are always with me, sister, you know that." Ondine stepped away and unslung her travel pouch from her shoulder. She sat down on the floor near the foot of the bed. There she removed a series of small suede bags and a pair of delicate leather gloves. "I wish Peaseblossom were here," she said.

"Now is not the time to think on faeries long gone," Titania said.

"Yes, of course." She pointed to a small black bag. "This is what we need. Shall I place it on the dog, or do we need to hold the stones?"

Titania closed her eyes and pressed her palms together. After a moment her eyes sprang open. "I'll cast a sleeping spell on them both. Then, Ondine, you'll need to place the crystal between the dog's legs."

Titania moved to the foot of the bed and took a deep breath. She'd been casting sleeping spells since she'd appeared in the world, but tonight, this whole summoning and call had made her uneasy. She could feel the portent of unintended consequences, as if there had to be other magic at play. The woman had called her name and spoken the key lines from the play. And she'd spoken them with intention, which is exactly what Shakespeare and that scoundrel Robin Goodfellow had thought would be so hilarious all those years ago. And yet, over time, the spell had seemed to weaken, as they do. She hadn't been pulled through the veil like this in a very long time. No matter. They were here, and they would not be able to leave until the summoning's desire was fulfilled. She held her hands out, wrists bent, palms up. A humming light appeared, oscillating through the red-violet spectrum. Titania shaped it into a single orb and pushed it gently toward the sleeping woman and her dog until it hovered over them.

"Restful spirits of earth and air, grant these two creatures, your humble servants, succumb to sleep's sweet succor and wake not until morning's light." Titania flicked her fingers outward and the light dissolved, falling softly over them covering them with lavender dew.

"That should do the trick. Ondine, the crystal." Titania took a deep breath. This spell might require a different approach and she would need Iolanthe's strength and restraint. Ondine slipped on the leather gloves and removed the stone, which was about the size of a large peach pit, from the pouch. She approached the sleeping dog. She had to lean over the woman to reach him, but they all knew that Titania's sleeping spell would hold them. After placing the stone between the dog's legs, she looked up at Titania. "Remember sister, this stone has elements of iron. Not so much as to cause you serious harm, but the sensation will be very unpleasant."

Titania nodded. This is why she'd chosen the Tangerine over the Tiger Iron, which probably would have worked better—but she would need all her strength to complete the final transformation and the Tiger Iron would make her ill. All faeries were allergic to iron. "Iolanthe hold my hand. Give me your strength." Iolanthe reached out and took her sister's hand. Titania slid her fingers between the dog's legs until her fingertips touched the edge of the stone. She squeezed Iolanthe's hand and Iolanthe turned her free hand palm up. In it a sparkling orb of chartreuse energy pulsed and sizzled. Titania's fingertips burned but she concentrated on the stone and the dog.

"Elements of earth and fire, metal, air, and water, heed my command. Restore this gentle creature to his rightful state of being." She inhaled sharply as the pulsing orb passed through Iolanthe and then to her and out through her fingertips.

Together they chanted: "Earth and fire blend your might, put this creature back to right. Air and earth, fire prevail, our command it shall not fail." For a moment the dog whimpered in his sleep, and Titania was afraid that they'd hurt him, but he remained asleep. Something warm and fuzzy pushed down against her fingers. The sensation didn't last long, but they could all see that the spell had been successful. She released Iolanthe's hand and nodded to Ondine. "You can remove the crystal now, sister." She smiled at them. "You were right, as usual, Iolanthe. One crystal was enough."

"Do you think we've made him happy?" Ondine said as she slipped the crystal back into its pouch.

Iolanthe laughed. "As a dog, he likely wouldn't care much one way or the other. But as a man, I'm sure he would prefer to not be a eunuch."

"And the woman," Titania said. "It is her wish after all."

"It is her wish," Iolanthe said. "But somehow, I feel as if something else is going on, too."

Ondine grasped Iolanthe's hand. "Yes, I feel it too. Something ancient and shadowy." She swallowed. "Something elvish."

Titania looked askance at her sisters. "Elvish? Don't be ridiculous."

A white cloud of mist started to gather around Ondine's head. "Don't discount me, sister. You know I carry trace elements of metal with me that allow me to see and feel things others do not."

Titania folded her arms and stared hard at her sister. "If only you could see things with a little more detail, they might actually be of some use to us." She waved her hand near her sister's head, dispersing the mist. "You are too dramatic, sister."

Ondine frowned. "And you are too skeptical."

Titania drew herself up. "Skepticism is a good quality in a ruler. Let's proceed so we can return to the Realm. The clutter of this abode depresses me."

"I think this animal will make a handsome man. I hope the woman is pleased," Iolanthe said.

"He already loves her. Even in their slumber anyone can see it," Ondine said.

"Perhaps," Titania said. "But what kind of love? Devotion, surely. But animals love their masters like children."

"What will happen when he becomes a man? Will his devotion be that of a child?" Ondine asked.

Titania waved her hands dismissively. "This is not our concern. I'm responsible for fulfilling the wish only. The consequences are their concern." Titania looked at her sisters. "I think we will need some water for this next spell. And I will need you both, all your strength and probably more. I don't believe the veil will open for us until we complete this task." She straightened her shoulders. "I for one have already spent more time here than I would like."

"Do you want the charoite or the malachite?" Ondine asked.

Titania closed her eyes and breathed deeply. "Charoite and amethyst." Ondine produced the stones as Iolanthe returned from the other room with a lavender glass bowl full of cold water. She set the bowl down on the floor. Ondine handed her the charoite and kept the amethyst. They each stood on one side of the bowl and leaned in over the water so that their heads touched. They grasped each other by the waist, forming a tight cone. The three sisters began by humming a choppy rhythmic tune. Discordantly at first, then coming into harmony. A swirling band of vermillion energy formed around them and from the center of the bowl of water a single strand of black energy rose up and through their heads. The vermillion ascended to combine with the black and when the two energies merged, it cycled through all the base elemental colors: green, red, white, blue, and yellow, and then transformed into a sparkling metallic gold so brilliant all three sisters had to close their eyes. Titania could feel its power as it filled the room. The choppy hum became a chant, and accompanied by her sisters, Titania spoke the transformative spell:

> *Now the happy dog must know,*
> *And a woman's gladness show.*
> *For her wishes to come true,*
> *We must turn this gold to blue.*

The metallic gold light flashed to a glittery midnight blue, shining as if it were made of crushed sapphires.

*Ancient power we command,*
*You to do as we demand.*
*Take this noble hound apart,*
*Bless him with a human heart.*
*Make his countenance as fine.*
*To the woman be sublime.*
*Ask us not the reason why,*
*Make it so or let us die.*

Titania felt her sisters' grip tighten. Likely they were not so happy about the last couplet. Neither was she, but these spells came to her from another place; she had no control over the wording. Together they repeated:

*For her wishes to come true,*
*We must turn this gold to blue.*
*Ask us not the reason why,*
*Make it so or let us die.*

The room filled with pulsing hues of gold and midnight and every shade in between. The light swirled and twisted, finally funneling, a gyrating vortex over the bed, swallowing the dog, engulfing him in a vermillion tornado of light and energy, shot through with electric strands of bronze and gold. In her sleep, the woman rolled over and away from the animal, her back now to the transformation occurring beside her. The room hummed and buzzed, vibrated and shook, and eventually the light faded, and the column of energy slid back into the bowl of water and away from the sisters, who collapsed into each other's arms panting and covered with a fine film of dewy midnight sweat.

Titania regained herself first and turned back to the bed. There she found the most beautiful man she'd ever seen, sitting up, staring back at her. His skin was smooth, his limbs long and muscled, his torso lean. The hair on his head was thick and his eyes were a soft brown, the color of fall leaves in the rain. Titania moved to him and cupped his chin in her damp palm.

"Tell me your name, sweet creature."

The man blinked, moved his lips as if he were not sure if he could speak.

"Take your time." She smiled at him and felt her own countenance soften. She'd seen many beautiful creatures in her life, many beautiful men: faerie, elfin, and human—but this man— there was something both beautiful and somehow familiar. He tried to speak again, and Titania nodded in encouragement.

"Oberon," he said at last. He seemed surprised by the sound of his own voice, which was silky and low, but also breathy from lack of practice. Titania blinked when she heard the name from the play. A name she'd never heard spoken anywhere else. The man smiled, revealing straight white teeth. He looked down at his body, rubbed his hands over his arms, his chest. "I?" He looked at Titania. "Did I speak wrong?"

Titania stroked his cheek. "It was the woman's wish."

"Jewell." He looked at the woman sleeping beside him. "My human."

"Sister," Iolanthe placed her hand on Titania's shoulder. "See how the veil thins. We need to go now. He is not for you."

Titania turned and faced her sisters, who stood behind her, also gazing at the man in wonderment. Her chest felt tight, as if her heart might escape her ribs and burst through her own skin. "He said his name was Oberon." Her voice trembled, and she reached out for Ondine to steady herself.

"What?" Ondine asked.

"He said his name was Oberon."

Iolanthe took Titania's hand. "It's the play. You know that. It doesn't mean anything. The woman invoked the play—that's what brought us here."

"Who?" Oberon asked.

Titania turned back to him. "I'm Titania," she said. She could see that her name meant nothing to him, but his face. His face said everything he did not know how to speak.

Iolanthe grasped Titania's arm and she turned at the force of it. "Sister. He is not for you," Iolanthe said.

"Who are you to tell me who or what is for me?" Titania wrenched her arm away and moved back toward the smiling Oberon. "What if he is for me?" She turned and looked at her sisters. "What if that's why we're here?"

"But that's not why we're here," Ondine said. She looked at Iolanthe with some urgency. "Sisters, our spell is cast. We must go."

Iolanthe reached into her pouch and blew a sparkle of chartreuse faerie dust into Oberon's face. "Forget," she said. "Sleep."

Oberon rubbed his eyes and fell back into the bed, his head landing softly next to Jewell's as Titania and her sisters shimmered back to the Realm.

# FOUR

HE SUN STREAMED in high through Jewell's bedroom window. She rolled over toward the light and sat up, then threw her legs over the side of the bed. Her mouth felt pasty and dry like she'd had too much to drink, but that's not what she'd remembered from the night before. What she remembered was a crazy dream. The details were as foggy as her head, but she felt sure they would come with some coffee and maybe some scrambled eggs. Oberon would need to go for a walk, but she needed some coffee first. She rubbed her palms over her eyes and stood up. "Come on, boy," she called. Normally, Oberon would be up, nudging her arm, running back and forth between the bedroom and the backdoor, but this morning, there was nothing. "Oberon? Buddy? Where are you?" Then she turned and saw him: tall, lean, and naked, and he was lying in her bed. She jumped backward, like a frightened cat, and crashed into the window blinds. The man finally stirred and rolled over toward her; the blankets tangled around his legs. He opened his eyes and smiled. "Jewell," he said. "My human."

"What the fuck? Who are you and how did you get in my bed?" Jewell said, backing around the edge of the footboard toward the bedroom door.

The man sat up and looked sad. "You know me. I'm Oberon."

Jewell reached behind her for the handle and opened the door. "Oberon is my dog. You are not Oberon."

He leaned forward, smiling again. He grabbed the footboard with both hands and rested his chin in between. He tilted his head slightly and looked at her with pouty eyes. This gesture so reminded Jewell of Oberon that she gasped out loud.

"Don't come near me. I'm calling the police." She looked around her room for a weapon and snatched her sixth-grade science fair trophy from her bookcase. She brandished it at the man in her bed. Instead of laughing at her, like she expected him to, he cowered at the head of the bed, curling into himself.

"Please don't hurt me," he said covering his head with his arms.

"Just stay where you are." He nodded. Jewell took a step toward the bed and set down the trophy. "I won't hurt you," she said. "I just want to know what you're doing here. Who are you?"

The man lowered his hands and looked at Jewell. Tears welled in his eyes. "I'm Oberon. Don't you remember? You wished for a man to love you, so here I am." He rubbed his eyes with the heels of his hands and then looked at them, confused. "What's happening?"

Jewell grumbled, "Good question." As she stared at him the fog lifted. Images flashed through her mind. What had Bobby put in that food? She'd had a pretty crazy dream. Swirling light the color of sapphires—so much light—then nothingness. She looked at the bed, at the man curled at the headboard, crouched atop her pillows. She must be losing her mind. "Stay right there," she said holding out her arm like she would when she told Oberon to stay. "I'll be right back." Then she turned and ran down the hall toward the living room looking everywhere for her dog. Where was he? That man in her bed could not be Oberon. This had to be a joke. She headed into the kitchen. Oberon's food dish and water bowl sat on the floor as usual. His leash hung on the doorknob. "Where is he?" She grabbed her hair in fistfuls, like it might help her think more clearly. "Here boy," she half whispered, half shouted. "Come to Mama. Come on boy. Let's go for a walk."

Nothing. The dog was gone. Jewell walked down the hallway back to her bedroom. The man sat in the middle of the bed, his legs crossed, the comforter pulled up over his lap. "I was cold," he said.

"I'll bet," Jewell replied. She swallowed and stepped further into the room. "Where did you come from?"

"First, I lived with a very nice family, but they moved away and left me at the shelter. Then you came and saved me. The other family called me Pumpkin, but you said that I deserved a more dignified name and called me Oberon." He leaned forward on his hands and knees. "I love you, Jewell. You are my human."

Jewell's knees buckled beneath her, and she reached for the footboard to steady herself. What was happening? This man thought he was her dog. She swallowed hard. Was he her dog? Why was she so ready to believe this?

"Are you okay, Jewell?"

She looked up and the man's face was inches from her. "I'm fine," she said.

He smiled and licked her cheek. Then he sat back on the bed, frowning. "That seems like a strange thing to do now," he said. "Why does that seem strange?"

Jewell stared at him. "People don't lick each other," she said. "At least not in this kind of situation."

"I'm not able to lick myself where I want to anymore either," the man said.

"No, of course not," she said. "Oh my god, what am I saying?" She backed away shaking her head. "Who put you up to this? Where is Oberon?" She picked up the trophy. "If you did anything to him."

"Jewell, I don't know why you don't believe me. You know in your heart it's true. Just last night, before you made your wish, we met a very nice man named Steve at the dog park. He smelled good. Not like that other one, Simon. He was all wrong. He always smelled like other women. Lots of other women."

"Who told you that?"

"No one. You. I was there."

"No. Oberon was there. Oberon is my dog. You are not a dog."

"Not anymore." He shifted toward her, gazed at her with pleading eyes. "Please believe me."

Jewell sighed.

"Jewell?"

"Yes?"

"I need to go out."

"Right, sure. Let me—crap." She stood up, smoothed down her top and went to her closet, suddenly self-conscious. She pulled on an old Penn sweatshirt and some leggings, then found a robe and handed it to the man—Oberon. The robe was big and fluffy and pink. He would look ridiculous, but it was better than having him sit there naked. She must be losing her mind. If this was a prank, it was epic. "You can put that on, so you won't be cold. Humans wear clothes." She gestured to her own. "Because we don't have fur, and because we're very uptight about our bodies." Oberon struggled to get the robe on. It was big on Jewell but was tight across Oberon's shoulders. She tried not to gawk at him as he raised up on his knees, the robe hanging open at his sides. Well, she thought, Oberon had been a beautiful dog and now he was a beautiful man. "Pull it around yourself." She mimed the action and Oberon did his best to imitate her. "Come here," she said. He scooted over to her at the side of the bed, and she tied the belt for him. "I'll get you some clothes later." She helped him off the bed. "One of the other things humans don't do is pee outside, unless it's an emergency. You've seen me go to the bathroom before. Come on."

She took him by the hand and led him to the bathroom. "Do you just have to pee?" He nodded. "I can't believe I'm potty-training a full-grown man," she said. "When you need to go come in here. This is a toilet." She pointed at the commode. "When men need to pee, they lift the lid and the seat." She nudged him a little closer so that he was standing directly in front of the bowl. "Then they, I think, I've never actually watched anyone do this, hold their penis and pee into the toilet." She looked at him expectantly, but he just stood there. "Go on." She untied the robe for him.

He looked over his shoulder at her. "What's my penis?"

She exhaled slowly. This is what she wished for? A man-sized toddler. "It's that thing that you wanted to lick but couldn't reach with your tongue."

He smiled. "Now I know what to do." And he did it.

Jewell turned away. When he was finished, she showed him how to flush and wash his hands. "This is what we do instead of licking ourselves," she said pumping soap onto her palms. "A person's immune system is different than a dog's. I don't want you to get sick."

She led him into the dining area and then went to use the bathroom herself. When she returned, she found him on the floor drinking water from his bowl, kibble scattered across the tile and stuck to his cheeks.

"It doesn't taste as good as I remember," he said.

"No, I suppose not," she said as she helped him up. "I'll make us some breakfast, then I'm going to have to go out and get you some clothes."

"I don't know that I like these clothes very much, Jewell." He waved his arms up and down, inadvertently exposing himself. Jewell turned her head.

"Well, if you ever want to leave this apartment, you'll have to wear some."

"I would very much like to go to the dog park. Can we go to the dog park, Jewell?"

"It might be kind of weird to show up there without a dog, but we can walk by there this afternoon."

After breakfast, she took a quick shower and threw on some yoga pants and a turtleneck. Then she dug in the back of her closet in desperate hopes of finding her old sewing kit. She was in luck. Inside she found loose buttons, spools of thread, a seam ripper, and her tape measure. She emerged from the closet to find Oberon asleep on her bed, lying across the bottom of it, like he would on any other normal Sunday afternoon.

She touched his shoulder. "Oberon . . .." She shook him again and he stirred. "Oberon, I need you to get up." He nodded and rose from the bed. She measured his inseam (strategically), arm length, neck, waist, and chest and wrote them all down on a sheet of paper. Then she looked at his feet. How was she ever going to get him to wear shoes? She kneeled and measured the length of his foot. Eleven inches. Now to figure out how that converted to an actual shoe size.

It occurred to her, as she took the measurements into the kitchen that she was about to go out and buy clothes for a man that was pretending that he used to be her dog. Not even Bobby could pull off a prank this epic, could he? Was she so far gone that she was ready to believe his insane story?

A few quick Google searches and she had all the information she needed. She was about to go back to the bedroom to tell Oberon she was leaving for a while when he appeared in the kitchen. "I'm not sure what to do," he said. "I thought I wanted to sleep, but I can't. I don't understand."

"Why don't you watch some TV?" Jewell said. "I have to go buy you some clothes and I don't want you to get bored or worried while I'm gone." She walked into the living room and turned on the TV. Oberon followed her. "You used to sit and watch TV with me all the time."

"I used to sit with you, Jewell. The world looks so strange to me now. There are all these colors I've never seen before. It's making my head hurt. And my nose is not working at all." He buried his face in her hair and inhaled, then stepped back, obviously disappointed. "The TV was just noise and blur."

Jewell frowned. "Let's take things slowly, okay? As a dog, you could only see blue and yellow, but as a person you can also see red and all the colors it makes combined with blue and yellow." She shook her head. "It must be overwhelming. No wonder your head hurts. Stay here, okay. I'll be right back."

She returned a moment later with two Advil and a glass of water. "Here, take these. They'll make your head feel better." She handed him the pills and the water. "Dogs can smell really well, but people not so much. I think this will take some getting used to, but you might actually like television, now that you can understand what's going on." She sat on the couch and patted the seat beside her without thinking, and Oberon sat down so close to her he was practically in her lap. "This is the remote," she said. "Push this button to turn it off and on, and this button to change the channels." She did it a few times to show him how and then watched him do it. "Think you'll be okay?"

He nodded. "I want to come with you."

"I wish you could, but you can't go outside dressed like that." She tuned the TV to Animal Planet. "Here, I think you'll like this channel," she said. "I won't be gone long. If you get hungry there is food in the refrigerator. Don't eat out of your old bowl, okay?"

He nodded and lay down on his side with the remote tucked between his hands and his knees tucked up under the robe. Jewell ran her hand through his hair, then bent down and kissed his forehead. She didn't know what else to do. Then she left.

## 2.

"Sister!" Iolanthe pulled on Titania's arm to keep her from rushing back through the closing seam of the veil. "He is not for you! You are bewitched." The three sisters had returned to the Realm and landed in Titania's royal bed chamber.

Titania turned on Iolanthe with force. "Nor is he for that— human! Surely you could see that. I could see in his eyes that he recognized me. Such eyes!" Titania marched across the room to the window hung with heavy brocade draperies. She stood for a moment and gazed over the vast meadow below filled with heather and lilac and lilies of the valley. "Look, Iolanthe. See all the flowers in the field have turned gold. What does this mean?"

Ondine stood behind Titania and rested her head on her sister's shoulder. "Who knows, dear sister? Perhaps the flowers changed color to welcome you back to the Realm. Such things have happened before."

Titania turned to her sister and embraced her. She reached for Iolanthe. "Now I know," she sighed, "the torment of human love. I feel quite unlike myself." Her eyes were wet with unshed tears. "How cruel I was to you both. I am filled with regret."

Iolanthe laughed. "You were never cruel to us. You accepted us home. You made us whole." She stroked her sister's cheek. "And we love you for it."

"Human love is what's cruel," Ondine said. "But Oberon is not truly human, is he? I mean, we made him physically human, but the rest seems up to her."

Titania broke free of her sisters' embrace and flung herself upon her bed. "I can see that woman is not up to the task."

"Perhaps not," Iolanthe said. "But that's not our concern, is it?"

"Since when do we care what humans want? It's been some time since I caused mischief in the human world. Perhaps it's time to get my hands dirty again," Titania said.

Iolanthe sat on the bed and stroked Titania's hair. "Weren't you just saying how much you regretted revealing yourself to Master Shakespeare? Now what do you want to do? Go back to that awful city where you'll be exposed to iron at every turn?"

"Robin has found a way to manage all these years."

"Maybe. We don't know for certain that Robin still exists." Ondine sat on the other side of the bed and pulled her knees into her chest. "Besides, you hate humans, Titania. Why would you torture yourself this way for a man, of all things, who used to be a dog?"

Titania rolled over and sat up facing her two sisters. "What you say is not wrong. I do hate Shakespeare and that damned play, but perhaps it was my fortune being told. Perhaps this is Hecate's way of showing me that my distaste for humans is wrong?" She buried her head in her hands. "I cannot forget his sweet face. It is too much for me to bear."

"Should we give you a forgetting draught?" Ondine said.

Titania looked up, wide-eyed. "No. Never! Please, swear to me you will not do that."

Iolanthe and Ondine looked at each other and then at Titania. "We promise," they said in unison.

"But only," Iolanthe added quickly, "if you promise to stay here in the Realm and not interfere."

"I don't know if I can promise that."

Iolanthe frowned. "Then I'm not sure I can promise to keep a forgetting potion out of your drink." She took Titania's hand in both of hers. "Please, sweet sister, give this woman Jewell a chance. She may decide on her own that he is not what she wants and then you can do as you wish."

"This is right thinking," Ondine said shaking her finger in agreement.

Titania gave them both a disgusted look and pulled her hand away. "May I observe their progress without fear of you poisoning me? Will you grant your queen this one small wish?"

"You are the most dramatic of all faeries," Ondine said. She rose from the bed and smoothed her pale-yellow skirts. "This must be what attracted you so to Master Shakespeare."

Titania dissolved from her bed and reappeared sitting on her private throne chair at the far end of the room. She reached out and ran her fingers over the silken baldacchino. "I've inspired more than the likes of Shakespeare, as you well know. And I am still your queen. Even though you are my sisters, you are bound by my command."

"Yes, Titania," Iolanthe said. She curtseyed deeply with her head bowed. "You are our queen, and I am bound by your command."

"Sister, please," Ondine said appearing on her knees next to the throne. "We will not give you a forgetting draught."

"I know you would not break a promise, Ondine," Titania said cupping her sister's chin. "It is our sister Iolanthe I do not entirely trust."

"I have pledged my fealty. Give me a command if you do not trust me," Iolanthe said.

"Let's observe for now, as you suggest. But, if things start to go awry, I reserve the right to intervene." She folded her hands in her lap as she always did when making a final decision. "If you make me forget and something goes wrong, I'll be of no help. We've never performed this kind of magic. Anything could happen."

"As always, you are wise, sister," Iolanthe said. "You are right. This magic could pose some challenges for us all."

Titania took in her royal bed chamber with its heavy draperies and ornate fixtures. Time passed so slowly in the Realm; it was as if it didn't pass at all. But time did pass. Things did change. Perhaps the time had arrived for her to change, too. This room was so vast compared to the woman's squalid living space. How could a creature like Oberon breathe in such a place? How fine would he look reclined against her damask pillows or seated in a throne chair of his own by her side.

# 3.

Jewell struggled with her packages and the key, and when she finally pushed open the door, Oberon fell upon her, nearly knocking her off her feet. "My god," she said. "Are you all right?"

"I was afraid you'd never return. I always feel that way when you leave. I don't know why. You always come back. But I forget." He helped her right herself. "Television doesn't make sense."

Jewell sighed. "You've got that right." She scooped up the packages and took them into the bedroom. Oberon followed behind her. He leaned in and inhaled deeply, pressing himself against her. She turned toward him and took a step back. He stepped in closer, her ratty pink bathrobe stretched tight across his chest, his face buried in her hair. Jewell had nowhere to go. She was pushed flat against the footboard. "What are you doing?"

"Smelling you makes me feel better." He laid his head on her shoulder and rubbed his cheek against her neck.

She patted him on the shoulder, gently pushing him back. "Come on now, let's get you dressed," she said. Then she explained to him the undergarments and why people wore them. She showed him how to put on socks and pull on the pants she'd bought him. He resisted the soft leather loafers, as Jewell suspected he would, but she assured him he only had to wear them when he went outside. She'd also gotten him some Nike gym slides like the guys in South Philly always wore. He liked those better. Teaching him how to tie shoelaces was probably best saved for another day. Most of the clothes she'd purchased at Target, but on the way home she'd stopped at Boyd's and gotten him a camel-colored cashmere turtleneck. When he put it on, her heart raced just a little. Whomever had played this trick on them had made Oberon a very handsome man. She'd been right. The turtleneck looked great. Oberon seemed to like it, too. He ran his hands up and down his torso.

"It almost feels like fur," he said. "It's so soft."

"I'm glad you like it," she said. "Now that you have clothes, we can go out together and buy some more things. Maybe not today. But eventually."

Oberon nodded.

"Are you hungry?"

"I feel like I'm always hungry."

Jewell fixed them some lunch. Oberon was confused by the sandwich when he saw Jewell pick it up with her hands. She explained to him that with some foods it was okay to eat with your hands, but usually using a knife and fork was best. "If you get confused," she said, "just watch and follow me." Jewell was happy to have the company, but once she finished explaining the ins and outs of cutlery use the table fell silent. Oberon looked up at her with expectant eyes between bites of his sandwich but said nothing. After he finished his sandwich, he managed to wolf down half a bag of potato chips in what seemed a matter of seconds.

"These are delicious," he said. "How come you never let me eat these before?"

"Because they're not very healthy," Jewell said.

"What does healthy mean?"

"It means that if you eat too many of them, they can make you fat or even sick."

Oberon set down the bag of chips. "It's too bad they taste so good."

"Yes, it is." Jewell stared at her plate. What now? "Let's go for a walk."

Oberon jumped out of his chair, knocking it over behind him. "Yes!" he said. "Yes! Let's go for a walk. That sounds like an excellent idea!" He paced in a tight circle then stopped and picked up the fallen chair. "I really do not like being cooped up in the apartment."

"It's okay," she said. "I don't like it much either."

Jewell grabbed her purse and the winter jacket she'd bought for Oberon. She showed him how the key and the lock worked, for when he'd be alone, and she was at work. As they walked down the hall toward the elevator, she started to laugh.

"What's so funny?" he asked.

"It just occurred to me that tomorrow I might wake up and there will be a dog in my bed dressed in a cashmere turtleneck."

Oberon tilted his head like he did not understand.

"What if I'm imagining all this?" she said. "Or what if tomorrow whoever did this shows up and changes you back?"

Oberon let out a long slow breath. "You are definitely not imagining anything."

She held the door to the building open for him, and as he stepped outside, she could see his entire countenance rise. His chest lifted toward the sun, and he wanted to sprint. She grabbed his arm before he took off into traffic. "It is a beautiful day, but you have to remember you're a man walking on a sidewalk. Please be patient and stick with me, okay?" She took his hand. "Once I get this all figured out, I'll get you some exercise clothes and you can go for a run."

"That sounds wonderful!" He grinned so hard Jewell thought he might hurt himself. "Can we go to the dog park now, please?"

Jewell nodded and led him down Locust Street toward the river. It was a sunny, crisp afternoon, not unlike the day before, but Jewell was not filled with hope, anger, or sadness—all the feelings she'd experienced yesterday in the park. Instead, she was filled with confusion. Perhaps this would all seem more real to her once Oberon interacted with some other human beings. Then it wouldn't seem like it was in her head somehow, either that or she would know she was crazy. She should text Melody. She would know what to do.

They crossed through the playground and in the distance, they could hear the dogs running in the park. Oberon dropped her hand and started to run toward the sounds, but Jewell held him back.

"I can hear Godzilla barking," he said. "She is so bossy. I always tell her to relax, but she says I don't know what I'm talking about."

"Godzilla, that's the Chihuahua, right?"

Oberon nodded.

"So, do dogs talk to each other?"

Oberon laughed. "Not exactly. Not like you and I can talk, which is very nice. We communicate in a much more general kind of way. I don't have to ask them how they're feeling—I can smell it. Tail high, good day. Tail not so high, not such a good day." He paused for a moment and looked in her eyes. "Life is very simple."

Oberon walked ahead to the fence and stood watching the other dogs. Godzilla came up to the fence and stood in front of him. She looked like she wanted to bark but didn't. Oberon turned to Jewell when she joined him. "I think Godzilla's confused. She recognizes my scent but doesn't understand what happened."

"I feel her pain," Jewell said.

"Look, there's the new dog, Fang," Oberon said. Fang was penned in, cornered by a bichon and a beagle. "Poor Fang," Oberon said.

"Do you have any idea what happened to him?"

"Not exactly. He was too shy to communicate much yesterday. But the other dogs scare him. They're too loud."

"He's very beautiful."

"He is. Maybe some faeries will come along and turn him into a man, too."

Jewell touched his sleeve. "Faeries?"

"Don't you remember? Last night. They tried to give me some forgetting dust, but it didn't work." He stared out at the river and Jewell noticed how the afternoon light reflected sparkles of gold in his eyes. "They were so beautiful," he said. "One of them had long lavender hair. I could never forget her no matter how much forgetting dust they gave me."

Jewell shook her head. "Wow, I am losing my mind. My dog just told me that faeries came in the middle of the night and turned him into a man."

Oberon stood close to Jewell, so close their shoulders touched. "They said you called them. That you cast the spell."

"What?"

He shrugged and looked away. "I'm sorry. I didn't really understand things last night like I do now. I'm learning all the time. Maybe tomorrow I'll remember better."

"It's okay," Jewell said. "We're both adjusting. Do you want to keep walking?"

"Look. Here comes Steve," Oberon said. "You know, Fang's human. We should stay and talk to him. He likes you."

"No, we should not stay and talk to him." Jewell turned to go but Oberon did not move from the fence.

"He smelled good."

"So you said," Jewell replied. "Come on."

"Hey, Jewell!" Steve called.

"Shit," Jewell said under her breath. She was caught now, but even still she put on a bright smile. Maybe Steve wouldn't think there was anything weird going on.

"Hi!" Steve said. Jewell couldn't help but notice how Steve gave Oberon a quick once-over. "Where's Oberon?"

Jewell elbowed Oberon before he could speak. He looked at her with concern but stayed quiet. "He's at the groomer's. Going to pick him up later."

"Well, it's nice to see you again," Steve said, looking more at Oberon than at Jewell.

"Nice to see you, too," she said. "This is my friend Ron. Ron Williams, from college. He's in town for a few days. He's thinking about moving to Philly." Need to stop talking. Too much to remember. She shoved her hands in her pockets and smiled at him like an idiot.

"Nice to meet you, Ron," Steve said extending his hand. Oberon smiled and grasped Steve's hand like a paw, enclosing his thumb, and shook it up and down several times.

"Nice to meet you too, Steve," Oberon said. He put his arm around Jewell and pulled her close rubbing his cheek against the top of her head. "This is my human, Jewell. Isn't she great?"

Steve stepped back and smiled, like he was repressing a laugh. Jewell could tell he thought they were both out of their minds. She pushed Oberon off her gently. "Ron is a total jokester. Sorry about that."

Steve shrugged. The corner of his mouth was upturned in a half-smile. He definitely thought they were crazy, but it didn't seem like he cared much. Jewell couldn't help but admire Steve in a way. For a Sunday afternoon he was well put together. Same trim jacket from the night before, but unlike some of the other men in the park, he was not dressed in stained sweatpants and mud-caked sneakers. Instead, he had on a nice pair of boots, not brand new, but well taken care of, and a pair of dark-washed jeans. Then she remembered the brush off from the night before. Maybe he had a date after his walk in the park with Fang. Her smile curved into a rueful knot.

"What made you stop by the dog park without your dog?" Steve asked.

Jewell paused and glanced at Oberon, who at the moment was leaning over the fence stroking the top of Fang's head. Steve noticed, too. "Wow, look at that. Fang never lets anyone get close like that." He looked up at Jewell. "This isn't the guy you were telling me about, is it?"

Jewell shook her head. "No. Ron just got in today. I guess he's just got a way with animals. Who knew?"

"So, Ron, what do you do?" Steve asked.

Jewell nudged Oberon and he looked up at her and then over at Steve. "Fang is very grateful to you."

Steve laughed. "He told you that, did he?"

Oberon smiled. "In a way."

Steve shifted his hands in his pockets. "What brings you to Philly?"

Oberon glanced at Jewell. Again, the angle of the light illuminated something golden in his eyes. For a moment Jewell found herself completely distracted, almost stupidly so, then Oberon turned his head back toward the dogs and she recovered herself.

"Like I said, Ron's an old friend from college. He's here to see me." She laughed and then felt silly. "We should probably get going," Jewell said, linking her arm through Oberon's. "It was really nice seeing you again. I promised to show Ron around the neighborhood."

"Well, I don't want to keep you." Steve knelt and scratched Fang behind his ears and then reattached his leash. "We need to head home, too."

After they started to walk away, Jewell stopped and called over her shoulder. "You should let me know how it goes with the dog trainer." She wasn't sure what had possessed her to say it. She should have just walked away. Let him think Oberon was her boyfriend. She felt a little light-headed suddenly and leaned on Oberon for balance.

Steve stood and rested his elbows on the fence. "I would, but I don't have your number."

"Right," Jewell said. She fished one of her cards out of her purse and patted Oberon on the arm. "Give me a minute, okay."

She walked back to Steve and handed him the card. "He really is just a friend from college. A bit of a goof, but harmless. I wouldn't have asked you for coffee if he was . . ." She looked down at the ground and then back up at Steve. "I wouldn't do that."

He shrugged. "I just met you yesterday. You don't owe me any explanations."

Jewell looked at Steve in his neatly tailored pea coat and expensive shoes. His eyes were clear and direct. She could tell he wasn't trying to be a jerk, but really wanted her to know she didn't need to feel weird about anything. Why couldn't she have met him six months ago? "You know, you're right," she said. "Not sure what my deal is. Call me, though, and let me know about the trainer. I might not be back to the park for a while with Ron here. I would like to know how Fang is doing."

Steve tapped the card against his hand. "Glad to know one of us made an impression."

She felt her face knot again. "You're the one who said you didn't want to be that guy."

Steve nodded. "True. And I don't."

"Which I admire," Jewell said. "So, you did make an impression." She smiled at Steve, then bent down and offered her fingers to Fang through the fence. He sniffed them tentatively then rubbed his cold wet nose up against her hand. She scratched his chin. "See you later, Fang."

# 4.

Titania sat on her gilded throne in the great hall of Castle Alfheim hunched over a glowing pool of water circulating in a large silver basin. Faerie courtiers, Elfin emissaries, and other citizens of the Realm mingled and murmured, giving their queen sidelong glances. Iolanthe and Ondine sat nearby doing their best to ignore the grumbling and whispering. Earlier, during the initial visioning spell an orc merchant had requested an audience, and Titania had brusquely turned him away. She'd been too focused on seeing Oberon, even if it was just a reflection of his life with that woman. How could she possibly be bothered to care what an orc might want? Ondine had gone after the orc, had managed to calm him with the promise of a royal visit the next day.

Titania spun her index finger around the edge of the bowl and sat a little straighter. "Look!" she said pointing at the pool. "See how she abandons him."

Iolanthe rose and placed a calming hand on her sister's shoulder. "Titania, be reasonable. She must clothe him. They are mortals. They cannot be together every waking moment. When I lived among the mortals, I was apart from my beloved for many hours every day. This is a part of the fabric of their lives."

"Maybe," Titania said, "but see how he longs for her. He is afraid without her."

"He will be fine."

"As a dog she would leave him all day," Ondine said. "Human women work jobs like men."

"How do you know such things?"

"I did some investigating." She squared her shoulders and raised her eyes to meet Titania's. "I consulted with Mustardseed, who's recently returned from an extended stay. The human world has made many advances since your last visit or mine for that matter. Human women are free to pursue anything they wish. They can vote, own property, engage in science and government."

Titania waved her hand dismissively. "Yes, yes. I'm sure it's all quite fascinating." She pinched the bridge of her nose. "It's nice that human men finally understand that women are their equal." Titania fussed with her jeweled chiffon sleeves.

"I'm not so sure I would go that far," Iolanthe said.

"So, what is this woman? A scullery maid, perhaps?"

"Jewell is an engineer, which is not unlike a magician. She builds things, uses science to change her environment."

Titania snorted. "She is no magician."

"Perhaps not," said Iolanthe. "You must give her some time. We thought of many things during our transformation spell, but I fear we may have forgotten some crucial elements."

"If only he had not looked at me with those mournful eyes. He was pleading for my love."

"He is a man. Pleading is in his nature," Iolanthe said.

"When did you become so hateful, sister?"

Iolanthe moved across the room and sat in a low tufted chair on the opposite side of the great hall. The courtiers and other guests shifted along with her, the fabric of their robes rustling along with their gossip. Titania seemed to sink in on herself. The lower she felt the darker her gown became, changing from ecru to mud brown, cycling through every shade in between.

"Your highness," Ondine said. She stood next to her sister's hunched form. "Calm yourself, please. If your mood becomes any darker a storm cloud will form above your head."

Titania scanned the court and courtiers. The faeries and other guests milled about in small groups stealing surreptitious glances at her. She glared at them, her lavender hair unkempt and her eyes wild and green. She turned to her sister and spoke in a loud voice. "I don't want anyone to worry about me." She laughed with forced abandon, bubbles escaping her mouth and bursting on impact with the air. "This is the Realm after all. We need to have a party, some revelry. I know, let's have a ball! Invite the goblins from the dale and the elves from the forest. All the creatures of the Realm will be welcome in Alfheim tonight, even the orcs." She rose and strode around the massive chamber, her gilt heels clicking against the marble as she marched toward Iolanthe. "Do you fancy a ball, dear sister?"

"I fancy anything that will please the queen and return her to good humor," Iolanthe said.

Titania turned to the court throwing her arms wide. "A ball it is, then, this very night!" Her voice echoed against the polished floors and rebounded off the grand staircase. "Go! Notify our guests and make ready. Summon the musicians!" She withdrew a sprinkle of glittery dust from the pouch at her waist and threw it up in the air. She stepped into it as it fell. Her gown transformed from muddy brown into an iridescent silver that fell in gossamer waves. A crown of dazzling diamonds appeared on her head atop row upon row of perfectly coiled curls. "Come!" she shouted. "We're faeries, let's not waste time." She flicked her wrist and a table laden with fruits and sweets appeared. She flicked her wrist again and a punch bowl of mead appeared on the opposite side of the room. Soon the musicians arrived, and other faeries began to transform their attire to match that of their queen.

Iolanthe rose and grabbed Titania's wrist before she could flick another table of treats into existence. "Go easy, dear sister, lest you rouse suspicion. I'm all for dancing and music, but there's no need to be manic in our pursuits."

"Ever the dampener of joy," Titania said. "Faeries are nothing if not manic. You've changed since your return."

Iolanthe shook her head. "No, sister. I was always the dampener of joy."

Titania took Iolanthe's hand. "Come. Let's dance. Musicians! Play a merry tune!" She turned to the orchestra and snapped her fingers. "Now you." She pointed her finger at Iolanthe. "It's time for you to change your tune."

Iolanthe sprinkled herself with faerie dust and as she twirled her clothes effervesced into a splendid spider web of blue and green and gold. "Better?"

"Much." Titania put forward her hand. Iolanthe placed her hand on top of her sister's, and they moved to the dance floor, forgetting for a moment, at least, poor Oberon as he pined for Jewell's return.

Festive gatherings of some sort occurred every night in the Realm, but rarely did they occur on such a grand scale. The goblins and elves and other inhabitants of the realm were happy enough to come eat the Queen's food and drink her wine, whether she had conjured it or prepared it with her own two delicate hands. By midnight every faerie still in the Glade was crammed into the palace and scattered along the grounds. The only prominent faerie not in attendance was Robin Goodfellow. He, like Iolanthe and Ondine, longed for the company of humans. He, however, did not linger with humans for love. His desire was mischief, or at least it had been. Titania hadn't seen Robin for many years—generations in the human world—not since the Shakespeare debacle. She'd banished him for what he'd done to her, although she wasn't sure it was much of a punishment. Either way, he was somewhere she wasn't, which is what she wanted. She was content to let him stay there and rot until the end of his days, which for faeries was a very long time.

As the days passed, the party continued to grow in intensity. Faerie musicians played every manner of gigue and bourrée, allemande and minuet. They danced in the great hall. They danced on the stairs to the upper balcony, in the formal courtyard, in the grassy dale, and the flowering meadow. They ate, got drunk, and fucked there, too. Then they slept where they fell, woke, and started all over again. Music filled Alfheim, echoed through the valley, and well into the forest. For a while, Titania was distracted enough that some of the flowers in the glade returned to their normal shade of yellow and pink.

After several days, she could bear it no longer and she slipped away from the festivities, and her sisters, and returned to her private chambers. She dismissed her attendants and told them to enjoy themselves. Once alone, she filled her private viewing basin with fresh water. She passed her hand over the surface and the water turned to mercury. In the flickering lamplight she could see her pale lavender hair had turned violet. This disturbed and pleased her at the same time. Iolanthe and Ondine had each had their own great loves. Now it was her turn. She could feel the hand of fate pulling her and no amount of drinking, dancing, and debauchery was going to dissuade her. Oberon was for her, and it wasn't because of the stupid play. There was something else at work, something ancient and mysterious—something that pricked at the back of her neck—like she should know what it was, but just couldn't remember. Maybe this is what it felt like to be glamoured. This thought made her smile, then she dismissed it. The Faerie Queen glamoured? By who? Ridiculous!

She passed her hand over the bowl again. There she saw Oberon and Jewell. Weeks had gone by in the human world, but time had hardly passed in the Realm. It moved at its leisure and was not dictated by such mundanities as the laws of physics or the movement of planets. This is why faeries never seemed to age. They did of course, just not in the same way as humans.

The human world was cruel in so many ways. That was why Titania had never had much desire to interact there. There had been Shakespeare, of course—she'd met him on a dare, a bet she'd lost to Robin Goodfellow. He'd been a charming distraction for a while, so charming that Robin had grown to regret his little joke, but by then it had been too late. She'd banished and abandoned Robin to his precious humans. She'd had her revenge. But now. Now, she longed to be a part of that cruel world, for what? A man? She clicked her fingernails on the arm of her chair. This seemed impossible, and yet he was a man of her creation. This appealed to her in a way she could not have imagined.

It wasn't just Oberon's physical countenance. Although for a human, even with his rounded ears and dull hair and skin, he

"Baby!" Bobby turned around and threw his arms around Melody and gave her a long dramatic kiss. Jewell smiled despite herself. She was happy for her friend, but if she was honest there was part of her, bigger than she wanted to admit, that was lousy with jealousy.

"You look fantastic, as always, Doc." Bobby looked Melody over. "What are you drinking? Never mind. Tell Gigi. I've got some great appetizers working for you. I'll be right back." He hurried off to the kitchen leaving Jewell and everyone else feeling out of breath.

Melody slid into the booth next to Jewell. "I always forget how high energy he is," Jewell said. "How do I always forget that?"

Melody shrugged. "He's the best."

"He's a faerie," Oberon said.

"What?" Melody looked like she wanted to hit him, then she turned to Jewell. "What have you been saying about him?"

"I haven't said anything about Bobby. Come on, Melody. Have you ever heard me say anything like that about anyone?"

Melody leaned in and lowered her voice. "Well, he had to learn it somewhere."

"He's home by himself all day and watches a lot of TV. I can't be responsible for everything."

Oberon smiled. "I didn't mean he was a homosexual. If I thought that I would have said it." Oberon shook his head. "No one says that anymore, do they? Faerie, used that way, is so old-fashioned and it's not very nice. I did hear it in a movie though, not too long ago."

Melody huffed. "Says the guy who's three weeks old."

"Technically, I've been human now for nearly two months."

"What can I get you to drink?" Gigi asked.

The three of them looked up at the smiling waitress. How long had she been standing there?

"Tell Max to make something up for us, okay? Something with a lot of Tequila," Melody said with a wave of her hand. Gigi nodded and turned to the bar. As soon as she was gone, Melody leaned back across Jewell. "You said faerie, *Ron*. What did you mean?"

Oberon sighed and clasped his hands on the table. "He's a faerie. Like the ones that turned me into a man."

"Are you sure?" Jewell asked.

"I've been living with that guy for over a year." Melody pointed her finger at Oberon. "Last week we decided to get married."

"Melody, that's great!" Jewell gave her a quick hug.

"Thanks. I'm pretty happy about it." Although Jewell thought, at the moment, she didn't look so happy.

"Why didn't you tell me?"

Melody nodded her head toward Oberon. "You've had other stuff to worry about, right? Plus, it was real spur of the moment. I don't have a ring and I thought I'd just wait."

"I guess. But still."

"Listen you," Melody said to Oberon. "The point is, I know my Bobby and he is not a faerie. Not a homosexual. Not a faerie with wings. He is a chef and a restauranteur and a goddamned great boyfriend."

Oberon looked at Melody and placed his hand on top of hers. Jewell, who was sitting between them, tried to make herself as small as she could. "He is also a faerie. But you know that, don't you," Oberon said. "Also, I don't believe faeries have wings, at least none of the faeries that I've seen, but Bobby is definitely capable of magic. I can see it all around him. I wish you could see it." Oberon leaned back against the cushions of the booth,

Titania looked down at him or tried to.

Bobby stopped drumming the table and looked her in the eye. "Save it for someone who gives a shit, will you?" he said. "We're not in the Realm, and I am not your subject. This is Philadelphia, PA, the birthplace of American democracy and Rocky. And in that same spirit, I am declaring my independence from you."

"Very well."

A waiter appeared with two glasses of cognac and dessert. "Thanks, Jimmy." He offered Titania a spoon. "Wait until you try this. It's going to blow your mind."

She took the spoon and dipped it into the dessert. Once the spoon was in her mouth, she looked at Bobby with wonder.

"I told you. Mind explosion. It's extra dark chocolate from Italy. My gelato guy has won awards all over the world. Who the fuck needs magic when you've got stuff like this to eat? Am I right?"

"I don't know what to say." She stopped and took another spoonful. "This is perhaps the single most delicious thing I've ever eaten, but I'm not sure I'm ready to renounce magic."

"Fair enough," Bobby said. "I think I have a pretty good idea why you're here. But you're going to have to tell me. I learned my lesson with you 400 years ago."

Titania resisted the urge to run her finger along the side of the dish and lick it clean. Instead, she sighed and weighed her options. Without Robin's help, when she did find Oberon, and really all it would take was one good wave over a viewing bowl and a scribe spell, she wasn't sure she'd have enough magic to get them both home. What if Oberon didn't want to go? What if he was so devoted to that woman that he wanted to stay with her? Everything was too uncertain. She needed some assurances from someone.

"Not going to tell me?"

She sighed again. "Are you going to eat that?" She pointed at Robin's half-eaten scoop of gelato.

He pushed it toward her. "Have at it."

"The truth is, I'm in love. My love is so strong it compelled me here against my better judgement. And I have you and that bastard Shakespeare to blame."

"That is so interesting. A guy that's been dead for four hundred plus years, and another who's been banished for the same amount of time, are somehow responsible for your lovesickness? Do tell."

"What makes you think you know why I'm here?"

"Let's just say it's been a very long time since anyone has seen me as a faerie and a few days ago, something like that happened, right here in this very place. I knew there was strong magic involved, but I had no idea it was you until you materialized in my kitchen tonight."

"Who recognized you as a faerie?"

"So how many of you did it take to pull off that stunt. Four, five?"

"Three."

"You, Iolanthe, and Ondine. Figures. Those bitches."

Titania bristled. "You say bitch like it's a bad thing."

Bobby laughed and sipped his Scotch. "You brought them back, forgave them. But me, your once and former lover, me you abandoned—condemned to banishment. Alone and without recourse."

Titania shook her head. "Puck, my dear, you, of all people, are never without recourse." She raised her hands to the restaurant. "Look at what you've made. Very impressive. Besides, if you wanted to ask forgiveness, all you had to do was summon me."

Bobby smiled. "Summoning's funny, isn't it? How often do you get summoned these days?"

Titania glared at him. "Not so much as you'd think. The summoning, as you know, must have heart-felt intention behind it, and most actors these days just can't rouse that kind of feeling with any real sincerity. But I have to say, convincing Shakespeare to include my name in the play, and so many variations on the summoning spell itself, was a splendid joke. A joke that I felt you would better appreciate here, among the humans."

"I'm guessing that's what brought you here on this most recent occasion? A good old Shakespeare-invoked summoning." His face was hard, his eyes tight with anger. "But there must have been something else. Something else that required the talents of your sisters. What could that have been exactly? And how did it go so terribly wrong?"

Titania rose, no longer wishing to play this game. He knew more than he was telling her, but he was only interested in taunting her, she could see that now. Eventually, he would help her if she needed him to. She was still his queen. She'd wasted enough precious time. She needed to find Oberon. "Thanks for dinner, *Bobby*. It was delicious, but I am here on business."

"Well, it's been good to see you, Sis. Stop in again soon!"

Titania moved toward the door without looking back, but she could hear the mockery in his voice, and it stung more than she wanted to admit. Time enough later for regrets. Right now, she needed to find lodging for the evening and a good silver bowl for her locating spell.

# SEVEN

## I.

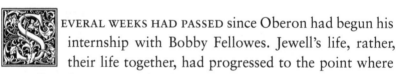EVERAL WEEKS HAD PASSED since Oberon had begun his internship with Bobby Fellowes. Jewell's life, rather, their life together, had progressed to the point where Jewell no longer thought about how Oberon, or Ron, as everyone else referred to him, had come into existence. He was just her very sweet, completely devoted, ridiculously handsome live-in boyfriend. He still made the occasional odd observation, but that had become part of his charm, or at least that's what her friends had told her.

The two of them had fallen into a routine of sorts, which surprised and disappointed Jewell. Her wish had been fulfilled, only for her to discover that her life, and the loneliness she felt, hadn't really changed all that much. Grief wasn't something you could wish away.

When Oberon returned home, late at night, smelling of dish soap and fryer grease, he still insisted that Bobby was a faerie. And he insisted that Bobby knew all about him—had since the two of them laid eyes on each other. He also talked about how he thought Bobby was hiding something from him, or that Bobby was hiding him from someone else—he couldn't figure out which.

Jewell had decided it was just easier to believe him than to convince him otherwise. Why couldn't there be faeries all around them? The empirical world that she thought she once understood completely did not really exist.

Jewell had tried to talk to Melody about all of this, but she was deep into wedding planning and had no interest in discussing anything but that. Anytime Jewell brought up magic or faeries, Melody changed the subject. Bobby had delivered on his promise and had bought Melody the biggest diamond solitaire ring that Jewell had ever seen. It was at least five karats. Despite this, Melody had been complaining about a woman skulking around the restaurant, who periodically showed up claiming to be Bobby's sister or something equally ridiculous. Jewell was tempted to give Melody a call even though it was late. She shuffled out of the bedroom to find her phone. The person she really wanted to talk to was her dad, but that was no longer an option.

When her father had been alive, she always called him when she needed to make a tough decision. She didn't feel on the cusp of a decision so much as she just wanted to hear his voice. He hadn't always given her the best advice, but he listened. She couldn't imagine how she would have explained any of this to him. She smiled thinking about it. But then again, maybe he would have understood. He'd had a magic of his own, a way with his music that could transport an audience to a different place even if just for an evening. No, he probably would have taken it all in stride and told her what he usually did. She needed to relax and trust herself.

Melody would likely tell her the same thing, and then launch into a diatribe about this mystery woman. Jewell dialed her number, anyway.

"Hey!" Melody said. "What are you doing?"

"Trolling my apartment like a zombie." She paused. She could hear music and the sound of people talking in the background. "Where are you?"

"Where do you think?"

Jewell heaved herself onto the couch. "Any sign of Cruella Deville?" This is what Melody had taken to calling the mystery woman.

"Not yet. You should come down. Help me keep vigil."

"I don't think I'd be very good company."

"Why? What's going on?"

"Too busy having a pity party. Plus, I'm already in my pajamas. You know how that is."

"Come on Jewell, throw something on."

"I don't want Oberon thinking I'm keeping tabs on him." Over the background noise Jewell could hear Melody's sharp intake of breath.

"Oh, you mean like I'm doing with Bobby?"

"Jeez, no. That's not what I meant at all." She stifled a sigh. This was how it was with them a lot now and she hated it. "See? Not good company. Oberon, Bobby, two completely different situations."

"I'm sorry. I know you didn't mean anything. Cruella's got me all on edge. All Bobby will say is that she's someone he used to know from the old neighborhood. He insists there's nothing between them, but I don't like it."

Jewell didn't know how respond. She wanted to tell Melody not to worry, but they'd both been burned often enough to know that maybe she should be.

"Jewell, are you there?"

"Just thinking how some of this is my fault."

"Don't be ridiculous. You didn't conjure Cruella, right? Hey, do you want me to come over?"

"No. It's okay. Pity parties are best celebrated alone."

"If you're sure."

"Totally. Try to have some fun. Sounds like the place is hopping."

"Yeah, every hipster in Old City is here, I think. I'll call you tomorrow."

Jewell said goodbye and hung up the phone. Had she conjured Cruella? She hadn't even considered that possibility. She looked around her apartment. Books, magazines, records—there was stuff everywhere. Her stuff. Oberon hadn't accumulated much. He said his needs were simple and his life to date had borne that out. Yep. What this pity party needed was some wine.

Oberon worked almost every night, and she was busy all-day long. She'd wanted Oberon to get a job, so he wouldn't be lonely and bored, and maybe so he wouldn't be tempted by other women. That seemed especially important after he'd confessed his daytime liaisons. But now he was still home all day, while she was at work. Albeit he usually slept until 11 or noon. Frequently he was out the door and off to work before she got home and didn't get home until well after midnight. Some days they barely exchanged a word. Working off the books was all she'd been thinking about. She hadn't considered the hours he'd be working and how much she'd miss him even though he was sleeping in her bed every night. As usual, she hadn't thought it all through like she should have. This was no way to get an actual relationship off the ground.

She stared at the clock hanging over the doorway to the kitchen. Half past midnight. She was determined to stay awake until Oberon got home. She could sleep in with him the next morning. She poured herself a glass of wine and took the bottle back into the living room. She turned on the TV. Animal Planet

no longer had the appeal it used to. She flicked through the channels and settled on a home improvement show. One where the
potential homeowners have such unrealistic expectations Jewell
wanted to shout at the TV. Well, at least she was awake.

When Oberon walked through the door at 1:30, Jewell had
drunk half a bottle of wine and had fallen asleep on the couch
with the TV on. She started awake when she heard the key in
the lock and sat straight up.

"Are you still awake, Jewell?"

She rubbed her eyes. "Barely."

"Why did you wait up for me?" Oberon kicked his kitchen
shoes off by the door and hung his jacket in the closet. He settled
on the couch next to Jewell and pulled her close.

"I missed you," she said. He leaned for a kiss, and she pushed
him back. "Have you been drinking?"

Oberon shrugged. "It's what restaurant people do after their
shift. I had one drink." He held up his finger as an illustration.

"Wow, really? Because it seems like maybe you started with
one but finished with several."

"Come on Jewell. Kiss me." He flung himself on top of her
and she pushed him away.

"I don't feel like kissing you right now." She got up off the
couch and sat in the armchair on the other side of the room.

"You are being super crabby."

"Super crabby, huh? Maybe you should have just stayed out
with your work friends."

"Getting this job was your idea. This whole thing," he gestured wildly, "was your idea." He stood up. "I was your idea.
And now you're so *mad*." He stretched out these last words as
if he were savoring them.

Jewell shook her head. "It was not my idea for you to get
drunk after your shift, come home, and slobber all over me."

He took a step toward her, wobbled, and then sat down on the couch again. "I used to slobber all over you. You used to love my slobber."

"Because you weren't drunk."

"How do you know I wasn't drunk? Maybe I was. Maybe dogs get drunk, and you don't even know it."

"Do dogs get drunk?"

Oberon waved his hand at her. "Of course not! Don't be stupid."

"Great. Now I'm stupid."

"I didn't say you were stupid." Oberon slowed his speech as if she might not understand him otherwise. "I said you were super crabby."

"Oh. My. God."

"Why did you even wish for me anyway, if I'm just going to annoy you?"

"Why do you keep saying I did this? I didn't do this." Jewell pulled her knees into her chest and rocked herself. Was she having this conversation or was she trapped in some bizarro fantasy world? "I was drunk and feeling bad, which you wouldn't know about because you never feel bad. And then I just sort of wondered out loud, wouldn't it be great if someone loved me the way my dog did? That's it. I didn't *do* anything."

Oberon lurched toward her. She reached out her arms to block his fall and he landed on his knees in front of her. "I do love you. I love you so much, I don't know what to do with all that love." He buried his head in her lap. "Do you want me to quit the job?"

Jewell took his face in her hands. "No. I am super crabby and very tired. And maybe also a little drunk myself." She pointed to the empty bottle of wine on the coffee table.

Oberon slid into the chair next to Jewell and put his arms around her. "Bobby says he can conjure me up a social security card and make me the lunch kitchen manager. That's why I had more than one drink tonight. We were celebrating."

"Conjure? Do I even want to know what that means?"

"Probably not."

Jewell curled into him. "Okay, well, congratulations. You've worked hard, and I know it hasn't been easy." She looked up into his face and for the first time she noticed little sprouts of gray at his temple. "Hey," she said sitting back. "What's this?" She ran her finger along his hairline.

"What's what?"

"I never noticed you were going gray."

"Am I really?" Oberon slid out from behind Jewell and headed toward the bathroom. Jewell followed him. He leaned against the sink and looked hard at his hairline in the mirror. "Wow, look at that," he said. "I really am going gray."

Jewell turned him toward her and away from the mirror. "How old are you, anyway?"

Oberon laughed. "In dog years, or human years?" His smile faded, and he gripped the sink.

"Shit," Jewell said.

"Shit," Oberon said.

"Well?"

"I have no idea." He looked at Jewell with panic in his eyes. "Don't you know?"

"I'm not sure they ever told me. Maybe I can find the adoption papers." Jewell hurried out of the bathroom and into the kitchen. Oberon followed close behind. She dug through her junk drawer, pulling out takeout menus, scissors, dead batteries, coupons and other miscellaneous stuff. She piled it all on the counter. "Not here. Maybe the desk." She started with the center drawer then moved to the larger side drawers. "Here it is!" she said holding the adoption certificate aloft. She turned, and Oberon was right on top of her.

"What does it say?"

"It says at the time of the adoption, Pumpkin is a three-year-old neutered, ACA certified standard poodle." She looked up at him. "Five, so Oberon the dog would have been about five." She paced the living room. "What do they say, seven human years to every dog year? Although I don't think that's really quite accurate. But let's just say—that would make you about 35. That sounds right." She tapped her chin. "Although most 35-year-olds do not have gray hair."

"That's true," Oberon said. "But some do."

"My dad started going gray in his forties. Maybe we've just miscalculated."

"Maybe." Oberon drew her to the couch, and they sat down. "You should come to the restaurant with me tomorrow. We should ask Bobby."

"Okay. Why should we ask Bobby?"

"You know why."

"Right, Bobby is a faerie, I keep forgetting."

"I know you don't want to believe me."

"I believe you, but you're right—I don't want to believe you." She pulled her hair back and stared at Oberon. "I don't know why this is freaking me out so much."

"It's freaking me out a little bit, too."

"Why? Gray hair is cool. It's even kind of sexy," she said. Although she wasn't sure who she was trying to convince.

"Sure."

"No. Really. Look at George Clooney or Eric Dane or John Slattery."

"Anderson Cooper?"

"Yes. Anderson Cooper. We could do this all night." She laughed. "At least we're not fighting anymore."

"Were we fighting?"

She stroked his cheek. "That, my love, was definitely a fight. Not a terrible fight, but a fight." She leaned into his chest. "If you're the lunch chef—"

"Kitchen manager," Oberon said.

"Right, kitchen manager. Will you still come home smelling like French fries?"

"Probably," he laughed. "But at least I will be home in time to make you dinner."

"That would be nice. I miss you."

"I miss you, too. So why were you really waiting up for me?"

Jewell wrapped her arms around him and thought for a moment about why she'd been so upset. Now it didn't seem that important. "I was really just missing you and feeling sorry for myself." She turned and kissed him. "Let's go to bed."

## 2.

The next morning Jewell made plans with Oberon to stop by the restaurant after work, so they could both talk to Bobby. If he really was a faerie, like Oberon kept insisting, maybe he would have some answers for them. Those gray hairs were nagging her for some reason. She'd woken up still thinking about them.

The weather had gotten warm. Winter had melted into full blown spring. Japanese Cherry trees blossomed pink and fluttery. Daffodils and forsythia bloomed yellow all around Jewell as she walked to the bus stop that morning. This was the kind of morning she really missed going to the dog park. The time she spent there, the excuse it gave her to talk to new people, to get outside herself, she'd cherished it. But that part of her life was behind her now and there were other, new things on the horizon. Soon there would be other reasons to go to the park, excuses to talk to new people, and she would cherish those experiences, too. At least that's what she hoped.

She decided to walk into work and hung a left on Locust Street. She could hear kids playing on the swings and the random bark of a dog. She paused and shook her head. Just go to work, she told herself. You've got other things to worry about. She spun around and found herself face to face with Steve Munroe. Fang sat by his side, looking calmer than Jewell had ever seen him.

"Look who it is Fang." Steve smiled at her. "How are you?"

"I'm great. How are you?"

"Good. Hey, I meant to call you to thank you for telling me about that trainer. Look at Fang. Can you believe it?"

Jewell shook her head then reached over and scratched Fang's furry ear. "He's such a beautiful dog." She bent down so she was close to his face. "I hope you're not letting Godzilla bully you anymore." She rubbed his head with both her hands. "Such a good boy." She blinked a few times before she stood up and looked at Steve.

"Is everything okay?" he asked.

"I'm fine. It's just kind of hard to talk about."

"That doesn't sound good."

What was she going to say to this guy? The last time they'd talked he was the one who said she didn't owe him any explanations, so why did she always feel like she did?

"It's okay. You don't have to tell me." He reached out and touched her shoulder. "Anyone could see how close you were to your dog. Not everyone gets to bond with their pet that way."

"You're right. I was lucky." She shoved her hands in her jacket pockets. "That day I saw you, when I was with my friend Ron? Later that same day, when we went to the groomer, he told me that he'd found a lump in Oberon's groin. The poor guy, he hung in there." She really thought she might cry just thinking about Oberon this way. Steve reached out and touched her arm. She blinked back a few tears and smiled.

"I'm so sorry."

"It's okay. Thanks," she said. "Looks like things are going great for Fang here."

"You were right. That trainer worked his magic on us."

"I'm so happy. Listen, it was great running into you."

"You too." He reached down and patted Fang, fiddled with the leash. "It's funny," he said, still not looking at her. "I've only ever run into you a couple of times, but I do think about you." He looked up at her. "I hope you don't think that's weird."

She shook her head. How could she say it was weird? The same was true for her.

"That woman I was seeing, when we first met?"

"You don't have to tell me."

"I know. It's just—it didn't work out. Turns out she didn't have the same ideas about fidelity that I did."

"I've been there."

"I guess we all have. Anyway, could I call you sometime?"

She pulled her jacket in closer to her, even though it wasn't chilly. "My circumstances have changed since the last time I saw you. I'm sorry."

"Just bad timing, I guess."

She nodded. "Listen, I've got to run to work. I don't want to be late. It was nice to see you. Take care." She reached down and gave Fang one last pat. "See you, Fang."

All the way to work, she couldn't help but think about Steve, about how differently things might have turned out if he had been free that first night in the park. What had Shakespeare said? "The course of true love never did run smooth."

# 3.

Titania's magic had worked well enough in the human world that she'd been able to secure herself the Commonwealth Suite at the Logan Hotel and a new wardrobe. Faeries could never be confident in how well their magic would work outside the Realm until they tested it out. Sometimes spells worked exceedingly well and sometimes not at all. Or a spell would appear to work, only to go awry later in some unforeseen way. Glamouring and viewing spells nearly always worked, as did cloaking or concealment magic. Conjuring, shimmering, and other types of procurement or transformative magic proved to be less reliable. The more powerful the faerie and the elements she was aligned with, the more likely it was that her magic would work.

Titania's magic had worked very well in almost all respects. She walked through the city like a woman of wealth and power. She even discovered that having lavender hair made her trendy, not conspicuous. There were women in this city who had hair far more strangely colored than hers. Robin had been right. These people had their own magic, but that didn't mean she couldn't still use hers to her own advantage. The only thing she was having trouble with was the one thing she really needed to work: her viewing bowl and her location spell.

At first, she thought it was some fault of hers, but eventually she began to suspect that something else was going on. Every other spell had worked just fine. When she'd attempted to pierce the veil with her viewing bowl to see what was happening in the Realm during her absence, all went as expected. She had been relieved to discover the revelry still in full swing. Iolanthe and Ondine seemed to be managing in her absence, but that wouldn't last forever. She needed to find Oberon, but someone was cloaking him. Fortunately for her, she knew exactly who that was.

When she marched into Pucks' Place that sunny afternoon, she had expected to find Robin Goodfellow toiling away in his kitchen, pretending to be a human. She did not expect to see him sitting in the dining room with Oberon and that sad little woman, Jewell.

When the hostess tried to stop her from entering the bar, Titania held up her hand and froze her still on the spot. Robin looked up, from what appeared to be an intense conversation. "Shit. Look who's here."

"I knew you were hiding him from me."

Bobby shrugged. "Would you mind unfreezing my staff, please?"

Titania glared at him. "When we're finished, and I have what I came for."

Oberon grabbed Jewell's arm. "Hey," she said. "What's going on? Who is she?"

"You don't recognize her?"

"She's very beautiful. Not sure about the hair, but no, I don't know her."

"Why would she know me?" Titania said. "She has no magic! Just look at her, so plain and pathetic."

Bobby stood and wrapped his arm around Titania's shoulder. He whispered loudly. "Come now my liege. Let's not have a scene."

He pulled out a chair. She sat down with a grand flourish then turned to Oberon, who sat across the table, her demeanor soft and demure. "My love! At last I've found you. I've been here for days, weeks even, who knows how time passes in this wretched human existence."

Jewell looked at Bobby, helpless. "What is she talking about? Wait," Jewell said, turning toward Titania. "You must be Cruella. Crap. I did conjure her."

"What?" Bobby said.

"Ask your girlfriend," Jewell said.

"I don't have time for human foolishness. Come Oberon, it's time to go."

"He's not going anywhere with you," Jewell said. She threw her arms out, blocking him, like a driver does for a passenger when they slam on the brakes.

Oberon took Jewell's hand. He tried to speak but no words came out.

"Look how he trembles in my presence. He's been waiting for me."

"Dial it down a notch, would you, Maleficent? We had a whole conversation going here before you barged in." Bobby paused. "Jewell, this is Titania, Queen of the Faeries and all the creatures of the Realm. Titania, this is Jewell, beloved of Ron. I think, my queen, if you look closely at Jewell, you will see exactly how beloved of Ron she is."

Titania barked out a laugh. "Why do you think I would care about a child?"

"A halfling probably."

Titania scoffed. "Myth. Legend." She shook her head. "Unlikely at any rate."

"Didn't your own sister give birth to a halfling?"

"Tread lightly, Robin Goodfellow," Titania said.

"A what?" Oberon said. He paused as if he was going to say something else, but instead leaned forward, clutching his stomach.

"Are you okay?" Jewell said. "You look like you're going to be sick."

"I think I might be." He pushed his chair back with a loud scrape.

"Go!" Bobby said. "If you get sick in here, you're fired."

Jewell stood to follow him, but Bobby motioned for her to sit. "You need to hang around. You haven't told him?"

She looked down at her hands. "Told him what?"

"That you're pregnant."

Her head snapped up. "How do you know that? I'm not even sure. I'm going to the doctor tomorrow."

"I think you'd better tell him." He nodded toward Titania. "The wicked witch of the west has arrived in Dodge. Who knows what kind of bullshit she'll stir up."

Titania pounded her fists on the table. The few diners in the restaurant turned and looked at her. "Someone had better tell me what is going on, before I turn everyone in here, including the two of you, into toads." She pointed her finger at Bobby. "You. Puck. Start talking."

"What is happen—" Titania raised her hand, pointed her index and middle fingers at Jewell, and when she snapped them together, Jewell could no longer speak, or open her mouth.

Bobby flicked his wrist and opened his fingers outward and Jewell opened her mouth but did not finish her thought. "Go easy, Titania. I know you're on a mission, but your magic has had some unintended consequences."

Titania shrugged. "So what. That's to be expected in cases like this."

"This one," she pointed at Jewell, "had a very strong intention. I haven't felt an intention that strong since . . ." She paused. "Since you tricked me, Robin Goodfellow. That's how strong her intention was. It pulled not just me, but Iolanthe and Ondine through, too." She tossed her hair over her shoulder. "We did the best we could. It's not science." She looked hard at Jewell. "It's magic."

"Well, when you restored your beloved, you and your fine sisters did not bother to compensate for the metabolic differences between a man and a dog."

"What are you talking about?"

"Science," Bobby said. "Which does, sometimes, intersect with magic. I've been here 400 freaking years. Don't think I haven't learned a thing or two."

"Dogs age much faster than humans," Jewell explained. "Oberon is aging before our eyes. It wasn't noticeable at first, but Bobby thinks it may be accelerating."

"All the more reason for me to take him back to the Realm where he will never grow old."

Bobby shook his head. "You don't know what will happen. I'm not even sure you could take him back to the Realm."

"He can't go," Jewell said. "Not now. I won't let you take him."

"You won't let me? That's a bold statement for a human. Why don't we ask Oberon what he wants," Titania said. "He might surprise you. Did you see the look on his face when he saw me? His love for you is old and obligatory. It's the love of a faithful pet, not a man. You were asleep with your mouth open, foolish woman, when he first gazed upon me and called me beautiful."

"Where *is* Ron?" Bobby said. He pushed himself away from the table. "I'm going to go check on him."

"I'm coming with you," Jewell said.

"As am I," Titania said.

Bobby turned to Titania. "You stay put."

"An army of goblins couldn't keep me here."

Titania and Jewell followed Bobby to the men's room. He appeared a moment later. "He's not in there."

"What do you mean?" Titania said.

"I mean, he's not in the bathroom."

"Maybe he went for a walk to clear his head," Jewell said. "He may be headed for the dog park."

"I know how we can find him without running hither and yon," Titania said. She turned to Bobby. "You must have a large silver bowl in this dump somewhere."

"Follow me." Bobby led them through the restaurant and into the kitchen, past the pantry station, where Oberon had started just a few short months ago, and into his office. Once they were all inside, he closed the door. The office was large, considering it was tucked in the back of the kitchen area, and remarkably tidy. A large bookcase stood against the wall next to Bobby's desk and was filled with cookbooks, journals, collections of poetry, and what looked like antique cooking utensils, one of which happened to be a large silver bowl. Bobby set the bowl in the middle of his desk. "I'll be right back." He dashed through the door and returned with two plastic pitchers full of water. He poured these into the bowl and stood back looking at Titania. "Do your thing, my queen."

Titania shot him an angry look then stepped forward. She passed her hand over the bowl and its surface turned to mercury. She closed her eyes and passed her hand over the bowl again. Jewell needed to sit down. She thought she might faint. Okay. *Magic*. Magic was real, she knew that already. Oberon was real. Sure. They were looking for him. But this woman, this faerie had magically sealed her mouth, and Bobby had just as magically unsealed it. It was all happening right in front of her. Now they were casting spells, looking for Oberon, when she knew exactly where he was. She wobbled a moment and then righted herself. "I've got to go."

Titania shrugged. "Suit yourself. You obviously don't care about Oberon like I do."

"Are you okay?" Bobby asked.

"I'm fine. I just need to go."

"Be gone then!"

Jewell reached for the doorknob then turned back to Titania. "Screw you, your majesty. I knew where he was ten minutes ago. You're wasting your time waving your hand over a bowl."

Titania spun toward Jewell, but Bobby grabbed her arm. "She's right, you know. Why haven't you found him?"

Titania snapped, "Because you've been cloaking him from me, you insufferable ass! Either unblock me or cast the view yourself."

"Oh, yeah, that's right. I have been cloaking him from you." He looked over at Jewell standing with her hand on the door-knob. "You should go." And she did.

# 4.

Jewell made her way back through the kitchen and out onto the street. She tried calling and texting Oberon, but he wasn't responding. She hailed a cab and soon was at the park. He could be anywhere, of course, but she went straight to the dog run. It was late afternoon, and the park was full of women pushing strollers, playing with toddlers. Cyclists and runners whizzed by on their way to the trail that ran along the river. The dog run was full of people with their dogs. She recognized a few owners and pets. Then she saw him. Sitting on the far bench, the one she used to sit on when she didn't feel like talking to anyone. He stared out over the river, just like she had. He did not look well.

"Ron!" He turned toward her when she called his name, but he didn't smile. She walked quickly toward him, jogging almost, terrified by his ashy complexion. "What's the matter?" She sat next to him, and he collapsed against her. His cheek felt cool and clammy. She tried to right him, but his eyelids flickered closed, and his full weight slumped against her.

"Someone help me!"

Several nearby dog owners turned to look at her with confusion.

"My boyfriend," she said. "He's very sick. Someone please call 911!" An older woman, who stood the closest to her took out her phone and dialed. Panic gathered like a fist in her throat. What was happening? The woman hung up the phone and came over to Jewell, placed her hand on Jewell's shoulder.

"The fire department's on their way," she said.

"Thank you. I'm so scared. I don't know what's wrong."

"He doesn't do drugs, does he?" the woman said.

"No!" Jewell shook her head. "No, that's not it. He's sick."

"I'm not judging," the woman said. "The cops saved my nephew's life with that Narcan stuff."

Jewell turned away from the woman and began to rock Oberon. She didn't know what else to do. He was still breathing, but his breaths were shallow and sour. Within minutes the Fire Rescue paramedics had arrived and had him loaded onto a stretcher. They allowed Jewell to ride in the ambulance, but once they arrived at the trauma bay at the hospital she was shuttled off to the waiting area.

After a few minutes a nurse appeared and handed her a clipboard and a pen. "We'll take good care of him," she said. "Fill this out as best you can." Jewell nodded. "I have to ask you. Has he taken anything that might have made him sick?" Jewell shook her head. "Are you sure?"

Jewell shrugged. "As sure as anyone can be, I guess. If he took something, I have no idea what it might have been. He drinks now and again, but he doesn't do drugs."

"Okay. I'll be back in a few minutes for the forms."

Maybe he had taken something. Maybe Titania or Bobby, even, had slipped something in his drink. Maybe this was just one of those unintended consequences of magic. Somehow something had gone terribly wrong and there was nothing she could do. If it was magical in nature, how could medicine help? She tried to concentrate on the form, but the words swam across the page. She left the clipboard in her lap and stared at the linoleum tile on the waiting room floor. Suddenly, the TV in the corner seemed impossibly loud. Some talking head shouting about politics or the economy. When she looked up to find someone to turn off the TV, she saw Bobby and Titania shimmering into view. No one seemed to notice them but her. She wiped her face with the back of her hand. "Nice of you two to show up."

"It took me awhile to remove my cloaking spell. I wasn't just blocking Titania, I'd also managed to keep myself from viewing anything. I guess I'm a little out of practice."

"You could have texted me."

"Would you have answered?" Bobby sat down next to her and slid his arm around her shoulder. Jewell sunk into his embrace and let herself cry.

"What if he dies?" she said, righting herself.

Titania tapped her foot. "This is so touching."

Jewell stood so quickly the clipboard clattered to the floor. She leaned in close to Titania. "Don't mess with me, faerie."

Titania took a step back but laughed. "You know I could brush you out of existence with the wave of my hand."

"That's a bit of an exaggeration," Bobby said.

Jewell sat back down and gathered the clipboard from the floor. "Wow. This is finally sinking in. You are a faerie. Oberon was right."

"Yes. That's what I was trying to explain when her highness marched in."

Jewell clutched the clipboard, suppressing the urge to hit Titania with it. "You did this to him," she said glaring at Titania.

"I didn't do anything to him that you didn't ask me to." She laughed. "This is your fault."

"Please, we're all worried about Ron. Let's try to stay calm," Bobby said.

Jewell took a deep breath and looked back at the form in front of her. Her anger helped her focus, and she was able to fill out the form with Bobby's help. He had managed to conjure up (probably literally) a social security number, a birth certificate, even health insurance. Jewell almost started to cry again.

"Try to hold it together, okay?" Bobby said. She nodded. "Oberon's not the only one you need to be worrying about."

"What is taking so long?" Titania said. "Human medicine still seems to be such a guessing game. Faeries get sick, we cast a spell, and they either get better or they die. It's so much easier." She sat down next to Bobby.

"They kept asking me if he'd taken anything," Jewell said. "Bobby, do you have any idea what this might be?"

He sat back and thought for a moment. He looked at Titania and then back at Jewell. "If I didn't know better, I'd say it was iron poisoning. But Oberon's not a faerie. He shouldn't be allergic to iron."

"Faeries are allergic to iron?" Jewell said.

"Everyone knows that," Titania said.

"Maybe 400 years ago they did," Bobby said. "No one thinks faeries are real anymore. They're just characters in fantasy stories and children's books." He sat back and crossed his legs. "They think we have wings and are four inches tall."

"What?"

"Sad, isn't it? It makes me so mad sometimes—all that 'bibbity-bobbity-boo' bullshit."

"Focus," Jewell said. "You can hate on Walt Disney later."

"I have no interest in any of this." Titania waved her hand dismissively. "What I do want to know is how have you managed to not get sick all these years."

"It was hard in the early days," he said. "I knew what foods and metals to avoid. I wore gloves a lot. Thankfully they were frequently the fashion. Then, as the world became more sophisticated and science advanced," he looked at Titania deliberately. "I found I was able to take some simple herbal supplements, including some chelating agents that have made life most comfortable. An old friend of ours mixes it up for me special."

"But Oberon's not a faerie, so it's probably something else," Jewell said. "Right?"

Titania stood, pointed her finger at the TV, which immediately went silent, and then turned back to Jewell and Bobby. "Unless, of course, he is somehow a faerie. Perhaps we didn't turn him into a man but something else."

"But he looks like a man," Jewell said.

"Yes. But looks can be so deceiving." She sat back down. "He is full of magic, so who knows what's happening." She looked pointedly at Jewell. "You named him Oberon. What was your intention?"

Jewell started to respond, but Titania held up her hand. "Don't tell me how much you loved that play, or I'll turn you into a slug. You think you know Shakespeare? *We,*" she waved her hand back and forth between Bobby and herself, "we *knew* Shakespeare. He had his good points, for a human. But he was terribly full of himself. Completely out of his depth."

They sat in silence for what seemed like a very long time. Jewell rested her head against Bobby's shoulder. He texted Melody, who arrived, worried and full of sympathy, 20 minutes later. Eventually, a doctor came to talk to them. "Which one of you is Jewell?" Jewell raised her hand. "He's asking for you, and I'll let you see him in a moment. I just wanted to fill you in on what's going on."

"Is he going to be okay?"

"I think so. He's in exceptional health for a man of his age." Jewell looked back over her shoulder at Bobby then back to the doctor. He was aging, that seemed clear now. "Has he been taking iron supplements for any reason? I know sometimes endurance athletes take them for recovery and to boost performance, but if you get the dosage wrong it can make you very sick."

Jewell swallowed and thought for a moment. "He is an avid runner. I don't know about any supplements he might be taking, but I suppose it's possible."

"Well, that would explain, in part, what's going on. He does have an excess of iron in his blood, and we can treat that with a chelation of deferoxamine. Once his levels are back to normal, we'll need to figure out exactly what caused the build-up in the first place." The doctor placed his hand on Jewell's shoulder. "His prognosis is excellent."

Melody and Bobby stood and hugged Jewell. "We'll need to keep him here for a day or so and run some more tests. But if you'd like to see him, you can follow me."

"Doctor, I'm over at Wistar in molecular oncogenesis," Melody said. "We're doing some research on the effects of mineral mega-dosing. Do you think it would be possible for me to take some blood?"

The doctor led them down the brightly lit hallway. "If the patient consents, of course. I'll have someone draw it for you and send it over."

"Great." Melody dug her card out of her purse and handed it to the doctor. "My lab's address is on here." The doctor slipped the card into his chest pocket and pushed open the doors to the emergency room bay where Oberon lay hooked up to several beeping machines. There was a nurse in the room with him who turned and addressed Jewell. "We're going to admit him, as I'm sure the doctor explained. You can talk to him for a few minutes while we get him ready to go upstairs, then you can visit with him during visiting hours." Jewell nodded and reached for Oberon's hand.

"Wow," Melody said. "I didn't realize you had any gray hair. Is that a symptom of the iron poisoning?"

The nurse frowned at them. "I don't think so."

"Maybe it's the light in here," Bobby said. "Ron's always had a little gray, right?"

"Right," Jewell said. "I think it makes him look distinguished." She ran her hand along his temple and saw that there was even more gray hair than yesterday. And were those tiny crow's feet under his eyes? Oberon smiled groggily at her touch.

"How are you feeling?"

"Better," he said. He sat up a little bit, pushing himself up against the pillows. "Where's Titania?"

Bobby shrugged. "Probably all this sentiment was making her sick."

"Hey, Melody."

Melody waved. "Glad you're feeling better."

The nurse interrupted them. "We're going to move him upstairs now. You can come back later and visit him."

"Before you take him, can I get a gander at his chart?" Melody smiled. "I'm over at Wistar."

"I can see that," the nurse said, indicating Melody's embroidered lab coat. "Mr. Williams, you have to give your permission. May Dr. Rodriguez look at your records?"

Oberon nodded and sank back into the pillow. Melody looked the chart over, nodded a few times and then handed it back to the nurse. "Thank you," she said.

"Okay. We really need to get him upstairs."

"Sure. Of course," Melody said.

Jewell leaned in to give him a kiss, and when she did, Oberon held her to him and whispered in her ear. "You have something you need to tell me, don't you?"

She stroked his cheek. "We've got time for that later. You need to concentrate on getting better, okay."

# 5.

Titania shimmered out of the hospital and back to her hotel room. She wasn't going to share Oberon with anyone. She'd had enough of this human foolishness. Now that Robin had lifted his cloaking spell, she could see him anytime she wanted, and she would wait until he was alone before she revealed herself to him. If she and her sisters had somehow imbued him with faerie qualities when they'd transformed him into a man, then she might not be able to control him. What she needed was some nectar from the love-in-idleness flower. At least Shakespeare, with all his fictionalizing, hadn't gotten that wrong.

Titania appeared at the concierge desk so suddenly that the concierge almost fell backwards when she looked up. "What can I help you with today?"

"I need an apothecary."

The concierge's smile didn't change. "I'm not familiar with that term. A what?"

Titania tapped her chin. "A druggist? An alchemist, perhaps? I have no idea what you call these people anymore."

The concierge nodded, but her eyes were blank—not a glimmer of understanding. The woman's stiff navy-blue suit jacket annoyed Titania. She suppressed the urge to turn her into a sheep wearing spectacles. "Do you want a drug store, where you can fill a prescription?" the concierge asked. "Or are you looking for someplace that has herbs and crystals and things of that nature?"

"Likely that second one. Specifically, I seek the distilled nectar from the love-in-idleness flower."

The concierge continued to smile and nod. "Okay. Give me just a moment." She tapped a few strokes on her computer and then looked up, finally something besides blank subservience in her eyes. "This looks like just the place for you. It's on South Street. Give me just a second." She tapped another computer key, turned around, and then handed Titania a piece of paper. "This has the name of the store and walking directions, or you can hop in a cab right outside the front door and be there in about five minutes. Shouldn't be more than a ten-dollar fare."

"Thank you." Titania stepped back into the center of the lobby, folded the piece of paper into four equal sections, closed her eyes then shimmered her way to South Street.

Once at her destination, she took in her surroundings. The street was bustling with pedestrians of all shapes and sizes and ethnic varieties. She saw more than one person with hair the same shade as hers, although some were dressed in ratty black clothes and looked as if they hadn't bathed in days. Many had metal rings and baubles protruding from their faces. Their skin, what she could see of it, was covered in colorful illustrations. Perhaps this was some new method of remembering spells and incantations. These humans surely needed all the help they could get.

A teenager riding on a tiny board with wheels breezed by her, nearly knocking her into the giant brass lion positioned in front of the store. Without considering the consequences, Titania's hand shot out and she flicked her index finger, causing the front wheel of the apparatus to fly off into the street. The teenager went down face first, skidding to a stop at the feet of a group of horrified tourists. Titania turned on her expensive heels and brushed past the lion, dragging her fingers across its burnished surface. What an odd place to put a statue of a lion. And yet, it made perfect sense. If nothing else, it would serve to remind people that powerful forces were at work.

When she stepped through the threshold a small man with ginger-colored hair and freckles greeted her. "Welcome to A Garland of Letters," he said. "May I help you find something?"

Titania took the man in. She sensed he could help her, but she also sensed other things in this store. She found herself surrounded by a sea of books on the occult and eastern philosophy, bins of polished crystals, jewelry that incorporated many of those same crystals. The vibrations of all those crystals bounced around her in waves, but more than anything it was the smell of the shop that made her feel seasick. Sandalwood, patchouli, lavender, bergamot, sage. The aromas layered atop one another. Oils, incense, and magic permeated the store. It was clear that these scents were being used indiscriminately by uninitiated fools and the residual effects made her wobbly. "I'm looking for the essence of love-in-idleness. There are so many smells in here I can't tell if you have it or not."

The man smiled and stepped out from behind the counter. "Purple pansy? I haven't heard anyone call it love-in-idleness for a long time." Did Titania detect a sigh in his voice or was she just woozy? He led Titania across the store, past open bins of polished and unpolished crystals, some of which called to her, others of which repelled her. "I don't have any essence of purple pansy, but I do have some other things that might work as well." He gestured to a set of narrow, locked shelves nestled between floor-to-ceiling bookcases. "What do you need it for, exactly?"

Titania narrowed her eyes and looked harder at the ginger-haired man. "Do I know you?"

The man smiled slowly. His blue eyes twinkled with faerie mischief. "My name's Thomas Peaseblossom, your highness. I'm surprised you recognized me, although I shouldn't be. Your powers can, of course, see through any cloaking spell."

Titania frowned thinking how Puck had managed to keep Oberon hidden from her. "Peaseblossom? How?"

"I never thought I'd see you here, in my humble store, asking for, of all things, love-in-idleness." He shook his head and sighed. "And yet, here you are." He bowed his head slightly.

"When did you leave the Realm?" Not that she cared, but she needed his help.

He laughed. "I followed Robin. I always followed Robin." He turned back to the shelves and took a small key out of his pocket. "Now, for your request. You haven't told me what you're using the love-in-idleness for. If I don't know, I can't recommend a substitute."

"It's an adoration potion. What else does one use love-in-idleness for." She narrowed her eyes. "You know that."

He shrugged. "I thought perhaps you had discovered some other use. I just wanted to be sure. It certainly wouldn't do to disappoint my queen, after all this time."

"No, it certainly would not."

Peaseblossom unlocked the cabinet. Inside were three shelves each lined with small brown bottles with hand-written labels. "I might recommend a few drops of civet oil with a dash of dragon's blood oil mixed into a glass of red wine. Or you could apply it directly to the eyes for maximum effect. I'd be happy to mix the oils for you, on the house."

"Why no essence of love-in-idleness?" Titania was still trying to make sense of yet another of her subjects here in this human city.

He shrugged. "You're free to go to a home improvement store and purchase as many purple pansies as you need and make the essence yourself, but I'm not sure in this day of hybridization and genetic modification the essence will do what you want." He took down the two bottles he'd suggested and relocked the cabinet. "I guarantee these oils 100 percent. I vet all my sources thoroughly, or I grow the herbs and flowers myself." He grinned. "All organic and non-GMO, of course. Pink shops here sometimes. Do you know Pink?"

Titania frowned. "Well, you always were a superior alchemist. I'll take your suggestions and pay you for them."

Peaseblossom guided Titania back to the front of the store where he mixed her oils. "Please, your highness, I could never charge you." He placed the potion in a small brown shopping bag lined with fancy tissue paper. Titania took the bag but didn't leave. "Why do you stay in this horrendous place?"

He laughed. His smile was wide and bright. She didn't remember Peaseblossom ever being so cheerful. "Why not?" he said. "We're all here. Mustardseed is a good friend, although she did just return to the Realm to visit her daughter. Cobweb, Moth, Brightkin, Moonwort," he laughed. "Even Patch and Pinch are here. It's so like you not to have noticed." He shook his head. "Robin always was our favorite. So much fun, so much mischief." He leaned in over the counter and lowered his voice. "Shakespeare loved him, too. Is that why you banished him?"

"Shakespeare loved me, for the record, and Robin's had his revenge." Titania inhaled sharply then regretted it. "I didn't banish you."

"No, you didn't." Peaseblossom looked at her with sadness in his eyes for the first time. "Good luck with your machinations, your highness. I'll give your best to the others."

Titania nodded. The others? How many faeries were here in the human world, and why hadn't she noticed? Perhaps she should ask Iolanthe and Ondine to conduct a census. She could always command them to return to the Realm. But how humiliating would it be if they refused? Perhaps she was not as beloved as she had assumed. No matter. She didn't have to be beloved to rule.

Outside, Titania shimmered back to her hotel room. Once there, she sat on the edge of her bed, clutching the brown paper bag tightly in her lap.

# EIGHT

## I.

BERON WAS RELEASED from the hospital after a few days, but the doctor recommended that he rest for a few more at home before he returned to work. He'd also need to return for some blood tests to make sure that his iron levels remained normal. In the meantime, Jewell had an appointment to see her gynecologist.

Before she left, she leaned over him and tried to fluff his pillow. "You're sure you'll be all right?" she asked.

Oberon sat up a little straighter. "I feel somewhat stupid sitting in this bed. I feel fine."

"I know but . . ." She stood next to him and rested the back of her hand on his forehead. "You feel hot. I should stay."

Oberon took her hand and kissed her palm. He looked up at her and for a moment, Jewell saw those eyes she'd been so used to seeing. Mournful, pleading, rimmed in white. "Please don't look at me like that," she said.

"Like what?"

She took her hand away. "You know what you're doing."

"I think you need to stop stalling and go to the doctor." He grinned. "I'm going to lie here in bed and watch reruns of *The Dog Whisperer*. You know how I love to heckle Cesar Milan."

Jewell rolled her eyes.

"What?" Oberon said. "Like a human could ever be the leader of a pack." He huffed. "Dogs are not wolves."

"Okay, okay. You're right." She looked at her watch. "You've convinced me. I'm going."

He smiled at her. "Kiss me before you go."

She sighed and leaned. "I'll be back soon."

"I'll be here."

## 2.

Jewell had put her clothes back on and had been ushered by a nurse into her doctor's office. The desk was stacked with files and papers and books. Unlike the waiting room, there was nothing for Jewell to read while she awaited the doctor with the test results. She felt sick to her stomach, but it wasn't morning sickness. She loved Oberon. What did it mean to be in love with a man full of magic? Would she love him, only to have him die of the rapid onset of old age? Or would he be done in by iron poisoning, or some other magic related catastrophe? Every day it seemed there were a few more gray hairs on his head. If he died, she'd be alone, again. Only this time with a baby, who might also age unnaturally, or fall victim to some other magical malady. How would she explain a third grader who looked 40? She shook her head. Selfish. That's what she was. Reckless. Selfish. Out of control. These thoughts were only about her. Maybe that's why she had only ever dated men who were dicks. They were what she deserved. And what about Oberon? Look what she had done to him!

She considered the room again, suddenly feeling like her clothes were too tight. It was hot. The doctor definitely needed to crank up the air. She would tell her that as soon as she got her lazy ass in here. How long was she supposed to wait anyway? She was about to get up and go say something to the receptionist when the doctor pushed open the door.

"Hi, Jewell. Sorry to keep you waiting. Busy day." The doctor settled herself behind her desk then looked at Jewell with concern. "Are you feeling okay? Do you need some water?"

Jewell shook her head and exhaled slowly.

"Well, the urinalysis confirms that you are pregnant. I won't have the blood test results for a couple of days, but based on your physical exam, I'm confident you're pregnant."

Jewell's shoulders sagged. "Okay," she said.

The doctor folded her hands on top of her desk. "So, I take it this wasn't anything you planned."

Jewell shook her head. "Not exactly."

"Is the father in the picture?"

Jewell inhaled. "Yes. He's great. The father is not the issue. Not really." She looked up at the doctor, wishing that the doctor could read her mind and then tell her she was not crazy.

"You don't have to have a baby, at least you don't in Pennsylvania."

Jewell swallowed. "I'm not sure I could do that."

"It's not a decision you have to make right away." The doctor leaned back in her chair and smiled at Jewell with sympathy. "Look, you're young and healthy. You are at a great age to have a child, if that's what you want. If this is not the right time to have a baby, then that's a decision you can make too, without any judgement from anyone in this office. Go home. Think about what you want and talk to your partner. The office will call with the official blood test results when they come in. I can also recommend a counselor if you want."

Jewell folded her hands in her lap and shook her head. She didn't feel like she was going to be sick anymore, but the doctor was right. She didn't have to have a baby if she didn't want to.

"In the meantime, I'm going to give you a prescription for prenatal vitamins." The doctor stood and handed Jewell the prescription.

"Thanks, Doctor."

"Do you have any questions?"

Jewell stared at her lap. "Did you notice anything out of the ordinary?"

"Everything looked perfectly normal." The doctor stood and patted Jewell on the shoulder. "You going to be okay?"

Jewell nodded. "I think so."

"Why don't we plan to talk again in a couple of weeks, okay? Tell Julie in the front you need a follow up."

Jewell rose and followed the doctor out of the office. Once outside, she texted Melody:

Meet me at the park? Really need to talk.

Melody replied:

See you in ten at the bridge. I've got some news, too.

# 3.

Jewell reached out and gave Melody a tight hug. "Thank you so much for coming. I really don't know what to do." She let go of Melody and tears stung her eyes.

"What's the matter?"

"Let's walk, okay?" She wiped her eyes with the back of her hand.

Melody reached into her purse and handed Jewell a tissue. "You always do that," she said, half laughing, half crying.

"What's that?" Melody said.

"You always have a tissue or a wet nap. You'd be such a good mom," Jewell said, then dissolved into tears.

"Oh, honey." Melody folded her into her arms. "It's okay. Please tell me what's wrong."

"I'm sorry." Jewell blew her nose. "I'll get it together, I promise."

"Come on," Melody said and linked her arm through Jewell's. The two women strode up the bridge that arched over the park and down to the boardwalk. "I love this so much," Melody said gesturing out over the Schuylkill River.

Jewell pulled Melody's elbow in closer. "With the sun shining like this, it all looks so sparkly, so grand." She bit her lower lip.

"Are you going to tell me what's going on?"

Jewell nodded and took a deep breath. "I'm pregnant."

Melody stopped short. "What?"

"I'm going to have a baby. Well, at least I hope it's a baby!" Jewell let out a short desperate laugh. "Jesus, it will be a baby, right?"

"This is Oberon's child. You're sure it's not Simon's?"

Jewell narrowed her eyes. "Come on."

"Wow." Melody stretched out the "o" like the news was just now sinking in. "A baby. A few months ago, you were just hoping to find a nice boyfriend."

Jewell started to tear up again. "I know. This is crazy." She grabbed Melody by the shoulders. "You've got to help me figure out what to do."

"What's there to figure out?" She pulled Jewell down the boardwalk, dodging a speeding cyclist as he whizzed past them. "Should I have this baby?"

Melody motioned to a bench that looked out over the water and they sat. "Is that really an option for you?"

"What do you mean? As my doctor said, 'in Pennsylvania at least, it's still my right not to have a baby.'"

"Of course, I know that, but you're in a unique situation. That baby could have magical powers or something." She grabbed Jewell's arm. "Oh my god, what if it's like *Rosemary's Baby* or the *Exorcist*?"

"Are you sure you're a doctor?"

"That's what my diploma says." Melody smiled.

"Well first, Oberon's a faerie, not a demon." Jewell leaned back into the bench. She studied the dancing reflections of the sun on the water, trying to work it all out. "I mean, humans and animals can't procreate. Not even humans and chimps. Genetically that's not possible, so the baby must be human. That's science. There's no getting around that, right? Oberon's a man. Man, plus woman, equals human baby. Right, doctor?"

"According to everything I know to be empirically true, that is correct." She paused. Jewell could see she was thinking hard about what to say next. Not that Jewell wanted her to add a big *but* to a statement that had the word empirical in it.

"I'm beginning to believe that magic is nothing but science that we don't understand yet." Melody squeezed Jewell's hand hard. "If we look at the nature of discoveries historically, this certainly holds true."

"Normally, I get excited when you talk all science-y, but today this isn't really making me feel any better."

"I'm sorry. Bobby and I have been discussing this a lot lately, for obvious reasons, I guess. Truthfully, I would love to write a big paper on this—do a study on Oberon, Bobby—whomever else would let me. But I'd also really like to keep my job."

"It would require outing them all, too."

"Yes. Well. There is that." Melody fell silent for a moment. Jewell could imagine how hard it was for Melody to not follow every path of inquiry. It was her nature and what made her so good at what she did.

"Well, what did the doctor say—besides talking to you about what's still legal in Pennsylvania?" Melody said at last.

"She said everything looks normal, but the blood work wouldn't be in for a few days." Jewell paused as a jogger pushing a stroller ran past them. "She said I should think about what I want to do."

"Have you told Oberon?"

Jewell shook her head. "He knows anyway. Somehow. So do Bobby and Titania, I think."

"Titania." Melody practically growled her name.

"Yeah, sorry. I don't really know what her deal is."

"Did you know she's their queen?"

Jewell nodded.

"Did you also know that she and Bobby used to be a thing?"

"No. Really? I can't see it."

"Bobby's being all cagey about it, but yeah, they were to-gether and then Bobby did something, and she got pissed and she banished him. She actually banished him! Who does that? I mean I guess I should be grateful. If she hadn't, I probably never would have met him, you know? And then I started thinking, what the hell? How long has he been here anyway?" She looked at Jewell and then looked away. "I mean how old is he?" She paused and when Jewell realized she was waiting for her to an-swer, all she could do was shrug. "Great. I was really hoping you might know that."

"If it helps, I don't think they are immortal exactly. I mean they can die—I think. They just live a really long time."

"Funny you should mention that. I was curious to look at Oberon's blood on a cellular level."

"And?"

"Well, it does look as if Oberon's cells are aging abnormally fast. Which is what we thought. I'm going to culture them to see if I can get them to replicate. That way I might be able to tell how fast they're aging and why."

"Basically, you're confirming what we've guessed at, but don't really know anything that might help him."

"Yeah. Sorry about that."

They sat together on the bench staring out at the water.

"Magic is fucked up," Melody said.

"You aren't kidding," Jewell said. "You need to talk to Bobby. Get him to tell you the whole truth."

"And you need to talk to Oberon."

"But we don't need to do that right this minute, do we?"

"No."

"Good."

They slumped together, their shoulders touching, their heads inches apart. Around them birds chirped and sang. Cyclists and joggers streamed past them in a long human blur. Melody held Jewell's hand. "Bobby talks about Shakespeare like he knew him."

"Yep."

She let go of Melody's hand and let her chin fall to her chest. "What in the world is going on?"

Melody put her arm around Jewell. "I think we're in a situation where we have to just accept as fact what we can see. If we start to question reality, we might just go crazy."

Jewell nodded.

"You are pregnant with what in all likelihood will be a baby with magic powers, and I have been sleeping with a man who is older than America. I'm just going to state things as truths and pretend like it's normal. I don't know that we have any other choice."

"No wonder Bobby loves you." Jewell sagged into her friend's embrace. "You are so smart."

Melody sat up and laughed. "Who says I'm smart? I think I have just given you the classic definition of denial."

Jewell smiled for the first time all afternoon. "Now that we've got that settled. What do I do about this baby—or whatever it is?"

Melody patted Jewell's arm. "It's a baby, don't get carried away. And with you and Oberon as the parents it will be a beautiful, loved baby that will probably be able to levitate furniture and travel through time and space."

"Those could be very helpful skills."

"Would save on airfare and furniture movers."

"There is that."

Jewell laughed. She was grateful that Melody was here. She knew that as much as she wanted to make this kind of decision on her own, she really did need to talk to Oberon. Knowing about the baby and discussing its realities were two very different things. Magical, half-magical—whatever this baby turned out to be—she was sure she did not want to terminate the pregnancy. She was smart, had a good job. She was able to support a child on her own, if she had to, though it was not anything that she'd ever considered. She'd always been so careful. Condoms. The pill. Must have been Oberon's magic sperm. Perhaps the universe was telling her that this was something she was meant to do. Maybe Bobby and Melody could figure out some way to reverse Oberon's rapid aging and the two of them could live a long and happy life together raising their child. Anything was possible, right?

"Hey," Melody touched her arm. "You okay?"

Jewell nodded. "Yes. Let's go home."

# 4.

Jewell waited for Oberon on the couch. She'd come home to find a note saying that he couldn't stand being in bed anymore and that he had gone to work. She was annoyed and anxious, but she couldn't blame him. It must be extra hard for someone like him to be trapped in the apartment all day. Around 10, she heard his key in the lock and sat up, curling her feet underneath her. She did her best to look relaxed, although she knew she probably wasn't doing a very good job.

"What are you still doing up?" He shrugged off his boots by the door.

"I thought we should probably talk. I was surprised you weren't here when I got home after the doctor's."

"Didn't you get my note?"

"I did. Your handwriting is so good, by the way."

He smiled and sat down next to her, that familiar smell of the kitchen filling the space between them. "Practice, practice, practice."

She took his hand. He seemed so tired. He shouldn't have gone in and now she was worried.

"What's the matter? Everything's okay with the baby, right?"

She let go of his hand and sat back. "How did you know I was pregnant?"

"What do you mean?"

"I mean that you and Bobby both made comments to me about being pregnant without me saying anything to either of you. Titania and Bobby talked about it like I wasn't even in the room." She folded her hands in her lap. "So, I want you to tell me how you knew."

Oberon shook his head. "I don't know exactly. It was the same way when I first met Bobby. I knew he was a faerie even before I saw him. It's like I could feel his magic. Titania, too." He paused for a moment, examining his fingernails. "It's hard for me to concentrate when I'm in the same room with her." He did his best to hold Jewell's gaze, but she could tell he wanted to look away. "It's like her presence pushes all the air out of the room. I swear I can feel her thinking about me even when she's not there."

"That doesn't sound good."

Oberon shrugged and looked away. "I don't know if it's good or bad. It just is."

Jewell touched him, encouraging him to continue. "You and I are connected. She and I are connected. I don't know what any of it means." He sighed. "Being human is hard." She reached out and stroked his cheek, and he let his face rest in her palm, looked at her with sad eyes. "Do you remember when you used to look at me and say things like, what a simple life you must have?" She nodded. "Now I know exactly what you mean." He paused, held up his hands, and examined them. "I mean, look at these things." He wiggled his fingers. "I mean really. This is magic. I can pick stuff up, make wonderful food, touch you and actually feel your skin with my skin." He brushed the back of his hand down her bare forearm.

She inhaled, needed to explain her feelings, but didn't know how to start. "I am pregnant, but you already knew that. Now we have to decide whether or not we want to have a baby."

He tilted his chin at her.

"I mean, just because I'm pregnant doesn't mean I have to have a baby."

"Where does it go?"

Jewell exhaled. "It doesn't go anywhere. I can have a procedure, at the doctor's office, so that I wouldn't be pregnant anymore." She could see the glimmer of recognition in his eyes, and he frowned.

"Is that what you want?"

"I'm not sure what I want, but it's not just my decision. I didn't make the baby by myself, and I don't plan to raise it by myself. I'm asking you what you want."

He leaned back. She could see him thinking and wondered if anyone had ever asked him what he wanted. She wasn't sure she had, and that made her feel awful. "I don't have much of a context for this. I know what a baby is. I know how the baby was created and that it's inside you, but I don't have any idea beyond that what any of this really means."

Jewell let out a short breathy laugh. "I'm not sure I do either. I always assumed that I'd have children and hoped that I'd be married, or at least have partner." She took his hand. "Are we partners?"

He pulled her to him. "Yes, Jewell. You're my human." He kissed her. "I love you."

She pushed him back, looked him directly in the eye. "But are we partners? You think things are complicated now. Having a child will only make things more complicated." She let her hand rest on her stomach. "I'm not sure I can do it by myself. I know I don't want to."

He shook his head. "I'm not going anyplace. Why do you think you'd be alone?"

"I'm worried about this." She brushed her fingers through his temples.

"Why, because I've gotten a few gray hairs?"

She curled into his side and let her head rest on his chest. "I'm worried because we don't know what's going to happen."

He laughed. "When does anyone ever know what's going to happen?"

"I suppose you've got a point." She sat up and looked at him. "Has Bobby said anything to you about any of this?"

He shook his head. "Not much. He's having a friend of his make up some of the anti-iron medication for me. I'll need to go pick it up in a day or so."

"That's good."

"He runs a store on South Street called A Garland of Letters."

Jewell sat up a little straighter. "I know that store. What a cool place."

"He said the guy's name was Thomas Peaseblossom."

"Seriously?"

"Why, do you know him?"

Jewell shook her head. "No. I've been in the store, but I've never met the owner. Peaseblossom is a character in the play."

"What play?"

"*A Midsummer Night's Dream.* It's the play I quoted that started this whole mess. Titania, Bobby or Robin, and this guy Peaseblossom are all characters in that play."

"Oh?"

"And so are you, by the way."

"What do you mean? I'm a character in this play?"

Jewell laughed. She'd never really thought about any of this before. She had nothing but questions for Bobby—about everything. Jewell jumped up and started to dig through piles of DVDs stacked against the wall next to the TV. "Maybe I've got a copy somewhere." She dug around some more but came up empty-handed.

"So, who was I?"

"There is a character named Oberon, but he is the—" She stopped short. But he was the king of the faeries and married to the queen. Whose name was Titania. She swallowed and turned towards him slowly. Oberon propped his feet up on the coffee table.

"Well?"

Jewell stood with her hands on her hips. "I had a dog once that was so regal and wonderful that I named him Oberon, after the King of the Faeries in a very famous play by William Shakespeare."

"I used to be the king?"

"I don't think so." She tried to sound convincing.

"Who was Robin?"

"Robin was Oberon's sidekick and hatchet man. His nickname was Puck. The two of them played a very dirty trick on Titania."

"What did they do?"

"They tricked her into falling in love with a very silly man who had the head of a donkey."

"Why did he have a donkey head?"

"Because Robin thought it would be funny. And also, it's kind of a metaphor."

"Robin turned this guy's head into a donkey head."

"Yes."

"I still don't get it. Why?"

"I guess they thought it would be funny—or rather Shakespeare thought it would be funny. It was silly. Elizabethan audiences responded to silly things. They did it because Oberon was mad at Titania for something she did." She sat down on the coffee table suddenly exhausted. "And because faeries seem to get bored easily and aren't terribly nice."

"What did she do?"

She shook her head. This could go on all night. "I honestly don't remember."

"I don't get it, Jewell. Why would he do something like that to her?"

She exhaled loudly. "Because he was a dick."

"I still don't understand."

"They were married, and he wanted something that she had, and she said no and so he and Robin played this awful trick on her."

"I was married to Titania?"

"Technically, a character named Oberon was married to a character named Titania. In the play. What went on in Faerieland," She made finger quotes around the word faerie. "I honestly have no idea. I guess we should start making a list of things to ask Bobby." She wanted to make him understand. But understand what exactly? She was as confused as he was. Were there parts of the play that were true? Titania and Bobby were real enough—and Peaseblossom, it seemed. Oberon looked so tired. She needed him to drop this and convince him to get some rest. "I guess we're not going to figure anything out tonight. Maybe we should just go to bed." Oberon straightened a little and looked around.

"What's the matter?" Jewell asked.

Oberon shook his head. "I don't think anything. Just had a weird feeling."

"You shouldn't have gone to work today. Are you taking your prescription?"

"Yes." He nodded. "Well, you're probably right." He rose, extended his hand to Jewell and they went to bed.

# 5.

While Jewell lay curled against Oberon's side and both were deep in slumber, Titania shimmered into their bedroom. She clutched Thomas Peaseblossom's potion tightly in her hand. She had other potions and powders in a pouch tied loosely at her waist.

Earlier that night, she'd made up her mind that she was tired of waiting and that there was no reason to delay. So long as Oberon wanted to go with her, getting him through the veil would not cause her any problems. That's where Peaseblossom's potion came in. Two simple drops in his eyes. That's all it would take. When he opened his eyes he would see her, looking resplendent as usual, standing over him, and he'd fall madly and irrevocably in love. Well, maybe not irrevocably, but in love enough to make him compliant. And, she'd decided, even if she couldn't get him through to the Realm, he'd at least be with her, not with this wretched pathetic human!

A sliver of light slid under the window blind illuminating a small fraction of the otherwise dark room. Titania tiptoed around the bed so that she stood next to Jewell. She looked at the woman's face. She had sweet but simple features, completely unworthy of the kind of beauty that Oberon possessed. Plus, she was human and would only get uglier as she aged. This was no kind of companion for someone as noble and beautiful as Oberon. Relations between humans and the magical always ended in tragedy. Look what had happened to her sisters! She was doing this wretched woman a favor. Anyone could see that.

She removed a pinch of faerie dust from the pouch at her waist and blew it over Jewell. "Sleep," she whispered. "Sleep deep and long." Once she was confident that Jewell would not wake, she moved to Oberon's side of the bed. He shifted in his sleep and Titania froze, afraid he would awaken and find her lurking in his bedroom. She needed to move quickly. She positioned herself near the head of the bed and kneeled, so that she was very near his face. She removed the stopper from the potion bottle and dripped a stopper full onto each of Oberon's closed eyelids.

She expected the potion to be absorbed immediately through Oberon's eyelids, but that's not what happened. Instead, the liquid rolled right off his eyelids and down the sides of his face. She inhaled sharply through her nose. Granted, it had been a very long time since she'd had cause to use such a potion. So long, in fact, she could not remember what the occasion had been. Perhaps she was remembering the effects of the drug incorrectly. Oberon rubbed his face but did not wake. She tried again, this time using two dropperfuls on each eye. The potion continued to run down Oberon's face.

Titania stood and paced the room, no longer caring if she woke anyone. Something was wrong. Peaseblossom had assured her that this would work just as well as love-in-idleness. She pulled the dropper from the bottle and held it to her nose. The scent was familiar. She held the dropper to her tongue and tasted it. As soon as the potion hit her tongue she gagged, loudly. Chamomile and valerian water with a hint of anise oil. Faeries could not tolerate the taste of licorice in any form. That damned Peaseblossom! He knew this wasn't an alternative to love-in-idleness. It was a sleeping potion! A sleeping potion that he knew she'd likely taste if it didn't work, so he added a drop of licorice! She looked at the worthless potion in her hand and hurled it across the room. The bottle smashed against the wall just next to Oberon's head. He woke with a start and sat up groggily.

"Who's there?" he said. His voice was thick, and he rubbed his eyes smearing the potion across his face. "Titania?"

Titania exhaled at the sight of Oberon's bare torso.

"Titania, I know you're here. You might as well answer me." He swung his feet over the side of the bed. He stumbled as he moved toward her, reaching out for the footboard. She swooped in to catch him before he fell, but he braced himself on the bed first. He wore pajama bottoms, much to her disappointment.

"What did you do to me?"

Now that Titania was this close to him, her senses went haywire. A buzzing, electric current ran back and forth between them. His scent enveloped her, and she felt lightheaded, even though he also carried the woman's scent on his skin. If she didn't regain her own equilibrium, they might both crash to the floor. Which was exactly what happened a moment later. Jewell moaned and rolled over but did not wake. Oberon groaned and pushed Titania off him. He reached for the footboard of the bed and pulled himself up. "I have to get out of here. I can't breathe," he said and staggered toward the bedroom door. "Don't touch me!"

"Wait, my love," Titania said. She rolled to her side and pushed herself up and followed Oberon out of the bedroom. She caught him at the door slipping on his boots and a jacket.

"You can't run away from me," she said. "Why do you try?"

He shook his head and steadied himself against the doorframe. "What did you do to me?"

Titania huffed. "It wasn't me. It was that incompetent Peaseblossom." She folded her arms across her chest. "I never should have trusted him."

"I can't think," he said. "I need some air." He grabbed his keys from the hook by the door and left. Titania stood in the living room, trying to decide what to do. Should she follow him? Perhaps his grogginess was not just a reaction to the potion. Maybe he was also having the same kind of physical reaction that she was having. She closed her eyes and could sense his presence just outside the building. She shimmered, reappearing at his side.

"Why won't you leave me alone?" His face was creased with desperation.

"You know why."

He turned away and walked down the darkened city street, his shoulders hunched forward. A cab drove by, slowing to see if Titania wanted a ride, and she waved the driver away, repressing a desire to turn him into a toad. Other than the lone cabbie, they were the only two on the street. Titania still had a hard time recognizing it as night. There was so much other light beside that of the moon. She wondered how humans ever slept with so much light around them. She hurried after Oberon, who had turned the corner and was headed for the park near the river. Titania could tell he found solace in that place, and she did not try to speak to him again until they reached it.

The park was darker. A place meant for daylight. She could sense the echoes of many humans. And something else, but what, she wasn't sure. Oberon sat on a bench and stared at a smaller fenced-in area. The moon glimmered off the river. A light breeze rustled the budding leaves in the park. Titania sat next to Oberon, but she did not try to touch him.

Oberon sighed and turned to her. "Please, just say what you came to say and then leave."

"Do you know who I am?"

"You are the faerie that turned me into a man."

"Yes, I am that, but I'm also the queen of all faeries, chosen to be so because I have the most powerful magic."

"Congratulations." Oberon slumped against the bench.

Titania laughed. "That didn't take long."

"What?"

"Your adoption of human sarcasm."

Oberon shoved his hands in his pockets and pulled his jacket close. "You didn't come all this way to tell me how powerful you are. I already know that, probably better than any human that's ever encountered you."

She paused for a moment. Why wasn't he more enthusiastic? He didn't understand what she offered. She gazed out at the darkened landscape. This world was so plain. It had its moments of color, but everything was either green or gray, or some boring hue in between. In the Realm the world was a kaleidoscope of color. The light was bright, the dark could be fathomless. Oberon could have anything he wanted. All he had to do was ask.

She reached out to touch him, but he turned away from her. She sighed. "You should come with me."

"I'm not going to do that."

"There's so much I can give you. In the Realm anything is possible." She sat up a little higher. "I don't think you understand that I am the queen. I want to make you my king." She touched his sleeve and he let her hand rest on his arm, but he did not look at her. "Don't you remember how you felt that night when you first laid eyes on me? I know what I saw in your eyes."

Now Oberon pulled his elbow in, so her hand fell to the cold wooden bench. Even in the dim light, Titania could see flecks of gold swimming in his irises. She'd known that he was magical. That they'd done more than transform him into a man, but when she saw his eyes spark, she understood why he'd had a faerie reaction to iron. "You can feel this pull between us," she said. "I don't know why you're bothering to fight it so hard. It's only making you old."

She saw disbelief in his face. "What are you talking about?" he said.

She waved her hand and some inadvertent faerie dust swirled around his head like glow-in-the-dark confetti. He swatted at it, but it landed on him and was absorbed by his skin. "This," she said. "You getting old. I understand it now. It's not just a side-effect of your dog to human transformation. It's the energy you're using to fight me."

"You're a liar."

She laughed. "Without question. But why would I lie about something like this? I want you young and beautiful, not old and gray."

"Because you lie about everything? Because you want me to come with you—I don't know. Because you don't know how to do anything else?"

"Ah, see, I'm right." She reached up and touched his temple and the air between them sparked. "There's another gray hair."

He brushed her hand away. "Please don't touch me."

She let her hand linger on his cheek. "Why? Because it's so hard to say no to me when you feel this current pass between us? Can you imagine what it would be like to make love to me?" She paused and concentrated hard, sending a pulse of energy through her hand, into his cheek, and down his spine.

"Stop!" He bolted from the bench and stalked toward the river.

She appeared at his side and attempted to link her arm through his. He stopped mid-stride and took her by the shoulders. "You need to go back to the Realm, or wherever, and leave me alone. I don't love you. I love Jewell. She's my human, and that's all I have room for. I will never love anyone else."

"You don't love that woman. You feel obligated to her. You love me. That's why you're so upset."

"Listen to me," he said. He shook her. Not hard, but enough to get his point across. "I will never willingly go with you. I belong with Jewell. You should go home." He didn't wait for her to respond but turned and walked away. He caught the lip of his boot on something in the dark and nearly stumbled. Titania was at his side in an instant and kept him from falling. He sighed. "Please, Titania." When he said her name, she felt a chill run through her. "Please just go home. If you care about me at all that's what you'll do."

"If only I could forget I'd ever seen you!" Titania said. "I don't think you understand. I'm not sure I understand, but I don't know if I could go home even if I wanted to. And I don't want to. Not without you."

He shook his head and turned away from the river back toward his apartment. "I'm done."

"You can't walk away from me—you know that, right?"

He turned and faced her, his hands angry fists. Titania could see, even at this distance, the gold in his eyes start to swirl and flare. He flung his fist at her and bolt of golden energy shot through the air and enveloped her. "Titania, be gone!"

And she was. In an instant she was back in her hotel suite. She found herself standing on her bed for some reason, as if she'd jumped up there on purpose. She felt queasy, not sure exactly what had just happened. The only other creature that had ever forcibly shimmered her somewhere had been Robin Goodfellow and that had been over 400 years ago.

# 6.

Jewell woke when she heard Oberon turn the key in the lock. She was groggy and confused. It was still very dark outside, and she wasn't sure how long she'd been asleep. The alarm clock on the nightstand blinked 3:30. "Oberon?" she said. "Is that you?" When he didn't reply she rose and slipped on her robe. She found him sitting at the kitchen table staring at a glass of water.

"What's going on?" she asked. He didn't respond and when she touched his shoulder, he looked up at her with the saddest expression she'd ever seen. She sank into the seat next to him and took his hand. "Are you going to tell me why you're up in the middle of the night with your jacket on?"

"She was here."

"Who? Titania?"

He nodded. "She tried to do something to me. Put something in my eyes while I was sleeping. She's not going to give up until I go with her." He reached out to Jewell, and she slid into his lap, wrapped her arms around his neck. He buried his head in her chest. "I'm so tired, Jewell."

She took his head in her hands and saw that he had tears in his eyes. If it was possible, he looked even older now than he had that morning. She brushed away his tears with her thumbs and kissed his forehead, his cheeks, his mouth. He wrapped his arms more tightly around her waist. "It's okay," she said. "We'll figure it out."

"I don't know if I can fight her."

"We'll fight her, together," Jewell said brushing her fingers across his cheek. She didn't care if it sounded corny. She meant it. He closed his eyes and rested his head on her shoulder. "Do you think she'll come back tonight?" she asked.

He shook his head. "Her potion didn't work. That's why I woke up. I tried to get away, but she followed me down to the park." He sat back. "Something strange did happen, though."

"What's that?"

"She made me so mad that I turned around and said, 'be gone!' and she disappeared."

Jewell laughed. "Really? That's a good trick." She stood and pulled him up with her.

"I don't think it was a trick at all," he said. "I think it was magic."

"Magic?"

He shook his head as Jewell led him back to the bedroom. "I can't really describe how it felt. Wait," he said, pulling her to a stop in the living room. He let go of her hand and shook out his shoulders. Then he set his jaw and clenched his fists. Jewell watched as flecks of gold swirled around his irises. His fists pulsed with a golden aura, and Jewell backed away from him, telling herself there was no reason to be afraid. Oberon extended his right hand and directed the golden energy at the coffee table. Jewell watched as the table slowly levitated off the floor. She stole a glance at Oberon and watched as his expression transformed from one of concentration to one of pleasure. He exhaled and extended his index finger making a clockwise circle. The table twirled in the same direction and Oberon smiled. As he lowered his hand, the table settled back on the hardwood floor.

"How did you do that?" Jewell asked.

"Magic, I think." Oberon laughed, but the laugh was ragged and devolved into a cough. Jewell could see beads of sweat on his forehead, and again, she swore she could see more gray hair.

"You need to stop," she said trying to quell the panic rising in her gut. "Please don't do that again." She took his hand and when he looked at her, his eyes were clear. "Let's go to bed," she said. "You're going to make yourself sick again."

He nodded and followed her into the bedroom. In the morning she would talk to Bobby. Maybe he would know better what was going on. Her hand rested protectively on her abdomen. Magic. Always magic. Oberon shuffled into the bathroom, washed his face, and then slipped into bed. Jewell curled next to him as he fell asleep, just as he had done so many times back in the old days. She hoped this brought him the same kind of comfort it had brought her.

# 7.

The next morning, as Oberon slept, Jewell rose early and called her boss. "Yeah, I'm not feeling that well," she told him. "I'll be in tomorrow no matter what." He said she should take as much time as she needed, which kind of surprised her. She also let out a little sigh. Her next phone call was to Bobby. His voice was thick with sleep when he answered, but once she explained why she had called so early, he seemed to perk right up. "Meet me at Patchwork in 20 minutes. It's in the Hyatt on Chancellor Street," he said. "I want to see if a friend can join us. You said Titania tried to put something in his eyes?"

"That's what he said to me." She hoped she didn't sound as desperate as she felt. "Do you think he'll be okay if I leave him?"

"Truthfully," Bobby said. "You couldn't stop her even if you stayed. I'll cloak his location, but now she knows where you live, so that will only work so well." He exhaled into the receiver. "Don't worry. She'll probably sleep until noon, too. These encounters will take things out of her as well." He paused. "She wants us all to believe she's invincible, but I know better than anyone that's not true."

Jewell cradled the phone against her shoulder and twisted the hem of her shirt. "I guess I don't have a choice. See you in 20."

Jewell pulled open the door of the restaurant and was welcomed by the warm aroma of coffee and cinnamon. Diners sat at long tables and in booths, heads bent low over plates of eggs benedict and omelets. Toward the back of the crowded restaurant, tucked into a corner booth, Jewell saw Bobby waving at her. Normally the smells of the restaurant would have had her mouth watering, but not this morning.

"You look positively green," Bobby said as she slid into the booth across from him and next to a ginger-haired man she didn't know.

She tilted her head and shrugged. "I'll be okay. Didn't get a lot of sleep."

Bobby frowned. "I can imagine."

"I suppose you're the one person who can." She looked sideways at the man next to her.

"This is Thomas Peaseblossom," Bobby said, gesturing to the ginger-haired man.

"Peaseblossom? Seriously? Oberon did get that right."

Thomas looked at her and smiled. "A fan of the play, are you?" He extended his hand. "I know we've never met, but I do know your whole story."

Jewell felt dizzy. She closed her eyes. What was happening? Was half the population of Philadelphia from the Faerieland? Was the whole world just a big faerie joke? In the periphery of her vision, she saw Bobby motion for the waiter, who returned with a large glass of ice water. Jewell clutched it with both hands and sipped until she felt her head clear.

"If you permit me, I can help you with that nausea," Thomas said. His voice was soothing, his countenance radiated calmness.

Jewell put her hand over the top of her glass as he produced a small vial from his jacket pocket. Bobby reached across the table. "It's okay," he said. "Let him help you. It's what he does."

Again, she felt calmness radiate towards her, this time from Bobby. She shook her head. "What are you two doing to me? I thought we were going to talk about Oberon."

Bobby sighed. "We can sense that you're not feeling well and we're just trying to help you feel better."

Jewell sat back in the booth. "Well, it's freaking me out!"

"Okay," Bobby said, "but if you start to feel nauseated again, Thomas can help."

Jewell unbuttoned her jacket and took another sip of water. "Let's just talk about what we're going to do about the princess of darkness."

Peaseblossom released a short chuckle and then looked at Bobby. He shrugged. "I'm sorry, it was funny." He turned to Jewell. "It's good not to say her name. That just makes it easier for her to eavesdrop, or worse yet, find us."

Jewell clutched her glass. "She can eavesdrop on our conversations?"

"Although I cloak myself, it's possible," Bobby said. "A lot of things are possible."

"And?" Jewell said.

Peaseblossom lifted his coffee cup to his lips, took a long swallow, and then slowly set the cup back in its saucer. "Her majesty was in my store looking for the love-in-idleness elixir. Since you seem to be so familiar with the play, I'm assuming you know what that is and what it does."

She nodded. "If you put it in someone's eyes while they are sleeping, they will fall in love with the first person they see when they wake up."

"Yes, that's the basic gist of it. So, obviously, I couldn't give her any, sensing what she intended to do with it. Robin's been keeping me abreast of all the goings on."

"So that's why it didn't work. You sabotaged her."

Peaseblossom smiled with satisfaction. "I am an excellent herbalist."

The waiter returned to take their orders. Jewell ordered toast and coffee, while Bobby and Peaseblossom ordered ricotta pancakes with sides of eggs and sausage and maple syrup. She shook her head. They must have magical metabolisms, too.

"Thomas and I are old friends," Bobby said. "I'm not the only one that Titania banished."

"Technically, that's not true," Peaseblossom said. "She never banished me. I stayed because I wanted to."

Jewell shook her head and poured some cream into her coffee. "What exactly happened to cause your banishment?"

Bobby and Peaseblossom looked at each other and laughed. "It's really a funny story," Peaseblossom said. "But Robin should tell it."

Bobby waved his hand like he was trying to be humble, but Jewell could see that he was dying to tell her. "Okay, okay," he said. "Lots of us, through the years, have enjoyed spending time in the human world. Titania will tell you that the Realm is so beautiful, and you can have anything you want, blah, blah, blah. But the truth is, faeries, as a species," he paused and looked at Peaseblossom, "present company excluded of course," Peaseblossom nodded, "are boring. So, so, boring. This is why we used to steal human children—"

"What?" Jewell said.

"Yes, of course. Come on now. You must be familiar with the myth of the changeling?" He made finger quotes around the word myth.

"I read a lot of Shakespeare, but I'm not really up on my Celtic mythology."

"Celtic, Scandinavian, Germanic. We're everywhere, baby."

"Sorry."

Bobby frowned. "Too bad. Makes for entertaining reading, some of it." He forked a quarter of a pancake into his mouth and started chewing, which did not prevent him from talking. "Titania and I used to have this thing." He nodded his head when he said *thing* and Jewell wasn't quite sure what he meant.

"Do you mean you were a couple?"

Peaseblossom laughed.

"Something like that." Bobby shot Peaseblossom a shut-your-mouth glare.

Jewell spread some butter on her toast and took a small bite. This baby was giving her some magical morning sickness, that was for sure. "Okay," she said. "And?"

"I always liked to keep tabs on what was happening in the human realm. You know how we can open windows to look at things in other places."

Jewell shook her head. "I didn't know that."

"Wow, for someone who managed to conjure the Queen and her sisters through the veil against their will, you know remarkably little," Bobby said. "I'm surprised."

Jewell started to reply but let out a low exhale instead. She pressed her eyelids closed and breathed through her nose.

Peaseblossom placed his hand on Jewell's. "Please let me offer you some relief," he said. "I promise it won't hurt you or the baby."

She sighed. If she was ever going to get through this morning, she needed to do something. Everything seemed louder than normal, the lights brighter. All her energy was being consumed by not throwing up. "Okay."

Peaseblossom removed the vial from his jacket and placed a stopper full of blue tinged liquid into Jewell's water glass. "Drink this," he said. "I promise you'll feel right as rain."

She watched the blue liquid disappear into the water and picked up the glass. "What the hell," she said and drank the whole thing. And she did feel better. Instantly. She turned to Peaseblossom. "You are an excellent herbalist."

He slid the bottle towards her. "Keep it. I made it especially for you. One stopper full is all you'll need. It should last 24 to 48 hours."

"Do you want to hear this or not?" Bobby said.

"Yes, sorry," Jewell said as she slathered her cold toast with some homemade jam.

Bobby leaned in over his empty plate, but before he started, he waved the waiter over to the table. "I think my friend wants to order some more food."

Jewell looked up from her toast at the waiter with her mouth full. She was hungry. Very hungry in fact. "I'll have what they had," she said, waving her finger at Peaseblossom and Bobby. The waiter nodded and left.

"Anyway, I was bored, nothing new," Bobby began. "And I'd been following this playwright, Shakespeare."

"You were watching him from Fairyland?"

"Fairyland?"

"How am I supposed to know what it's called," Jewell said.

"Officially, our realm, which exists parallel to yours, is called Eventyrlandungen," Peaseblossom said. "But we all refer to it as the Realm. It's just simpler that way."

"Do you want to hear the story?" Bobby said. Jewell nodded. "Okay, okay, so back to Shakespeare. It's a very simple spell. All you need is some water and a bowl. Silver is best, but glass will do."

"Who knew?" Jewell said. The waiter arrived with her breakfast, and she tore into it like she hadn't eaten for days. "You can watch people like you can turn on a television?"

Bobby laughed. "Kind of. You don't always get an HD picture or sound, but you can see where they are, what they're doing, who they're with. Most faeries use it for locating people, other faeries, or lost objects, but you can watch people."

Jewell swallowed some pancakes and licked her lips. "You were watching Shakespeare and you got an idea."

Bobby clapped his hands together. "Exactly! You know how I love a good joke, and I thought, maybe I could shimmer on over to England and convince this Shakespeare fellow to write a spell into one of his plays."

"Why would you do something like that?" she asked.

"That's what I said to him," Peaseblossom said. "Titania never had a sense of humor. She takes herself rather seriously. And getting summoned through the veil is not the most pleasant experience." Peaseblossom poured Jewell and himself some more coffee from the thermal carafe on the table. "I knew she'd be angry."

"But you did it anyway," Jewell said.

"Obviously," Bobby said. "I just wanted to liven things up. Titania is a stiff. All that power and she never wanted to have any fun." Bobby rolled his eyes. "The thing was, once Shakespeare met Titania, he was enthralled by her. He decided he had to write a whole play about her. He put all of us in it, which I was okay with. At the time, she was okay with it, too." He pointed at Jewell. "If she tells you she wasn't flattered, she's a liar. The thing is, she took a liking to that Shakespeare, but he didn't want to come to the Realm with her and she got mad and banished all of us."

"Well, just you really," Peaseblossom said.

"Okay, just me."

"So how many of you are here?" Jewell asked.

"From that time?" Bobby looked a Peaseblossom and shrugged. "You might know better than me."

"There's myself, Robin, Mustardseed just went back, Moth, Blossombum—he's my cousin—and Bottom, who was also a faerie."

"I did not give Bottom a donkey head by the way," Bobby said. "That was all Shakespeare. Elizabethan audiences loved that shit."

"Good to know," Jewell said. "Still, I'd hate to be the victim of one of your pranks."

"There are quite a lot of us, actually," Peaseblossom said. "Over the years, which pass very, very slowly in the Realm, others have slipped through the veil, but Titania never paid any attention. She was too tied up with all that business with her sisters."

"Her sisters?"

"That is a story—actually stories—for another time. Although . . ." Bobby shook his head. "No. Back to the matter at hand. If you're really curious you can Google them. Iolanthe and Ondine. Not that you'll get the whole truth, but generally the mythology gets the gist of it right."

"What about Oberon?" Jewell said.

"Oberon was your dog," Bobby said.

"No, I mean the real Oberon. Shakespeare's inspiration."

Bobby shrugged. "I have no idea. Shakespeare was a writer after all. He made a lot of stuff up."

"I kind of always assumed," Peaseblossom said, "that Shakespeare was Oberon. He fell hard for her, but then there was that whole fling he had with you."

"What?" Jewell tried not to choke on her coffee.

"Don't be so judgy, J.J. We live in a very fluid world."

"Who's judging?"

"It was a juicy little triangle, but we can talk about it later." Peaseblossom tapped his chin. "There is a chance Shakespeare got the name, anyway, from that old elf legend."

"How would he have known about that?"

Peaseblossom shook his head. "You love to tell that story. The drunker you get the more outrageous the version."

Bobby shook his head. "I never told him anything. That wasn't it. At least I don't think so." Jewell could see that Bobby was processing, but then he waved it off. "I think she was terrified to get involved with a human, even one as lovely as Shakespeare," Bobby said. "But she did love him. Of that I am convinced."

"Wait, weren't you two involved?" Jewell asked. "Weren't you jealous? I mean, if Shakespeare was Oberon, then what did that make you?" She leaned in over her empty pancake plate.

"Faeries don't really get jealous."

"Right," Peaseblossom said. "There was a bit of a row, which is what precipitated the banishment. Everyone, it turns out, was sleeping with everyone. You know actors."

"And faeries, it seems," Jewell said. "Well, this explains a lot, but what I need to know now is what I can do to stop her from taking *my* Oberon back to the Realm with her."

Peaseblossom and Bobby exchanged glances. "What?" she said. "What aren't you telling me? I thought this was the whole reason why you convinced me to come down here this morning."

She pushed her plate away. She'd lost her appetite again, but not because she was feeling sick.

"Thomas and I have been discussing this," Bobby said. "We're not sure what to do."

"Great," Jewell said. "I hope you're paying for breakfast. I could have stayed in my apartment and felt hopeless."

"No one said the situation was hopeless."

"Seems pretty hopeless to me." She rubbed her eyes. She did not want to cry in front of these two. "I swear every hour Oberon gets older. Titania told him it was because he was fighting her so hard. Could that be true?"

Peaseblossom and Bobby looked at each other but said nothing.

"He also said that last night he was able to shimmer her away." She looked up at them. "Isn't that what you call it?"

"He did? How did he do that?" The waiter came to the table to drop the check and Bobby handed him his credit card.

"I was kidding about paying."

Bobby waved her off. "Please. I've been accumulating wealth for the last 400 years. I can afford breakfast."

"Tell me what he did," Peaseblossom said.

"I wasn't with him in the park, but later in the apartment he showed me. He made his hands into fists and concentrated hard. This gold light swirled around his eyes and his fists, and he made the coffee table levitate."

"Gold?" Peaseblossom let out a slow breath. "Well, that's unexpected."

Jewell let her hand rest on her still flat stomach. "Do you think the baby will be magical?" She felt panicky. She'd been sitting in this booth too long. It was clear to her that these two did not know any more than she did. "Stop looking at each other like I'm not sitting here and can see you," Jewell said a little more loudly than she'd intended. "If you two can't help me, I am totally screwed."

"It'll be okay." The waiter returned with the credit card slip and Bobby signed. "Let's take a walk," he said.

The three of them left the restaurant and headed down Chancellor Street toward Rittenhouse Square. Bobby put his arm around Jewell's shoulder, and she found some comfort in this gesture. Magic. Damned magic. There were times when she thought she was losing her mind. That she must be trapped inside a twisted fantasy of some kind. Her boyfriend had impregnated her with a magic baby and the Queen of the Faeries wanted to kidnap said boyfriend. Meanwhile, her two allies were a couple of faerie jokesters who didn't know anything more than she did.

They paused for the light to change at 18$^{th}$ and Walnut Streets and crossed into Rittenhouse Square. As usual, there were lots of people in the park ranging from the homeless to the ultra-rich. Curtis Institute of Music students played frisbee or sat chatting with friends on one of the many park benches that edged the sidewalks. Young moms pushed strollers down those sidewalks making wide arcs around the few unwashed men slumped in the grass or asleep on a bench. An older woman, sitting on a bench near Walnut Street, rocked back and forth talking to herself. Three toddlers, not too far past the old woman, chased a small dog around on a patch of grass, under the watchful eye of their nanny.

"I've always loved this park," Peaseblossom said.

"Me too," Jewell said.

"There are a lot of faeries in this city," Peaseblossom said. "We're drawn to it because it's old and there are people here who still believe in magic."

"If you're talking about the sports fans, I think you might be confusing magic with miracles." Jewell smiled a little.

"At least you haven't lost your sense of humor," Bobby said.

Jewell came to a stop near the fountain. She stared at the bronze face of what she always assumed was Zeus. Water poured out of his mouth like he was angry or sick, she couldn't decide. The three of them sat on a bench facing the fountain. Children and their parents scurried around them. Rich ladies walked their tiny dogs. A lone trumpet player had cracked his or her practice room window across 18th Street at Curtis, and now faint strains of a baroque trumpet voluntary floated on the breeze. Jewell closed her eyes and took a deep breath. They had to figure something out. Peaseblossom took her hand, and she opened her eyes and smiled at him.

"If you can read my mind, please don't tell me," she said.

"I can't read your mind," he said. "But your face is easy enough to read."

Bobby stood up and faced them. "We need reinforcements. Someone who was at the scene of the crime. Someone who can tell us exactly what we're up against."

"What do you mean?"

"I mean, I can't really formulate a strategy without all the information. If Oberon has magic in him, then that changes everything."

"For the better or the worse?" Jewell asked.

"Can't say, J.J.," Bobby said. Jewell started to protest, but Bobby held up his hand. "Let me finish. We've forgotten all about the queen's precious sisters."

"Are you sure about this Robin?" Peaseblossom shook his head. "What if by bringing them here, we're only reinforcing her power?"

Bobby paced in front of the bench like a general making a war plan. "It might be a chance we have to take."

Jewell stood and blocked his path. "What about Melody? Maybe she can develop a serum or vaccine that can reverse this. She tested his blood. I mean, this is what she does, right? She said she wanted to write—"

Bobby held up his hand and she stopped mid-sentence. "My Melody is a certified genius, as you well know, but how many years does it take to create drugs and vaccines in the real world? This isn't an episode of *Star Trek*."

Jewell sat down, defeated. "Do you have to summon them?" Jewell asked. "Can you communicate with them with that bowl thingy?" Peaseblossom and Bobby looked at each other. "You're doing that thing again where you look at each other like I'm not here," Jewell said. Peaseblossom rose and stood next to the closest corner of the fountain. He closed his eyes and waved his right hand in a circular motion. Jewell rose to get a better look. "What's he doing?" she whispered to Bobby.

"That bowl thingy," Bobby said. His smile did little to reassure Jewell.

"It'll work in a fountain?" she said.

Bobby shrugged. "Guess we'll find out."

They stepped up behind Peaseblossom as an image began to form in the corner of the fountain. Jewell could not believe what she was seeing, even after everything she'd already witnessed. The water turned opaque, almost mirror-like. In the center, the image of a woman's face appeared. She looked strikingly like Titania, only her hair was ombré shades of green. It looked almost like seaweed. Her ears rose to gentle points and her skin seemed to glow with a kind of opalescence. Not sparkly, like those movie vampires, but swirly, like mother-of-pearl. Jewell couldn't decide if this was how she really looked or if it was an effect of looking at her through the fountain. The woman smiled out at them like she was looking in a mirror, not at anyone in particular.

"Is this a two-way thing?" Jewell asked, tugging on Bobby's sleeve.

"We'll see," he said. "Thomas knows what he's doing."

Peaseblossom bent down and tapped the water, only it looked as if he were tapping the woman's forehead. She looked up, as if startled, then looked around her. They could see her lips moving but could not hear what she was saying. Peaseblossom tapped the water again, only over her mouth this time. Suddenly Jewell, and anyone else standing within 10 feet of them, could hear what the woman was saying. "Who's there?" she said. Bobby looked at Jewell, who motioned to a homeless man sleeping on nearby bench. The man stumbled awake, lurching toward them. "It's me, baby!" he shouted. Bobby closed his eyes and made a fist. Jewell watched as a ball of amber light appeared to glow around his hand. As surreptitiously as possible, Bobby flicked his wrist outward, making a circle of light around himself, Jewell, and Peaseblossom. Jewell looked at him and raised her eyebrows.

"Hey!" the man said and then sat down heavily on the bench.

"Dome of invisibility," Bobby said, like that explained everything.

"Oh."

"We don't need any eavesdroppers, now do we?"

"Certainly not." She leaned in closer to Peaseblossom. "Who is she?" Jewell asked.

"Iolanthe," Bobby said. "Titania's sister. One of them, anyway."

"The practical one," Peaseblossom said.

"Coming from you, that's a compliment, I guess," Iolanthe said.

"Shit." Jewell clutched Peaseblossom's shoulder. "She can hear us!"

"Yes, I can," Iolanthe said. "It's been a long time, Peaseblossom. I assume Robin is with you?"

"You can," Peaseblossom said. "Although I prefer to be called Thomas these days."

"Very well, Thomas. To what do I owe the pleasure?"

Bobby moved in closer so that the woman in the water could see him too. "Long time no see, 'Lanthe. What's it been four, five hundred years?"

"Probably longer," Iolanthe said. "I can't imagine that you miss me. What do you want?"

"We need to know how to stop Titania," Jewell said.

"You!" Iolanthe said. "If it weren't for you, my sister would be back here where she belongs. The goblins and orcs are plotting an uprising. The sprites are talking about secession. Meanwhile, most of the Council has taken up residence in the Grand Pavilion and are refusing to leave, the drunken idiots. Things haven't been this bad in a millennium. Why should I help you?"

"Simple. Because we want Titania to go back to the Realm as much as you do," Jewell said.

"Robin, what's going on?" Iolanthe said. She brushed her multi-colored hair over her shoulder and stared hard into whatever it was she was looking through.

Bobby moved Jewell aside and bent directly over the fountain. "It's good to see you princess."

"Yes, yes. Get on with it."

"Will you and Ondine come? We need your help."

"So, I've heard."

"There are things going on that Thomas and I don't know how to counteract."

"I hope you know I've no argument with you, Robin. I've actually been lobbying on your behalf."

"I appreciate that, but I don't really care about going back to the Realm. I like living with humans as much as you did."

"That's only because human women are more forgiving than human men. You look pretty good by the way."

"Thanks," Bobby said. Jewell tugged on his sleeve and pointed at the small crowd that had started to gather at the edges of the invisibility bubble he'd created. People could see that the space was empty and yet they could not pass through it. "I can't really get into details right now. Can you come?"

Iolanthe sighed. "One of us has to stay and keep an eye on the goblins and the orcs. You know how they can get."

Bobby shrugged. "I have some vague memories of my parents telling tales about their previous uprisings. Nothing like the old stories they told about the war with the elves, but still."

"Such a mess. The Glade was in ruins. They turned all the trees in the forest black. They actually stormed the castle," she said. "Who knows what will happen when they finally figure out Titania is gone!"

"Yes. I know. It sounds horrible," Bobby said. "All the more reason for you to help us."

"You really don't think you can handle things without me?"

Peaseblossom leaned in. "It seems that you three did more than transform Oberon into a man."

Iolanthe pursed her lips and folded her arms across her chest. "It's magic, not science."

"You said it, my friend," Bobby said. "Will you come?"

"I will," she said. "But you might not like the outcome."

"What does that mean?" Jewell said.

Iolanthe narrowed her eyes. "It means that what's happening might be outside of anyone's control. You'd better prepare yourself for that."

"Bring it," Jewell said.

"Determination. Interesting. No wonder you got under my sister's skin so easily."

Bobby put his arm around her shoulder. "Jewell, we need Iolanthe's help."

Jewell looked away and then back at the woman's face floating in the fountain. "I'm sorry. I'm scared. I don't want to lose Oberon any more than you want to lose your sister."

Iolanthe bristled. "My sister is the Queen, the most powerful of all the faeries. Oberon on the other hand, I'm not sure what he is, but I will come."

"Thank you," Bobby said.

Jewell looked around at the number of people pushing at the seemingly empty space in front of them. It was starting to look like a convention of mimes. "We need to wrap this up before someone calls the police."

"We'll see you soon," Peaseblossom said to Iolanthe. She nodded and the shimmering window into Realm disappeared.

"Let's get out of here." Bobby snapped his fingers and the dome disappeared. A woman fell forward toward them, gasping in surprise.

Jewell could hear the whispers and feel the stares as the three of them moved through the park. "Can't you make them all forget or something?" she said her chin tucked into her shoulder.

Bobby snorted. "Not enough faerie dust in the world for that."

"Well, at least she said she'd come," Jewell said.

They crossed the park in silence and stopped at the crosswalk at 19$^{th}$ and Walnut. "I need to get to the restaurant," Bobby said.

He looked over Jewell's shoulder at Peaseblossom for a moment then took her by the shoulders. "Iolanthe was right. You need to prepare yourself that there may not be anything we can do."

Jewell looked from Bobby to Peaseblossom and back again. "About what? What aren't you saying to me?"

Bobby shook his head. "I don't know. We can probably convince Titania to return to the Realm, unless there's some magical force compelling her to stay that we don't know about. Who knows? But we might not be able to slow Oberon's aging. If a dog ages approximately seven years for every human year, then he should be?"

"Thirty-five," Jewell said. "Or there about."

"He looks older than that to me," Bobby said.

Jewell bit her lip and crossed her arms. "Lots of people get gray hair in their thirties."

"Yes, but usually—"

Jewell interrupted him. "Titania said it was because he was fighting her. That it was the magic that was making him age. We just need to figure out how to counteract that."

"Maybe," Bobby said. "Didn't Melody say his cells were aging rapidly?"

"Yes. But she couldn't tell how fast."

Jewell turned to Peaseblossom. "You're the apothecary. You must have a potion or spell that can fix this."

Peaseblossom squeezed her arm. "I will try."

"Go home, Jewell," Bobby said. "Keep Oberon close and make him rest. Tell him if he tries to come into work, I will fire him." He gave her a quick hug then steered her towards the crosswalk. She turned and looked at Bobby and Peaseblossom standing on the sidewalk and wondered again what exactly it was that they weren't telling her.

# NINE

## I.

HEN JEWELL RETURNED, she found Oberon asleep in bed. She doubted he'd stirred the entire time she'd been gone. She watched him for a bit, resisting the urge to stroke his cheek or let her fingers linger on the curve of his neck. When a person is so deeply asleep, she thought, when his face is so free from worry or stress, it should be easy to see their younger, simpler self. But Oberon had never been a child, not a human one at any rate. Melody was right. This was her new reality. She let her hand rest on her abdomen. Would they ever have a chance to be a real family?

She left Oberon a note taped to the back of the door letting him know that she was going for a walk, just in case he woke and wondered why she wasn't there. It was early afternoon when she left the apartment building. The park called to her from across the street. She felt her phone buzz in her pocket, and when she took it out, she saw a text from Melody:

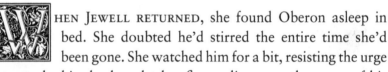

r u ok?

She responded:

been better

Lunch?

Not hungry.

Friend?

Always.

R u at the park?

Where else.

Be there in 10.

K. on the boardwalk.

Jewell meandered across the street and through the park. She could hear the dogs barking at the dog run and wondered if Steve might be there with Fang. What would someone like him think of all this? What would anyone think? There were days when she expected to wake up and realize it had all been a stupid dream, to find Oberon curled at the end of her bed, looking at her with his sad brown eyes, his head tilted to the side, as if he were questioning her sanity. But that kind of thing only happened in bad TV shows and in crappy romance novels. She found a bench near the entrance to the boardwalk and watched a jet skier fly up the Schuylkill. She shook her head. She'd lived in, or near, this city her whole life. As a kid, most people talked about the river the way people talked about the canals in Venice—too polluted to go anywhere near—and now people were out on jet skis. Who said the world couldn't change for the better? She slipped on her sunglasses and let her head rest against the back of the bench. The sun felt warm on her face, and she thought she might not leave this spot ever again when Melody tapped her on the shoulder.

Jewell smiled at her friend. "I suppose you spoke to Bobby." She nodded and sat down. "Has what's-her-name," she paused for a moment, "Iolanthe showed up yet?"

"I don't think so," Melody said.

"I feel like there's something that Bobby and Thomas are not telling me. Do you know what it is?"

Melody shrugged. "Bobby hasn't said much to me. I mean, I knew when I got involved with him, we were going to have our challenges, but I didn't exactly expect this." She sat on the bench and stared out at the water. "Can you believe people are riding their jet skis out here now?"

"I was just thinking the same thing," Jewell said. "Wait. What do you mean?"

"What do you mean, what do I mean?"

"Don't do that, Mel. How long have you known Bobby was a faerie?"

Melody turned away from her. "Since Oberon told us."

"Bullshit."

"Jewell, come on."

"Seriously Mel, how long?"

"He told me a couple of months after we started going out."

"And what, you just forgot to tell me?"

Melody's mouth was a stiff straight line. "No. I made a conscious choice not to tell you, because I didn't want you to think

I was nuts. I love Bobby and I just want to spend whatever time I can with him. He's had lovers before me and he'll have them after, and I'm okay with that."

"So, all your reactions to everything—Oberon, Titania, all of it was just acting?"

"Not really."

"What do you mean, not really?"

"I mean that for a very long time I was in denial. I accepted what Bobby told me, but I didn't exactly believe him. I mean, I would see him do stuff. I saw the way people reacted to him, but I just kept telling myself that it was sleight of hand, like a stage magician, not actual magic. That is until Oberon showed up and sort of proved, without a doubt, that magic exists." Melody looked a Jewell. "And then there were the blood tests."

"You mean the ones you did on Oberon?"

"No. The ones I did on Bobby. I really did think it was just an eccentric game. Then Oberon showed up and then I started thinking, what if it isn't magic. What if faeries, and all the rest, what if they're just another kind of humanoid. I mean genetically we're close enough to each other to procreate. Like dogs and wolves, horses and donkeys. Bobby said he didn't mind, so I took some samples and ran some tests."

Jewell knew her mouth was hanging open. "And?"

"I have a lifetime of work ahead of me. Work that I will never be able to publish. Still, you know me. I have to figure it out. If I do before I die, I promise I will tell you all about it. In the meantime, there seems to be a continuum of cellular aging. Faeries are on the slow end, humans are in the middle, and then there's Oberon."

"Were you going to tell me this?"

"I think I just did." Melody crossed her arms. "I should have trusted you and told you about Bobby, but like I said, I was afraid you were going to think I was out of my mind." Her eyes were damp with tears. "Can you forgive me? Please?"

The truth was Jewell couldn't afford to be mad. She needed Melody and the thought of losing her was more than she could bear. "You know your boyfriend slept with Shakespeare."

Melody shrugged. "I know. Crazy, right?"

"You're okay with all of this?"

"I guess," Melody said. "Everyone's got a past. Bobby's is just a little longer and more colorful than most."

"I'm not sure I could do it."

Melody laughed and threw her arm around Jewell's shoulder. "Have you forgotten that your baby daddy used to be a dog?"

Jewell smiled. "True."

"So."

"So." Jewell paused. "Do you know much about faeries? Other than their super slow cellular aging? I mean their history, what the rules are—how the magic works?"

"Bobby loves to tell me stories about the people he knew and the places he's lived but doesn't really like talking about being a faerie all that much. I honestly don't think they know how the magic works. What about you?"

Melody looked directly at Jewell. "Do you know much about faeries? I mean, have you ever read any stories or myths or anything?"

"Not really. I watched *Jonathan Strange and Mr. Norrell* on BBC America, does that count?"

"I thought that was about magicians."

"It was, but there were faeries in it, too." Jewell sat up a little straighter and pushed her hair back over her shoulder. "Why? What are you getting at?"

"I don't know," Melody said. "Maybe I've just watched too many episodes of *Buffy the Vampire Slayer*, but I feel like we should be in a library somewhere doing research or something."

"Maybe it's because you do research for a living?"

"Point taken." Melody crossed her arms. "Bobby says in the Realm they live for what might be thousands of years because time passes so slowly. Hardly anyone ever dies of old age, and babies are born, but not very often. They're not immortal, exactly. They just age so slowly they might as well be." She paused.

"And you've seen this borne out under the microscope?"

"In very preliminary examinations, yes."

"But you still don't understand why or how."

"Not a clue."

"Titania could be right. Oberon has magic inside him and every time he tries to combat her, it ages him—burns him out a little more—because his metabolism is different than a normal human's or faerie's."

"Because he used to be a dog."

"I guess." Jewell shrugged. "My god this is a bizarre conversation."

Melody took a breath. "Did you know that when humans go to the Realm, they also stop aging? Or rather, their aging slows significantly."

"What? How do you know that?"

"Bobby. He said that the slow passage of time affects all creatures in the Realm, even humans."

"Even humans that used to be dogs?"

Melody squeezed Jewell's hand. "I didn't ask him that."

"But maybe that's what they're not saying."

"I know that Bobby will do whatever he can to help you and Oberon stay together and stay here."

Jewell stood up and looked down at her friend. The bright sunshine highlighted her curls and made her cheeks glow. "You're saying that the only way to save Oberon might be to let Titania have him."

"No." Melody stood, too. "No. What I'm saying is that if Oberon were in the Realm—if any of us were to go there—our aging would slow significantly. I didn't say anything about letting Titania have him. Last I checked he wasn't anyone's possession."

"What's that supposed to mean?"

Melody looked down at her watch. "I have to get back to the lab. I didn't mean anything, you know that." She patted Jewell's arm. "Walk me to the corner?"

Jewell nodded. "Sure."

## 2.

Titania lay on her bed with a cold washcloth over her eyes. This human world was giving her a headache. She would have asked Peaseblossom for an herbal remedy, but after his little stunt with the love-in-idleness potion, she wouldn't trust him to hand her a glass of water. She sensed Iolanthe shimmering through the veil before she appeared. She raised herself up on her elbows and let the cold cloth slip down her face and onto the bed. "What took you so long?" she said with a sigh.

"I'm not sure you're going to be so happy to see me, sister." Iolanthe sat on the edge of the bed. "You look terrible, by the way."

"Good to know I look how I feel." Titania propped herself up against the headboard and took a good look at her sister. It was strange the way the passage of time here in the human world had affected her. She felt like she hadn't seen her sister in a millennium, when it had only been a few weeks. Or had it? She couldn't tell anymore. "You're going to want to change your costume before you go anywhere." She waved her index finger at her sister and her glittering blue-green faerie gown transformed into a similarly colored peasant blouse with sparkly beads and a pair of form-fitting jeans.

Iolanthe looked down at her new clothes and then back at her sister. "Thank you?"

"You're welcome. Trust me, it will go with your hair."

"I see that your hair is still lavender."

Titania shrugged. "Humans don't seem to care so much about things like hair color these days." She sighed. "So, why are you here?"

Iolanthe crawled up the bed and sat next to her sister. "You know why I'm here."

"I suppose I do." She grasped her sister's hand in both of hers and squeezed it. "I cannot describe how I feel when I'm with him. Now I know why you fought so hard to stay with your own sad human."

Iolanthe brushed back a stray hair from her sister's face. "Humans have a magic all their own, don't they, sister?" Titania nodded and felt the inexplicable urge to cry. She blinked hard a few times and leaned into her sister. Two tiny lavender tears dripped down her cheeks, and she decisively brushed them away. "So," Iolanthe said at last, "tell me what's been happening."

"You haven't been following along?"

"I've been too busy trying to run the Realm in your stead. Orc uprising. Always a risk when you invite them to the party."

"Well," Titania said. "I didn't see that coming, but I suppose I should have."

"Ondine has things under control for now," Iolanthe said. "But the Council is also getting anxious, wondering why they haven't seen you what with the orcs threatening to burn the place to the ground."

"Should I be worried about the crown?"

"I don't think we're there just yet." Iolanthe smoothed the edges of her blouse with her free hand. "But I suppose worrying about maintaining power is part of the job."

"I've been a pretty lousy monarch."

"You've maintained the status quo, which is what I believe most of your subjects want. A sort of loosely controlled anarchy where they can essentially do what they want so long as the outcome isn't too disastrous."

Titania leaned against her sister. "You should be queen. You're much wiser than I am."

"Ah, but I don't draw power from all four elements like you do, sister. Earth faeries give good counsel, and that's what I'm here to do."

Titania kissed her sister's cheek. "I'm grateful. Robin and Peaseblossom are working against me."

"I'm sure it feels that way."

Titania sat up and released her sister's hand. "What do you mean?"

"They want me to convince you to come home."

Titania turned so she could look her sister in the face. "I want to go home. You have no idea how much. This world is not for me. But the man. He is in my mind every waking minute. When I fall asleep, I dream of him. I am consumed."

"Have you tried glamouring him and just taking him?"

Titania shook her head and rose from the bed. "Doesn't work. He is glamour-proof." She opened the mini-bar and removed a tiny bottle of Absolut vodka. "Have you ever seen such things?" She held the bottle out to her sister. Iolanthe shook her head. "Would you like one? It contains alcohol and it's delicious."

"Yes, I suppose I would," Iolanthe said.

Titania removed several more bottles and poured the vodka into two tumblers sitting on top of the bar. She twirled her finger over the top of the glasses and ice appeared and tiny wedges of lime. She flicked her finger toward her sister and the glass floated across the room. Iolanthe appraised the glass and then took a sip. "Have you tried a relocation spell?" Iolanthe said. "This is delicious, by the way."

"So much better than mead, don't you think?" Iolanthe nodded and sipped while Titania sunk into the overstuffed armchair next to the mini-bar. "I have tried everything I can think of to either get Oberon to the Realm or for me to forget him. He is more than just a human. Something else is going on. Not only can he block me, but he also forcibly shimmered me."

"Impressive." Iolanthe took another sip.

"Yes," Titania said. "I'm not sure even you could do that."

"I see what you mean."

"Also, the woman is pregnant."

Iolanthe frowned. "I suppose that does change things."

"Why should it change anything?" Titania rose from her chair and threw herself into an armchair opposite the bed. She propped her feet up on the end table.

"You know how attached humans are to their children," Iolanthe said. "What if the child is a halfling?"

"Yours wasn't."

Iolanthe sighed. Titania knew better than to bring up Iolanthe's son, but she did it anyway.

"True," Iolanthe said. "My son inherited none of my magic, which is why I felt it was better to leave him with his father's family." Iolanthe fixed Titania with a stare both hard and sad. "Leaving my son behind was the most difficult thing I've ever had to do."

Titania smiled. "Yes. And then when you went back to make sure he was properly married that turned out to be quite a fiasco, didn't it?"

"It all worked out in the end." Iolanthe shrugged.

"These humans are so easily scandalized. How people did not recognize you as the boy's mother, I'll never understand."

"He had a hard time believing I was his mother." Iolanthe set her drink down on the low table between them. "I did not come all this way to rehash old times and my misadventures with humans, or my son, whom I miss every day."

"If you'd brought him to the Realm with you, he'd still be alive."

Iolanthe's eyes darkened. "Perhaps. You know how it goes for humans in the Realm. It rarely ends well for them."

"But you would have been there to protect him."

Iolanthe stood with her fists clenched. A blue aura swirled around them. "How? By glamouring him? By altering his reality forever? Humans weren't meant to live such lives. You know this, and yet you torment me. Is cruelty the only thing that brings you pleasure?"

"You're right, sister. I am not myself. Please, sit. Calm yourself. I'm only now beginning to understand why you made the choices you did."

Iolanthe took a deep breath and the aura around her fists faded. "Come home with me for just a little while," she said. "Deal with the orcs, get some perspective, and then come back. The man is not going anywhere."

"And how much human time will pass while I'm away dealing with Greibon and his motley horde? Is that what you want?

Do you think if I go back to the Realm I will forget?" Titania's eyes glowed with swirling crimson light.

Iolanthe stood and moved toward her sister. She reached for Titania's hand, but then pulled away when she saw the swirl of light coming toward her. "Sister, I am no match for you." She kneeled on the plush carpet. "I won't defend myself. Do what you will."

Titania exhaled and her eyes returned to their normal violet. "I'm not myself."

"Clearly." Iolanthe stood and when Titania sat back down, she did, too.

"You have to help me, not work against me." Titania drained her drink.

"Always, sister. You are my queen." Iolanthe took both of her sister's hands in hers and kneeled again. This time right in front of her sister. She pressed her forehead to the backs of Titania's hands and then kissed each one as if they were home and Titania was sitting on her throne. "My fealty is yours forever." Iolanthe paused, but kept her head bowed. "May I make a suggestion?"

"Of course." Titania had not seen such a display from her sister in a very long time. In fact, the last time her sister behaved with such contrition, she had been begging to be allowed back into the Realm after the death of her human husband and the birth of her half-human son. She thought her ability to read her sister was infallible, but now she wasn't so sure. "What's your suggestion?"

Iolanthe raised her eyes. "I sense more is going on here. You're not saying it, but I can feel it and I think you must, too. Before I can offer any possible suggestions, I need to see exactly what's happening. Can we conceal ourselves?"

Titania squeezed her sister's hands. "We can try."

"Good, then let's go to Oberon. I want to see for myself what's happening between the two of you."

"They've hidden him from me again. And the woman. If I were human, and knew how to do such things, I suppose I could just find their location with a map, but I've never read a map in my life."

"Robin and Peaseblossom haven't hidden Oberon from me!" Iolanthe said with a laugh. "I know exactly where he is." She took her sister's hands again and stood very close. She raised her hand above her head and drew a circle. The air sparkled for a moment and then they shimmered into Jewell's apartment, where Oberon was sleeping.

# 3.

When they materialized, Titania instinctively stepped toward the bed, but Iolanthe reached out and held her back. "Sister, what are you doing?"

Titania shook her head as if she were trying to rouse herself from a dream. "I don't know. I have an indescribable urge to touch him, like a magnet to metal. I don't know how else to explain it."

Oberon rolled over in his sleep, pulling the blankets with him, revealing his long-muscled back. "Have you ever touched him?" Iolanthe asked.

Titania looked at her sister and cocked her head. "Yes, but not for long. There's been very little skin to skin contact."

"Well." Iolanthe looked down at Oberon. "Let's see what happens."

"Are you sure that's a good idea?"

Iolanthe shrugged. "I'm not sure at all, but I am curious. Perhaps all you need to do is satisfy that desire and it will go away."

"Or it will intensify."

"Good point." She stood back and tapped her chin. "What if I touch him?"

"Do you feel any kind of unnatural desire around him?"

"Desire?" She smiled at her sister. "He is a most attractive human. But nothing stirring within me feels unnatural." Then, without further consultation, Iolanthe reached out and placed her hand on Oberon's bare arm. Without thinking Titania reached out to stop her, but when she connected with her sister, a tremor of electricity, or something very like it, coursed from Oberon, through Iolanthe, and into Titania, who staggered backwards, unable to let go of her sister. Titania couldn't catch her breath. It was as if an orc were standing on her chest.

Oberon sat straight up in the bed with an exaggerated inhale, his eyes wide open. He also seemed to be gasping for breath. Iolanthe stood perfectly still, anchored between the two of them. She stared straight ahead, her eyes fixed and covered with a semiopaque aqua film. She mumbled a few incoherent words as a golden aura formed a halo around her body. Oberon inhaled violently. He jerked his arm from Iolanthe's grasp and Titania fell to the floor clutching her chest. Iolanthe sputtered back into consciousness, the halo disappeared, and she reached down to help her sister to her feet. She blinked several times, clearing her vision.

"You!" Oberon had scrambled over the other side of the bed and stood in his boxers with his back pressed against the far window. He reached for a sweatshirt that had been lying at the foot of the bed and pulled it over his head. "When will you just leave me alone?"

Titania slumped into a chair. Her head fell to her hands and her shoulders shook. When she finally looked up at Iolanthe, pale lavender tears trailed down her cheeks. "Sister?" she said. "What is happening?"

Iolanthe was beside her in a flash, brushing the tears from her cheeks. She stroked her hair and placed her arm around Titania's shoulder. "I don't know what we've done, but you need to come with us." She pointed at Oberon and a thin aqua beam of light shot across the room toward him. He raised his palm, as if to block the light, and shielded his face in the crook of his other elbow. Titania and Iolanthe watched as a gold flicker of light surrounded Oberon, repelling the magic. All of this happened in an instant. Titania looked up at her sister. She was not crying anymore.

"Look what he can do," she said under her breath.

"I've never seen anything quite like that." Iolanthe stepped closer to Oberon but did not attempt to touch him again. "There are stories about the Elf King and the powers he possessed."

"The Elf King!" Titania sat up straight, her eyes flashing crimson. "The elves have lived without a sovereign for over a millennium. Our ancestors fought those wars and now the elves live peaceably as part of our kingdom." She gripped the arms of her chair, her knuckles white. "Elf King. I've never heard anything so ridiculous."

Iolanthe turned to her sister. "Perhaps we somehow tapped into the Elf King's essence when we transformed Oberon? The legend says at the end of the conflict his very quiddity was dispersed into the plane between our world and this one." Iolanthe paused and took a hesitant step toward her sister. "And that one day, he and the Faerie Queen—"

"Stop right there," Titania said. "Those stories are nonsense. You know it as well as I. No one believes them."

Oberon stepped toward Iolanthe, the golden sparkle dissipating to a shadow. "Why won't you leave me alone?"

"My Lord," Iolanthe said. She faced Oberon and kneeled.

"What? Stand up!" Oberon said. "I'm nobody's lord. I want you two out of my house before Jewell comes home."

"Get up, sister," Titania said. "You're being ridiculous."

"Am I?" she said still on her knees. "Wasn't there a prophecy, one that foretold the coming of a new king? One that would bewitch the queen and put to rest a mighty upheaval in the Realm?"

"Tales spun by wizened male faeries who were frightened by the prospect of female leadership. Our parents never put any stock in such stories, and neither do I."

Iolanthe rose. "No, but our uncle did."

"My case in point. Misogynist old fool." Titania pushed her hair over her shoulder. "Besides, there is no uprising in the Realm."

"Have you not been listening to me? Greibon is massing an army of orcs."

"You said that Ondine had it under control—that it was nothing."

Iolanthe bowed her head but did not respond.

"Ondine does have it under control, right sister?"

Iolanthe remained mute.

"Sister do not play games with me. You cannot have it both ways. Is there a credible uprising or isn't there?"

"There have also been some grumblings amongst the goblins and trolls, who've stated that they might be forming an alliance with the orcs to move against us."

"To do what?"

Iolanthe stood and faced Titania, splitting the space between her and Oberon. "What does any insurgent force ever want?"

"Ridiculous!" Titania stamped her foot and the whole room shook.

"What are you talking about?" Oberon said.

"My sister now thinks that you are the re-embodied spirit of the Elf King. She is deluded in her desperation to help me. Now she tries to convince me with lies of open rebellion and insurrection in the Realm." Titania glared at Iolanthe.

"Help you do what?" Oberon asked.

Titania stepped forward and her eyes glowed. "Either conquer you or forget you. I cannot go on this way."

Oberon swallowed and gripped the brass footboard. "So, there is more than one option available."

"Yes. I would prefer to forget you, but there is magic compelling me, and I have no control over it. This compulsion began the night I first saw you and now plagues me like a nightmare. At first, I thought it was love. This does sometimes happen to faeries. Now I know that it's more than that. There are powerful forces at work that no one quite understands."

Oberon sank onto the bed and let out an audible sigh. "Why didn't you say that from the beginning?"

Titania moved toward Oberon, but Iolanthe stepped in between them. "I understand what's happening. You don't want to accept it," Iolanthe said.

"You know nothing."

"I saw it all, sister. When I was connected to you, I had a vision of him, of the Elf King."

"Liar."

"Sister, you wound me. Why would I lie about such a thing?"

"Look at him!" Titania said. "Look how fragile and weak he is. He is no elf! He is far too beautiful." She dismissed her sister with a wave of her hand and turned all her attention to Oberon. "You understand nothing of magic, do you?"

Oberon shook his head and gazed up at her, his soft brown eyes too sad and mournful. Titania stood too close. Without considering the consequences, she reached out and tipped his chin up toward her. "Sister, don't!" Iolanthe said, but it was too late. As soon as Titania's finger made contact with Oberon's chin, the room began to hum. Oberon lifted his face to Titania and rose. Iolanthe stumbled backwards and did her best to balance herself against the dresser. Oberon drew Titania into his arms and kissed her, and as they embraced swirls of lavender and gold light entwined and danced around them. The room no longer hummed but had begun to shake. Iolanthe closed her eyes and did her best to summon Robin and Thomas Peaseblossom. Within moments Peaseblossom appeared and soon after, Robin shimmered into the room with Jewell.

"I didn't know you were strong enough to bring a human with you," Iolanthe said to Robin.

"I can do a lot of things." He released Jewell's hand and stepped toward Oberon and Titania.

# 4.

Upon shimmering for the first time, Jewell found herself unsteady and not sure where she was. It didn't take long though, for her to realize that she was in her bedroom and that Titania and Oberon were locked in a passionate embrace. The floor of the room vibrated as pulses of light entwined Oberon and Titania, who almost seemed fused together.

"What's happening?" Jewell shouted. When no one responded she pushed past Bobby and used her shoulder to wedge herself between Oberon and Titania. She shoved Oberon's chest as hard as she could, and he let go of Titania, stumbling backward away from both women. "Oberon! What are you doing?" Jewell shouted.

He staggered away from her, the residue of golden light still pricking and dancing off his skin. "Jewell, I—"

"Look at him," Peaseblossom said. "All his gray hair is gone. His skin is glowing."

Jewell moved toward him, touched his cheek. "How do you feel?"

Oberon shook his head. "What just happened?"

Jewell turned to look at the other people in her bedroom, placing herself between them and Oberon. "Yes. What just happened?"

Bobby looked to Iolanthe, who shook her head. Titania stood where Oberon had left her, her eyes wide, her mouth slightly agape. "It's you," she said at last, pointing at Jewell, her hand shaking. Her voice was rough and low. "He can't leave with me unless you let him go. And he must come back. I know that now."

"What are you talking about?" The room tilted around Jewell.

"This is why he's aging. He's using all his strength to fight me, because you are keeping him in this world where he does not belong."

"Is she right?" Jewell asked looking toward Bobby.

"I don't know," he said. "Anything is possible."

"I think when we made him," Iolanthe said, "we somehow invoked the essence of the Elf King."

"What?" Peaseblossom said. "Why would you say something like that?"

"Because. Earlier I came between them, and an energy ran through me like nothing I've ever experienced before. I had a vision. I could see things."

"Like what?" Bobby said.

"I saw a picture of the before time," Iolanthe said. "I saw the Elf King, in this world, long, long ago, stealing his final child, which now lies there." She pointed at Jewell's abdomen.

"But that would have required so much magic. All four elements converging." Peaseblossom looked at Bobby. "I thought you said you had nothing to do with this."

Bobby furrowed his brow. "I didn't."

Peaseblossom paced the bedroom. "It doesn't make sense. Titania is queen. Her primary element is fire, yet she has secondary elements of earth, air, and water, which is why she is queen. Only one faerie every generation can access all four elements. But that shouldn't have been enough. All four individual elements should have been present. Ondine is a water faerie, Iolanthe, like me is connected to earth." He looked at Bobby again. "They would need you. A powerful faerie connected to air to complete such magic." He gestured toward Oberon. "I mean turn a dog into a man, okay. Not so easy, but it would not require all four elements. Reincarnate the Elf King? That would definitely necessitate four elemental faeries."

"I'm telling you. I wasn't here." Bobby's eyes sparked bright yellow, and he shook his head as if the surge of emotion had caught him off guard.

Jewell had never seen Bobby angry before. His face seemed to morph slightly, like a mask was falling away.

"Wait. Wait a minute." He shook his head again. "No. No, no, no." He grabbed Titania by the arm and shook her. She looked up at him as if roused from a stupor. "The night you cast the spell did you eat anything here? In the apartment?"

"What are you talking about?" Titania looked around confused as if Bobby were speaking a language she didn't understand.

"Did. You. Eat. Anything?"

She glared at him. "No!"

"Yes." Iolanthe spoke up from the other side of the room. "Yes. I saw her. She ate at least one mushroom from the woman's plate that night. She said she didn't, but she did."

"Those mushrooms where delicious," Oberon said. "Jewell fed one to me that night, too. She was feeling so sad. Then she started to eat, and she felt so happy." He looked at Bobby. "You made that food. Jewell ate a lot of it."

"Oh my god," Jewell said. "That was the night of my father's memorial." She flew at Bobby and slapped him in the face. He recoiled slightly but stood his ground. Peaseblossom put his arm around her before she could hit him again. "You did this. You put magic in that food."

"I was only trying to make you feel better. You were so sad. Just like Oberon said. I can't stand to see anyone sad. How was I supposed to know you were going to make that stupid wish?" Then he turned on Titania. "And how was I supposed to know that you'd show up and eat the damn things, too? How is any of this my fault?" He paused for a moment and let his hands rest on his hips. "But you must admit, it is pretty impressive." He smiled.

Jewell struggled to get at him again, but Peaseblossom held her back.

"Yeah, maybe not the time to be boasting about my culinary prowess. Sorry."

Jewell took a deep breath and Peaseblossom released his grip.

"In essence, you were part of the convergence, since all the principle parties ingested food infused with your magic. This would make the quadrangle complete. Fire, water, earth, and air." He looked at Titania. "We all know this is why quadratic spells are forbidden. With all four elements at play, and the power of the queen behind the spell, the outcome would be entirely unpredictable. There are just too many variables." He let go of Jewell and stepped back to address the whole room. "Congratulations. I believe it's very possible that you have, in fact, reincarnated, reconstituted, revived, whatever you want to call it, the Elf King."

The room fell silent. Jewell stood next to Oberon, who sat on the bed and rested his head against her hip.

"None of this will ever be right," Titania said, "until you decide he can leave." She pointed at Jewell. "Otherwise he will wither and die, and it will happen before your child is born."

Jewell shook her head. She didn't know what to think or say. "This is insane. How do I know you're all not trying to trick me?"

"Ask him," Titania said, indicating Oberon.

Jewell turned to Oberon. "Is she right? Oberon?" Jewell grabbed his sweatshirt and pulled him closer. "Oberon, answer me."

Finally, he looked at her. "I don't know." He shook his head. "Maybe."

Jewell jerked away from him and turned on the others in the room. She didn't care that they had magic powers or that maybe they would hurt her. She wasn't thinking about any of that. She was thinking about Oberon, about the father of her child, about this whole fucked-up situation, and if they all didn't get the hell out of her apartment, she might lose her damn mind.

"Get out!" she shouted. She pointed at the bedroom door, while they all stared at her open-mouthed. "Did you hear me? Get the hell out of my apartment!" She lunged at Titania. "You can fly, you can shimmer, you can crawl on your belly like a snake. Just get the hell out."

Again, no one moved. "Go, or I will call the police."

Bobby reached out to her, but she dodged his grasp. "All of you. Out. I need to talk to Oberon alone."

First Peaseblossom shimmered away and then Iolanthe followed. Jewell looked at Bobby. "Get her out of here."

Bobby shook his head. "I can't make her do anything. She's my queen."

"I can make her go," Oberon said. "Are you going to make me do that, Titania?"

"You need to tell her," Titania said. "I'm not leaving until you promise—"

Oberon raised his arm and held his hand out in front of him, palm forward, then pushed a ball of golden energy at Titania. She shimmered, mid-sentence, her atoms sparkling away like dust motes in a shaft of light.

"That was impressive," Bobby said. "Seriously. Titania is the most powerful faerie in the Realm. This is why she's our queen. I don't think Iolanthe, Thomas, and I together could do such a thing. Although I managed it once, with some help." He stepped toward Oberon. "We need to talk."

Oberon looked hard at Bobby. "No. Jewell wants you to leave, and so do I."

"But, Oberon, this is important."

Oberon held his hand out in front of him. "Please don't make me, Bobby. I get so tired."

"Okay, okay. I thought you just got your battery charged." He laughed, then looked at Jewell, who scowled at him in return. "Yeah, so maybe that was a shitty joke. I'm going." He edged toward the door. "It's okay. When you need some answers, want to know who the Elf King is—you know where to find me." And with that he shimmered away in a haze of yellow mist.

Once they were alone, Jewell crumpled onto the end of the bed. "I can't believe you were kissing her."

"Neither can I." Oberon sank onto the bed next to her. "However, and I really don't want to admit this, but I do feel better than I have in weeks."

Jewell frowned. "Maybe you did recharge your battery."

"Maybe."

"Well, what are we going to do now?" she said. She let the full weight of the image of Titania and Oberon locked in a preternaturally passionate embrace fall on her. She felt sick to her stomach in a way she hadn't in a long time. Jealousy, rage, betrayal, emotions that always cycled back to feelings of inadequacy and worthlessness. She tried to tell herself this was different. What was happening was beyond Oberon's control and had nothing to do with her. And for once, instead of feeling powerless and accepting things the way they were, she was going to do something.

# TEN

## I.

EWELL AND OBERON stayed up most of the night talking. Jewell did not know, because Oberon did not tell
her, that while he'd shared that embrace with Titania,
he had been filled with a vision, much like the one that Iolanthe
had so briefly described. He knew that the time was long, long
ago, even though Oberon had very little context for the passage
of time. In the vision a dark desire had overwhelmed him, and
it had been very, very cold. He'd been traveling in the human
world, during a time of the year when the days were short. Frost
clung to the ground and to the few leaves left on the trees. He
could see his own breath in the moonlight and feel the prick of
winter on his cheeks. In the distance, he'd seen some travelers: a
father and son on horseback, riding at a canter through a forest.
The images had been gauzy and dreamlike, and he hadn't understood them at all. Conflated with this vision was the essence of
Titania, warm and light in his arms, and from her he had drawn
strength, but not love. He did not tell Jewell about the vision. He
did his best to reassure her, to tell her that what had drawn him
to Titania was magic, nothing else. He did his best to convince
her that since his iron allergy was under control and some of his

youthfulness had been restored, he would be able to hold out longer against Titania and the magical forces at work against them—but that was hardly the whole story. There had been a time, not so long ago, when he wouldn't have been able to lie to Jewell. Now he understood that telling the truth was not always the best thing to do. This realization made him sad in a way that he didn't know was possible. Duplicity seemed to be a state of being reserved for humans and faeries. He had been incapable of such a thing, but now it slipped over him like an old t-shirt. He did not like how comfortable he felt.

As they lay in bed later that night, after they had exhausted themselves with talk, when Jewell was tucked safely in his arms, he realized he would rather die than give her up. He'd had no choice in his transformation, and the things that continued to happen to him were not of his choosing. This he would choose. Titania had been right. For him to travel to the Realm, Jewell would have to release him, but Jewell didn't know this or understand the ramifications. He didn't want her to. She held the key to completing his transformation, because she was the owner of the wish. Faeries were bound by such things even though they pretended they were bound by nothing. Oberon had become human enough that he could lie, but he was also human enough to know Jewell's face was the last one he wanted to see before he was gone from this life forever. The child she carried frightened him for some reason, and somewhere, in those gauzy memories of that long-ago time, he thought it might be better for everyone if he never saw that child born. This too made him profoundly sad, but he pushed those thoughts aside and drifted off to sleep.

## 2.

When Jewell awoke the next morning, she felt hung over. She let Oberon sleep, thinking he likely needed it. His boss was magical, hers was not. She needed to get to work and accomplish something. Maybe today would be normal. Maybe if she stared at enough science she could forget about magic. Maybe. She went through her regular morning routine and eventually found herself sitting at her kitchen table staring at a plate of cooling scrambled eggs. Eat, she told herself. Do it for the baby. The sourness in her stomach faded as she ate her last bite of toast and took her last sip of tea. As she grabbed her jacket from the hook near the door, she saw Oberon shuffle out of the bedroom.

"Off to work?" he said.

She shrugged. "My boss doesn't give a crap about faeries and their problems."

He smiled and kissed her on the mouth, then drew her to him in a tight embrace. "Are you going to be okay?" she asked.

He nodded and kissed her again. "Don't worry about me. I just miss you when you're at work. I always have."

"I miss you, too." She touched his cheek. "Promise me you'll stay home and rest today. You're starting to look like your old self again. Maybe you should stay away from that whole crew."

"I don't know that they'll stay away from me, but I won't go into work. I doubt Bobby is expecting me."

"Right." Jewell kissed him quickly. "I'll call you later," she said and then she left.

A block from her house she pulled her phone out of her bag and called Melody.

"I heard you had a hell of a night," Melody said.

"Please. I really don't want to talk about it. Not now anyway."

"Fair enough. What's up?"

Jewell asked Melody what she was doing after work.

"Why?" Melody asked.

"I was thinking it might be time to take a trip to the library," she said. "Want to come with?"

"Absolutely," Melody said. "Finally, some research. I live for this shit."

Jewell laughed and that felt good. They decided where and when to meet and then Jewell went to work with a clearer head than she'd had in months.

# 3.

Iolanthe woke to find her sister staring at her from the end of the bed. Titania wore a fluffy white robe, the kind provided by the hotel with an embroidered insignia on the breast pocket. Her hair was pulled back in a long, wet ponytail and her skin was bare.

"Did you sleep at all?" Iolanthe asked.

"Some," Titania said with a sigh, "but I had disturbing dreams."

Iolanthe pulled the comforter up over her chest. "I can imagine."

"I suppose you can," Titania said. "You did have a vision of the Elf King, didn't you?"

"Why would I make something like that up? You did, too. I can see it in your face."

"It was most disturbing." Titania rose and poured herself some orange juice from the minibar. "First the orcs take to the Dale, demanding whatever it is that they're demanding."

"Fairer compensation," Iolanthe said.

Titania looked down at her fingernails. "Is that all?"

"I believe so, sister."

"For that they're willing to sack the palace and throw the entire Realm into an uproar?"

"It has been a long time coming. Don't forget about the goblins and the trolls."

"What do they want?"

"Better working conditions and an increase in bridge tolls."

Titania rolled her eyes. "Ondine will take care of all that, won't she?"

Iolanthe nodded. "She is an excellent negotiator, but what does this have to do with your vision of the Elf King?"

Titania sighed. "If the orcs can get themselves so worked up over something as minor as wages, imagine how the elves will feel when they realize that their king has been reborn."

"The legend says that the king will bring unity and peace to the Realm for 1000 years. That doesn't sound so awful. Maybe a little boring . . ."

Titania stared hard at her sister. "Does it say anything about a dog in that legend of yours?"

Iolanthe shook her head.

"Don't we have unity and peace now?"

"I guess you'd have to ask the goblins, trolls, and orcs how they feel?"

Titania paced across the room, gesturing with her glass of juice. "I mean and then what? A thousand years. It's not like we're human where that might actually mean something." She turned and pointed her finger at her sister. "No one believes these archaic tales anymore, do they? It's not like the old days when magic ruled both planes, here and in the Realm. Back then you could make up any old kind of story you wanted. Whisper it down the lane. Spook a few humans, and voilà, a legend is born, stories that change and morph with time and the retelling. If they're good enough they inspire literature and art. But humans don't believe these things anymore. Why should we?"

Iolanthe shrugged. "Because we're not human? Because we know better?" She slid out of bed and started for the bathroom. "Is there another robe for me?" Titania waved her hand and a robe appeared hanging from a hook on the bathroom door. "Thanks," Iolanthe said, slipping it on. "One thing humans do understand is luxury."

"Yes, I suppose," Titania said. "The robe is quite comfortable."

Iolanthe slouched into one of the chairs and rubbed her bare feet across the plush carpet. "I mean this," she said nodding toward the floor. "Why don't we have this?"

"Now that you know you like it so much, you can have whatever you want. Can't you?"

"Of course. But why didn't we think of it?"

"Because we can't think of everything! I don't know, sister. Sometimes you are insufferable."

"So I've been told. More than once. By you."

Titania stopped pacing and stared at her sister for a moment, and then sat down on the floor next to her and rested her head against her sister's legs. "I am quite beside myself."

"I can see that." Iolanthe stroked Titania's hair. "That's why I'm here."

"What are we going to do?"

"I think our only course of action is to convince Jewell—"

"I see you use the woman's name now."

"Yes, Jewell. I think we must convince her that she needs to release Oberon so that he can choose."

"But what if he chooses to stay with her? Will I be left feeling this way forever? I don't know that I could remain sane for long in such a state."

Iolanthe sat up and Titania moved so that she could see her sister's face. "If Oberon chooses to stay and you feel no relief, we'll think of something else." She pushed back a stray piece of hair from Titania's face. "You were right, though. I felt it, too. If he stays, he will die."

"Robin's been among these humans for so long now, he thinks like they do. Perhaps we should talk to him."

"You are probably right. Jewell will not want to talk to us. After last night, I doubt she trusts Robin anymore either, but he does know her better than anyone."

Titania stood. "Yes, that's true. And isn't Robin's human companion a good friend of the woman's?"

Iolanthe frowned. "You've been here longer than I have, so I'm going to say yes."

"Good. Let's go talk to him then."

Iolanthe stood up. "Can we eat first, and maybe have a few more of those tiny bottles of alcohol?"

"It's so early, are you sure you want to consume alcohol?"

Iolanthe smiled. "You have been here too long. We're faeries—what do we care what time it is?"

# 4.

Jewell met Melody on the steps of the Philadelphia Free Library at a quarter past five. Together they entered the expansive lobby, which Jewell thought always felt like it should somehow be brighter. The library itself was an extravagant example of Beaux Arts architecture. The Carrera marble floor stretched before them for the length of half a city block, ending in an equally grand marble staircase. The cove ceilings were 20 feet high and crisscrossed with decorative plaster moldings. It was hard not to feel humble in such a space.

"I haven't really been here for books since I was a kid," she said.

"Really?" Melody said. "You're such a book nerd."

"I'll own that," Jewell said. "I mean I come to readings when I can, especially if it's a favorite author. I like to buy books instead. I know it's weird, but once I read something, I don't want to give it back."

Melody laughed. "That is kind of weird." She pulled Jewell toward the stairs. "Let's go talk to the reference librarian. Librarians love to answer questions."

Melody paused at the base of the steps and laid her hand on Jewell's arm. "Bobby told me everything. Well, he said he told me everything. Are you okay?"

Jewell nodded. "I'm better than I should be, I guess. Seeing Oberon kissing Titania made me want to punch her—and him— but I don't know." Jewell struggled to find the right words. "I was terrified, angry, hurt, confused. All of it mixed together. And to find out Bobby was the catalyst for all of it. Mel, I'm really pissed at him."

"I know," Melody said. "But he really was only trying to make you feel better. He didn't know this was all going to happen. How could he? He's spiked people's food before, and it's always been fine."

"Did you know what he'd done?"

Melody looked away. "Not exactly."

"Geez, Mel." Jewell started to walk away, but Melody stopped her.

"Come on, Jewell. Be fair. When this happened, I still wasn't 100% convinced that Bobby hadn't been playing some big joke on me. Part of me wanted to believe him, because I didn't want him to be crazy. When Oberon said he thought Bobby was a faerie, I just about choked on my pickled sombrero, or whatever it was we were drinking." She paused, took a breath, and searched Jewell's face for signs of forgiveness. "Who is going to be Xander to your Buffy, except me? If it makes you feel any better, I'm here because I don't entirely trust Bobby and would like to find out some stuff for myself, you know?" She waved her engagement ring at Jewell. "Who knows where this thing came from?"

"You aren't a faerie, are you?" Jewell gripped Melody's arm. "After all this, you'd tell me, right?"

Melody laughed so loudly the security guard at the front of the building turned and shushed them, wagging her finger.

"You've known me since we were kids. Be serious."

Jewell thrust her chin at Melody.

"No. I am not a faerie." Melody made an X over her heart. "Cross my heart."

"Okay. Just please, don't ever let Bobby do anything like that again."

"Like I could stop him."

Melody grabbed Jewell's arm and pulled her up the marble stairs to the second floor and then led her to the reference section. The massive room was filled with people studiously hushed and bent over books or staring into computers. The whir and click of the microfiche machine echoed from the back as someone scanned old newspaper articles. Jewell stopped and took a deep breath. She had forgotten the way the library smelled, old books, unwashed street people, fresh brewed coffee.

Melody marched right up to the counter and rested her elbows on it. "Excuse me," she said.

The librarian had her back to them and was focused on her computer. When she heard Melody, she turned around and smiled. "What can I help you with?"

"Hi!" Melody said again. Jewell stood behind her and let her do her thing. "This may sound a little crazy, but we're looking for historical texts or reference books that have information about faeries."

The librarian thought for a moment. "Do you mean fairy tales?"

Melody turned and looked at Jewell. "I don't think so," she said. "I think we're more interested in the historical folklore kind of stuff."

The librarian smiled. "Yes, of course. Well, there is a lot of material. Which part of the world were you interested in?"

Again, Jewell and Melody exchanged glances. "What do you think? England, probably. I mean the way they're always talking about Shakespeare and everything."

Jewell half-nodded at her, wondering what the librarian was thinking. Melody made a face that said, *lighten up*, and she smiled awkwardly at the librarian. "Yes. I think probably England. So, yeah, British Isles, Ireland—maybe Scandinavia? They have elves and faeries, too, right?"

"Most cultures have faerie-like creatures in their folklore. There's a lot of debate about the origin of faeries and faerie myths. Britain is probably a good place to start." The librarian motioned for them to follow her. She moved out from behind the reference counter and led Melody and Jewell toward the back and down a long stack of books to the right. "Here you go ladies," she said. "Also, you can check the reference databases at any of the computers to find specific articles that might be of interest. If you take something off the shelf and don't want to check it out, please put it in one of the carts." As she turned to go, Jewell tapped her arm. "We were also looking for information about the Elf King?"

The librarian stopped and turned around. "Well, that depends. Are you looking for translations of the Goethe poem, or are you looking for translations of the original tales of an Elf King? You know, the work that inspired Goethe, which *was* Scandinavian, I believe. You might want to read the *Chanson de Geste Huon de Bordeaux*. Of course, it's French and gets overlooked sometimes because there aren't many good English translations."

"Okay, thanks," Jewell said, thinking it was too bad she didn't read French.

"Maybe we could start with the Goethe and then move on to the legends?" Melody said.

"Well, you'll find the research material in this area here." The librarian gestured toward an area just a few shelves away. "The Goethe will be with the German Romantic Poets, downstairs in the literature department. But if you're just looking for a translation, you can find that online." She smiled at them, tacitly asking them if they had any more questions.

"Thanks so much," Melody said.

"You're welcome," the librarian said leaving them to their inquiry.

Once she'd left, Melody nudged Jewell. "Bobby told me that they think Oberon might be this reincarnated Elf King. That's crazy!"

"Is it any crazier than anything else that's happened?"

"I guess not."

They paused and scanned the shelves. Nothing stood out to either one of them. "Why don't you keep looking," Jewell said.

"I want to go Google that Goethe text. I don't want to leave empty-handed."

"Sounds good."

Jewell left Melody in the stacks and settled herself at a computer. Why she hadn't thought to do this earlier, she wasn't sure. She typed in Goethe, Elf King and 27,500 pages popped up. In all her love of literature and books, she'd never been big into German Romanticism, and now she kind of regretted it. How could she have never heard of this poem? She clicked on the Wikipedia page and scanned the article.

Melody came up behind her and dropped a book on the desk next to her with a loud thwack. Several nearby patrons raised their heads to scowl in their direction. "Sorry," Melody mouthed. She whispered in Jewell's ear. "So, did you find anything good?"

"Yes. Looks like a start anyway. Why I didn't think of this earlier, I don't know. I'll print it out."

Melody read aloud over her shoulder:

> *"Willst, feiner Knabe, du mit mir gehn?*
> *Meine Töchter sollen dich warten schön;*
> *Meine Töchter führen den nächtlichen Reihn,*
> *Und wiegen und tanzen und singen dich ein—"*

She put her hand on Jewell's shoulder. "What the hell?"

"Do you speak German?" Jewell asked.

"*Ein bischen*," Melody said smiling. "The Germans are doing a lot of good research in my field."

"The things you learn when you go to the library."

"I remember this poem now," Melody said. "It's messed up. Find a translation."

Jewell hit the Google translate tab. The two of them read the poem and slowly exhaled at the same time.

"God, that is messed up," Jewell said.

"I told you," Melody said. "And that's not even a very good translation. There's a lot software can't handle."

"There's a lot I can't handle."

"Yeah—and there's this, too."

"What is it?" Jewell said, pointing to the book.

"It looks like it has some pertinent information, and we can check it out. *Faeries in Tradition and Literature.*"

Jewell looked at her watch. "Shoot. I told Oberon I'd be home by now. Just let me text him."

"Of course. Meet me when you're ready," Melody said and headed back to the stacks. Jewell bent down to dig her phone out of her purse and when she sat up, she saw the whole gang shimmering to view: Bobby, Peaseblossom, Titania, and her sister Iolanthe. Jewell stifled a groan.

"To what do I owe this awesome pleasure?" she said, not bothering to try to hide her bitterness.

"Just checking in on my girls," Bobby said with a weak smile.

"I'm nobody's girl, Bobby."

"Right, of course," Bobby said. "It's just an expression. Where's Mel?"

"Couldn't you see her in your crystal ball?"

"I told you this would be a waste of time," Titania said.

"Patience, sister," Iolanthe said.

Melody bounded around the corner holding another book. "Look what I found. Hey! What are you doing here?" She rushed to Bobby, who greeted her with his usual kiss.

"Look, why don't you all sit down, since you've come all this way." Jewell said. "You're making me nervous standing around me like Lurch or something." The four of them, along with Melody, slid into chairs at a nearby table. Jewell joined them.

"Who's Lurch?" Titania asked.

"Lurch is a character from a very old television show," Jewell said. "He was very tall and used to just stand and stare at people."

"Plus, he kind of looked like Frankenstein," Melody said.

"Who's Frankenstein?" Titania asked.

"Listen," Bobby said turning to Titania. "We don't have time to explain every cultural reference since the time of Shakespeare to you. If you really want to know, take notes and go home and look it up. Or better yet, we're in a library—go find a librarian."

Titania looked at Iolanthe. "Do you have any idea what they're talking about?"

She shook her head. "Television is the magic picture box, yes?"

"Yes," Bobby said.

Peaseblossom reached around Melody and tapped Bobby on the shoulder. Then he cleared his throat and nodded toward Jewell.

"Yeah, right. Sorry. So, ladies," Bobby said. "How's the library?"

Melody looked first at Jewell and then at Bobby, a sweet smile on her face. "You know. It's the library," she said.

"Did you know that Melody speaks German?" Jewell said.

"Wow, really babe? You are amazing," Bobby said, squeezing Melody's shoulder. "Are you reading German in the library today?"

Jewell smiled and blinked at him a few times. "Why yes. A very famous German poet. One that I could not believe I'd never read before, considering I am such a book nerd."

Bobby shook his finger at her. "You're a funny girl, Jewell. That's why I like you so much."

"I'm nobody's girl, Bobby. I thought we established that."

Bobby laughed nervously. "You know what I meant. Don't be so uptight. So you read some Goethe, so what?"

"I didn't say we were reading Goethe. There are lots and lots of German poets."

Titania exhaled loudly. "What are you two talking about? Please! Also, I'd really like a beverage of some sort. Coffee, perhaps? Or maybe one of those tiny bottles of vodka? Yes, I'd much prefer the vodka, but whatever you can find in this dreadfully decorated palace will suffice. I didn't see any servants. Would one of you be so kind?" She looked around the table until her eyes fell on Peaseblossom, whose smile did not do a very good job of hiding his annoyance.

"Nothing would make me happier, my queen," he said. "Would anyone else like anything?"

Bobby smiled. "I'd love some coffee, dude."

Jewell reached out as Peaseblossom swung by her. "Let them conjure up their own beverages. We're not in the Realm. You're not their servant." She narrowed her eyes at Titania. "Besides, you can't bring drinks up here anyway."

Melody leaned forward. "That's right. These librarians will kick your ass."

Peaseblossom smiled at Jewell, turned to Titania and shrugged, palms up. Then he sat back down.

"You speak German and Spanish," he said. "You impress me every day, honey bunch." He leaned in and kissed her on the temple.

"Seeing as you're at least 400 years old, I bet you speak lots of languages, too, honey bunch."

"Funny and smart. Lots to love."

"What I don't get is this. You," Jewell pointed around the table at Bobby, Titania, and Iolanthe, "said the Elf King had dissipated to the four corners of the universe or something ridiculous a long, long time ago. And for the likes of you, I'm guessing that is an extremely long time. So, what's with the Goethe?" She frowned and crossed her arms. "I mean, of course it was Goethe. But is it the same Elf King? That poem was written in 1782, long after Miss Thing here was messing with Shakespeare. And you," she pointed at Bobby, "Hadn't you been banished?"

"What poem are they talking about, sister?" Iolanthe said.

"I have no idea," Titania said. "I guess we'll have to look it up, whatever that means."

Peaseblossom leaned forward. "Robin and Goethe were drinking buddies," Peaseblossom said. "Robin always had a thing for playwrights and poets."

Bobby smiled. "Goethe was a fun guy. Seriously. He knew how to party."

"Is there no one you wouldn't stoop to corrupt?" Titania said.

"What do you care? You didn't know him," Bobby said. "Besides, Johann was not the kind of man you could corrupt. Trust me, he had plenty of ideas of his own. I was just along for the ride."

"What's the story?" Jewell asked.

"You know how it goes. You're sitting around Auerbach's Keller in Leipzig, everyone's drinking their schnapps, having a good time—"

"He got drunk and told the story, sort of. And Goethe made up the rest," Peaseblossom said. "The usual. There are so many. Hoffmann, Byron, Poe." Peaseblossom shook his head. "Speaking of *Frankenstein*." Bobby shot him a look and he stopped talking.

"Was the Elf King punished for stealing that child?" Jewell asked, still not sure she was following.

Bobby waved his hand. "No, no. At least I don't think so. All that business with the Elf King happened long before Titania or I were born. Besides, faeries and elves used to steal children a lot, right, T? I mean it was a thing we used to do back in the day. Not so much now. Am I right?"

"Are you speaking to me?" Titania said. "I've never stolen a child in my life, and my sister gave birth to a halfling, so why in the world would she need to steal one?"

"I'm just saying, it wasn't such an uncommon thing."

Peaseblossom sighed. "Unfortunately, he's right. I don't know how often it happens anymore, since there is very little traffic back and forth between worlds."

"You could have fooled me," Jewell said.

"Really, this is quite an unusual circumstance. Nothing like this has happened in a long time," Peaseblossom said. "The point is that because it is so difficult for faeries and elves to have their own children, they used to, occasionally, come here and take a human one."

"Nice," Jewell said.

"I was reading in one of the books I found," Melody said hoisting the tome aloft, "that in Celtic cultures it was not uncommon for townspeople to leave a sick baby in the woods to die, believing it was a changeling."

"What's a changeling?" Jewell asked.

"A faerie baby left in the human world," Iolanthe said. "We never swapped out sick children. That's a myth. Sometimes we were able to rescue those sick human children, whose parents had abandoned them to die, but we never took a human child and left one of our own in its place—that just doesn't make sense."

Melody shrugged. "I'm not judging. Humans are the ones who left their kids in the woods to die. Pretty barbaric if you ask me."

Jewell took a deep breath and pushed back her chair. "Can someone please just give me some straight answers about what is going on with the father of my child? I don't care who tells me, or what you say, so long as it is the truth. I honestly don't know how much more of this jibber-jabber I can take." She sat back and crossed her legs. "Thomas, you seem like the guy with the least likely reason to lie to me. Please. Tell me what the hell is going on."

Peaseblossom folded his hands on the table and leaned toward them. "None of us knows for sure exactly what's going on." His voice was even and steady and Jewell thought she could believe him. It didn't feel like he was trying to influence her, like in the diner. "We suspect that ancient faerie and elf forces may be at work. Forces that none of us realized were still relevant. Robin and I have been living among humans so long, we go days, weeks even without using any magic. Why Titania and Iolanthe have grown so disconnected from their own culture, I can't tell you. I haven't been back in over 400 years, but the inhabitants of the Realm, I suspect, are not so unlike humans in that after a period, certain beliefs fall out of fashion. What was once believed to be true and irrefutable becomes just another story. First it is doubted and then dismissed." He paused for a moment and looked at Jewell. "Would you like me to continue?"

"Please," she said.

"Faeries and elves are related, and not as distantly as some would have you believe." He shot a quick glance at Titania. "At some point during our creation history, all the creatures of the Realm settled into their respective territories. Orcs, trolls, and goblins had their territories. Faeries and elves had theirs."

"Don't forget about the sprites and the brownies," Iolanthe said.

"Yes, of course. Everyone," Peaseblossom said. "These lands all border on each other, so there was an occasional skirmish. We each have our own set of skills and magical capabilities, but in the end, probably because faeries and elves are so much alike, our two races tended to square off against each other more often than the rest. Although, I hear the orcs are currently on the move forming a possible alliance with the goblins and trolls."

"Ondine has things under control," Iolanthe said with a grimace.

"I have no doubt," said Peaseblossom. "At any rate, it is said that at one time the elves had their own king—the one depicted so darkly in the poem by Goethe. He was fond of stealing human children for his daughters. They refused to marry and were not interested in trying to have children of their own, and their father, who cared nothing about humans or their children, only about the cruel happiness of his daughters, had no problem taking what he wanted. He also thought that he should rule all the Realm, and not just the Elfish territory, so he gathered a magical army and attacked the Glade. The faeries were able to resist him in no small part because of our alliances with the other inhabitants of the Realm. Because the faeries were victorious in this battle, and neither the orcs, trolls, nor goblins were interested in leadership beyond their own backyards, it was decided that a faerie be named the ruler of the Realm, whether that be a king or queen, and govern all the land to maintain the general peace."

He paused, smoothed out his jacket lapels, then began again. "The Elf King was so distraught at this prospect and having come to the realization that in his desire for power, he'd committed unforgiveable acts of cruelty, not just in the Realm, but also in the human world, he decided to disassemble himself, spreading his essence out into the space between the human world and the Realm. Of course, before his body turned to sparkling ash, he prophesied his own return, stating that one day he would be reborn. When that happened, he would come to woo the Faerie Queen and bring 1,000 years of prosperity and unity to the Realm, thereby earning his absolution."

Everyone sat in silence for a moment taking in the scope of Peaseblossom's story.

"Do you think that's what's happened? That Oberon is the Elf King reborn and it's his magical imperative to woo Titania and rule the Realm?" Jewell said. Her stomach churned. She did not need to hear Peaseblossom's answer.

"Yes, we think that's what happened." Peaseblossom reached across the table for her hand. She let him take it. "We think that your invocation or spell, unknowingly boosted by quadratic magic, has reincarnated the Elf King in Oberon."

"I—" She looked at all of them staring at her and suddenly didn't know what to say.

"Are you okay?" Melody asked.

"Honestly? I don't know."

"This is quite a tale," Titania said. "And explains why I have felt this overwhelming desire to be with him." She looked at Jewell with pity in her eyes. "I care little about human beings and their feelings."

"I would have never guessed."

"However," Titania continued. "I do not enjoy being at their mercy. If I could have found a way to leave this world and Oberon forever, I would have done so by now."

"And what about my child?" Jewell reflexively placed her hand on her abdomen. "Am I even going to have a baby, or is it going to come out with green skin and pointy ears?"

"Elves don't look like Vulcans, Jewell," Bobby said.

"Well, they do a little," Peaseblossom said.

"Please, just tell me."

"The child should be beautiful," Iolanthe said. "And a boy. He will be a brilliant combination of you and Oberon. If you're asking if he will be magical, no one can say. This is uncharted territory for all of us."

"You should tell her, Iolanthe," Peaseblossom said.

"Tell me what?"

Iolanthe took in a deep breath and looked at Jewell for the first time. "I believe you are carrying the spirit of the last child the Elf King stole from the human world. I believe this because of a vision I had when I was connected to Oberon and Titania and their energy flowed through me."

"What does that mean, exactly?"

"I don't know that it means anything except that it's a gesture on the part of the Elf King to make amends for his past mistakes. I think it's a very good sign."

"Or it could mean that the child is destined to destroy Oberon," Titania said. "All the more reason why Oberon should come with me, and you should stay here with your child."

"This gets better and better. I thought I was just having a child by a man that used to be a dog. It turns out that I'm having a child by a man who is the reincarnation of an evil Elf King that used to steal babies for fun."

"Well, when you put it like that," Bobby said, "it doesn't sound so good." Melody elbowed him. "What? Chances are pretty good that kid will have some magical abilities. That'll be fun, right?"

"Bobby, seriously?" Melody said.

Jewell ignored him. "How do I fix this? I mean, how do we fix this. How do we get Titania back to the Realm where she

218

belongs? How do I keep Oberon from ageing? Is there a spell, a potion, Thomas? Please, someone tell me."

"You need to release him," Peaseblossom said.

"Release him?"

"Because you cast the spell, you need to release him from it."

"Okay, so how do I release him?"

"You should just be able to say, 'I release you,' " Bobby said. "But you have to say it directly to him."

"Seriously? It's that simple? No magic words? No powders or potions?"

"It should be that simple."

"Then what happens?" She turned to Titania. "Do you go back to the Realm?"

"Nothing would make me happier," Titania said.

"You should know," Peaseblossom said, "that once you release him, he may choose to leave."

"Why would he do that?"

"We don't know what he'll do, but once you release him, he can choose. Right now, he can't. The compulsion to be with Titania may also disappear with the release, but it might not," Peaseblossom said. "If it's the essence of the Elf King that's compelling Oberon to be with Titania, when he loves you so obviously, he might not be able to stay, no matter how much he wants to."

"Either way, unless he comes to the Realm he will continue to age, and he will die," Titania said.

"Is that true?" Jewell looked to Peaseblossom who had become her savior in all this.

"Yes," he said. "It does seem that his life force is draining at an accelerated pace. This confluence of magic, both intended and unintended, has made for great deal of uncertainty."

"You don't know anything for sure."

"We don't know anything with a one hundred percent certainty."

"I just look at him, say, 'I release you,' and see what happens?"

"Yes, that's about it," Peaseblossom said.

"Anything else anyone want to tell me?"

"I'm so sorry, Jewell. This is the worst," Melody said.

"You said it." Jewell stood and surveyed the group huddled around the table in the middle of the cavernous Philadelphia Free Library. To anyone else they must look like a typical group of Center City dwellers, their heads bent deep in conversation, their clothes fashionable, their books scholarly. If only the world knew what was really going on. "I guess I better get home," she said. "Wish me luck."

# ELEVEN

## I.

EWELL PUSHED OPEN the door to her apartment to find Oberon on the couch watching *The Amazing Dr. Pol* on Nat Geo Wild. As usual, Dr. Pol had his arm up the backside of a cow, and the sight of this and the wave of nostalgia that came with it sent Jewell reeling.

"Jewell?" Oberon turned just as she hit the floor. In a moment she was sitting up and feeling stupid. "What's the matter?" Oberon asked as he helped her onto the couch.

"It's nothing," she said. "Just over-tired, I guess. Pregnant lady stuff."

"Are you sure? Let me get you some water."

She nodded. Soon he was back and handing her a glass of ice water. "Did you eat dinner?" She shook her head. "Let me get you something."

"Oberon, really, I'm okay. I'll get something in a minute. You're supposed to be resting, not running around fussing over me." She set the glass down on the coffee table and shrugged off her jacket. "So how are you feeling?" she asked.

"I feel great. I think I should go back to work tomorrow."

"Really? I thought you were going to steer clear of Bobby and those guys. Now that you've got some experience and Bobby made you those fake papers, you could work anywhere." She took his hand. "Wouldn't you like to meet some new people? Maybe ones that don't have magical powers?"

"Turns out I've got magical powers." He shrugged. "Bobby's helped me a lot, and he's funny. Why are you so down on him?"

"I'm not down on him. I just—"

"What?"

She shook her head. "It's not important. Which episode is this?"

"The one where Dr. Pol goes out in the cold and ends up sticking his arm up a cow's butt. Oh, wait, that's every episode."

"If you don't like it, why are you watching it?"

"I didn't say I didn't like it. I love Dr. Pol. It's our show, right? The one we were watching the night everything happened."

He turned from the TV and looked at her. All the wrinkles and gray were gone. His skin was aglow with youthful vigor. Maybe she should just leave well enough alone. What the hell. Those stupid faeries really didn't know any more than she did. Maybe it was all a trick. Could she trust any of them? Thomas maybe, but even Thomas had tried to glamour her.

"Are you sure you're okay?" he asked. "You seem kind of out of it."

She turned away from him for a moment. She looked at her record collection. Her father would have loved this man sitting next to her. She could just hear him telling her: *He cares about you as person, not just a woman, or a partner, but as a human being. This is a guy worth sacrificing for—he'd do the same for you.* But her father wasn't here. "Do you ever just feel like you're going crazy? I swear I'm barely holding it together. When I walked in and saw Dr. Pol on the TV and you here on the couch, I think my brain short-circuited."

"Jewell, we don't have the same point of reference. I don't think about how none of this makes sense. For me it just is."

They stared at the muted screen for a while, watching as Dr. Pol and his son delivered a baby goat. The weather was miserable, cold and snowy, and the two bickered and groused the entire time, but when that little goat came spilling out of its mother onto the dirty straw strewn across the barn floor, they smiled and hi-fived each other in celebration. Mission accomplished. The world was right again. The beauty of nature had won the day, and at the end of the episode, they drove off down the snowy wind-swept Michigan road toward another adventure.

"Oberon—"

"Don't, Jewell."

"How do you know what I'm going to say?"

"You were with them tonight, weren't you? All of them. That's why you were late, why you missed dinner. Don't bother denying it. I can smell them on you."

"I suppose with what you've got left of that sense of smell I'd be hard pressed to hide anything from you." She couldn't meet his gaze. His question sounded like an accusation, but she couldn't blame him. "Yes. I was with them."

"You were making plans about me."

"Yes."

"They told you that you need to release me."

"Yes."

"What if I said I don't want you to."

"What are you talking about?"

"I don't want you to release me. I'm afraid if you do, I won't be able to resist Titania." He gathered her up in his arms. "Please," he said burying his face in her hair. "I'm afraid."

She untangled herself and held him at an arm's distance. "But if I release you, I might also release her. Then she would go back to the Realm and you and I can live in peace like normal people. Well, relatively speaking."

"But you don't know for sure."

"We don't know anything for sure. But she says she wants to go and that she would rather go alone."

"She's afraid, too."

"Of what?"

"She's afraid that I am the Elf King."

"Oh, they're all pretty convinced you're the Elf King. Why didn't you tell me?"

"I didn't know how to explain it in any way that made sense. All I had was a feeling and some images that made me very uncomfortable."

"The whole thing makes me uncomfortable. Turns out that not only was Bobby all buddy-buddy with Shakespeare, but he also used to party with Johann Wolfgang von Goethe."

"Wish I knew who that was," Oberon said. "Was he famous?"

Jewell settled back into the cushions. "This man, Goethe, wrote a poem called *Der Erlkönig*, which in German means *The Elf King*. Turns out he got the idea from Bobby one night when they were sitting in a bar drinking. I guess these are the kinds of things you can do when you're virtually immortal. I heard a lot of elf and faerie history tonight. If you can call it that. Melody and I went to the library and the rest of them followed us there, like a stupid episode of *Scooby Doo*."

Oberon cocked his head.

"Never mind." She sighed. "You know, it's too bad they don't have a president in the Realm, because I would vote for Thomas Peaseblossom. He's the sanest one of the bunch."

"Yes, I like Tom, too," Oberon said. "Will you read the poem to me?"

"Are you sure?"

"Maybe it will help me understand what I saw."

"But Thomas said that Bobby was just telling an old elf story and that Goethe made most of it up."

"I want to hear it."

"Okay." Jewell retrieved her purse. There were two sheets of folded paper jammed between her wallet and her phone. She pulled them out and sat next to Oberon, who threw his arm around her shoulder.

"Melody helped me with a literal translation. Did you know she speaks German?"

He shook his head.

"No, why would you. I didn't know until today. Anyway, in German it rhymes and flows much better."

"I wouldn't know the difference," Oberon said.

"Sure you would," Jewell said. "Poetry is also about how the words sound when they're read, not just what the words mean. A poem is supposed to invoke a feeling or emotion, not just images in your mind. It's kind of like visual art in that way. Does that make sense?"

He nodded.

"Okay. Here goes," she said.

"The Elf King

> *"Who rides, so late, through night and wind?*
> *It is a father with his child.*
> *He holds the boy well in his arms*
> *He holds him safely, he keeps him warm.*

" 'My son, why do you hide your face in fear?'
'Father, do you not see the Elf King?
The Elf King with his crown and cape?'
'My son, it's a streak of fog.'

" 'You dear child, come, go with me!
I will play the most lovely games with you;
We've many colorful flowers on the beach,
My mother will give you a golden robe.'

" 'Oh father, my father, can't you hear
What the Elf King quietly promises me?'
'Be calm, stay calm, my child;
It's just the wind rustling through the fall leaves.'

" 'Do you, fine boy, want to go with me?
My daughters shall take good care of you;
My daughters lead the nightly dance,
And will rock you and dance you and sing you to
        sleep.'

" 'Oh father, my father, don't you see there
The Elf King's daughters in that gloomy place?'
'My son, my son, I see it clearly:
It's just the shimmer of the old gray willows.'

" 'I love you! Your beautiful form entices me;
And if you're not willing to come with me, I will use
        force.' "

Jewell looked away from the poem. "That sounds familiar."
Oberon removed his arm from around Jewell's shoulder and
let his hands rest in his lap.
"Please, Jewell, keep reading."

She nodded and continued.

" *'Oh father, my father, he's touching me now!*
*The Elf King has done me harm!'*

*"This horrifies the father; he rides like the wind,*
*He holds his moaning child in his arms,*
*With hardship and difficulty he reaches the farm;*
*And in his arms, the child is dead."*

When Jewell finished reading the poem, she looked at
Oberon who had his head in his hands. She thought he might be
crying. She tried to comfort him, but he shook her off and then
sat up. His cheeks were wet, but his eyes were angry.

"So. This is who I am?"

"Oberon, please," Jewell said. "It's just a poem. Goethe was
fascinated with darkness and melancholy like all the Romantics.
He wrote a play that's 500 pages long about a man who sells his
soul to the devil. He's a writer. Writers make stuff up."

"But you don't understand. I remember this."

"What do you mean you remember it?"

"I stole that child because my daughters wanted someone
to dress up and play with. It was so long ago, long before this
poem was written. They were cruel because I was cruel. When
they tired of the boy, they let him wander off into the Glade
where he died for real." He rubbed the sides of his head with the
heels of his hands, as if he was trying to push the memory back
into that part of his mind where he couldn't access it anymore.
"What I saw in my mind wasn't like watching something on TV.
It was all so dark and hazy. It was more like I felt it than saw it.
I do believe, though, that may have been the last time I was in
the human world. Something else happened that kept me in the
Realm, and then there's nothing." He stood, clenching his fists,

and for a moment Jewell saw something she did not recognize. He seemed to be trying to keep it together. He paced a few steps, turned and glared at her. The air around him crackled with a golden energy. The light flickered in his eyes and then was gone.

"Please sit down." She reached for his hand, but he did not take it. "There was a war, which the Elf King lost. You are not the Elf King." Again, she tried to take his hand, but he wouldn't let her and so she retreated into herself.

"Am I evil?"

"How could you ask such a thing?" Jewell wanted to touch him so badly. "You are the most beautiful person I have ever known. You may have this Elf King's essence in you, but you are not him. You are my sweet, smart Oberon."

Oberon's fists were still clenched against his thighs. His mouth a hard, straight line. "If you loved me so much, how could you do this to me?"

"What do you mean? I didn't do anything to you."

"Yes, you did. We were so happy together, weren't we?" He turned away from her and stared out the window. Jewell followed his gaze and saw the darkening sky. "We could be at the park right now," he said. "If you'd just been patient, that man Steve, who liked you so much, would have asked you out. He probably would have married you. Maybe you'd be having his child now. And I'd be here, too. Content to share you, sleep in the same bed with you, love you both." When he turned back around, his face was wet again, but she couldn't tell if they were tears of sadness or anger. "Look what your wish did to both of us."

Finally, she could take it no longer and she stood and threw her arms around his shoulders. He did not push her away, but gathered her up as she whispered, "I'm sorry." She kissed his cheeks and held his face in her hands. "Can you forgive me?"

He nodded. "I have to," he said. "I love you too much."

"I'll figure out a way to make this right. I promise."

He took both her arms and didn't quite shake her but made her pay attention. "Don't do anything." He looked at her hard. "You don't understand. I would rather die here with you, than live forever in the Realm. And now that I've lived this life, held you in my arms, I could never go back to what I was before. I just hope that I die before the baby is born."

"My god! Why would you say something like that?"

"Because I'm afraid of this Elf King, too."

"Oberon that's crazy. You are full of light. Enough light to obliterate any dark force that might be part of the Elf King. Thomas says he did what he did to redeem himself. I don't know why everyone is so afraid. He didn't say he was going to come back and lay waste to the Realm. He said he would come back, woo the Faerie Queen, and bring 1,000 years of prosperity and unity."

Oberon shook his head. "You didn't see what I did. I felt it in my soul."

"Maybe he realized that to be good, he had to reassemble himself in someone like you. Someone full of light. Someone who could balance out his darkness." As she said this, she felt it must be true—that this is what had drawn the Elf King's essence to Oberon during his transformation. She was sure the rest of them had it all wrong.

"Doesn't that make the most sense? The reason these things frighten you so much is because you don't have any real experience feeling bad about anything. I mean, I live with you, so I know you feel sad sometimes, maybe feel guilty. Genuinely dark thoughts are not part of your nature—but for most humans, they are. We can imagine all kinds of horrible things. Some of us are even capable of enacting them. This understanding of evil, or darkness, or whatever you want to call it, and then our ability to resist it, is part of what makes us human. But because of who you are, and how you came to be, you don't have this capacity for evil. It just doesn't exist in animals—or in you."

Did she see relief in Oberon's face or fatigue? There had been a time when she could have read his every expression, but every day he was becoming more of a mystery to her. Her silly selfish wish had set him on this path. Now this simple sweet man was caught up in forces beyond anyone's understanding. This wasn't fair. But she also was beginning to understand that his devotion to her was no less harmful than the overwhelming attraction that he felt for Titania. She did not want him to be a pawn in this game any longer. He needed to be able to make his own choice.

"You look exhausted," she said. "I can see how all of this has upset you. Why don't you go to bed?"

"I am tired," he said. "But I haven't seen you all day, and we can't seem to talk about anything but this."

"I know. I'd love a little normalcy for just one night."

"Well, let's be normal. Right now. I know you're hungry." He tapped the side of his nose. "How about I make something to eat, and we sit right here on this couch and watch something stupid. Together."

"Are you sure?"

"Yes."

"Okay, then," she said. "Let's do it."

## 2.

Later that night, after they'd stuffed their faces full of macaroni and cheese and bowls of chocolate ice cream and salty pretzels, after they'd watched a marathon of *My Cat From Hell*, and Jewell had told Oberon some funny and sad stories about her parents and how much she missed them both, after they'd had sex for the first time in weeks, and had fallen asleep in each other's arms, Jewell awoke from a dream about the future. A future that did not include Oberon. She couldn't tell from the dream if this future outcome was because she'd done nothing, and he'd aged and died, like all the faeries were telling her would happen, or if it was because she'd released him, and he'd gone off with Titania to fulfill his destiny as the reincarnated Elf King. Either way she knew that he would be gone. In one scenario he'd be dead and in the other he'd be in another world with another woman. She tried to push these thoughts out of her mind, and go back to sleep, but she couldn't. She needed to decide. So her restlessness would not wake Oberon, she slipped out of bed and into her robe and huddled on the couch to think.

She did not want him to go to the Realm. She wanted him to stay with her. She loved him, as a man, as a beautiful, kind man, but she also felt responsible for him. At this point, maybe those feelings were a little ridiculous, but she felt them none the less. He had been right when he'd blamed her. If she had known her silly selfish wish could come true, would she have made it anyway? The truth was, she probably would have. Feeling the way she had that night, not realizing how much she still missed her parents, how alone she really was, and that awful rejection from Simon. Simon—she hadn't thought of him in months, not even when she looked at the print he'd given her. She did still think about Steve Munroe sometimes, and the fact that Oberon had mentioned him, meant that Oberon still thought about him, too.

What would her life had been like, if she'd only been able to hold out a little longer? But that kind of thinking was pointless.

And now she was trying to decide Oberon's fate. She wanted to respect his wishes. He'd begged her not to release him, even if that meant his death. If she did nothing this was a near certainty. If she released him, he might go with Titania, but he might also stay with her. If he did stay, it would be his choice, not hers. If he left, at least he would be alive. In the end, there was only one thing to do.

She rose from the couch and tip-toed back into the bedroom. She removed her robe and slid back into bed, but she didn't snuggle back in next to Oberon. Instead, she took a deep breath and gently shook him awake. He roused slightly and blinked at her a few times with sleepy eyes. "Is something—"

She shushed him by placing her finger on his lips. His eyes opened wide, but she said it before he could stop her. "Oberon," she said. "I release you from my spell. I love you and I want you to be able to choose."

# 3.

Across town, in her penthouse hotel suite, Titania sat straight up in bed, which woke her sister, Iolanthe.

"What?" Iolanthe said. "What's happened?"

Titania looked at her sister. She felt surprised, but she did not feel happy, exactly. "She did it. She's released him."

"So now what?"

Titania shook her head. "I have no idea. I guess it's up to him."

# TWELVE

## I.

S SOON AS THE WORDS slipped out of Jewell's mouth, all the youthful magic that surrounded Oberon vanished, as if she'd snapped her fingers or waved a magic wand. Before her eyes, the deep-set wrinkles around his eyes returned, the gray that had started at his temples spread upward through his otherwise dark hair. His skin paled and his cheeks lost their plumpness. As his muscle mass contracted, the skin on his arms and chest lost its elasticity and drooped ever so slightly in tiny, papery folds. She thought the transformation might never stop—that he might turn to dust right there in their bed—but eventually the transformation slowed and then stopped. Oberon said nothing, but stared at her, his eyes wide with disbelief. When it was all done, he looked like he could be his own grandfather.

"Why?" was all he could say as he propped himself up against the headboard.

"My god—I had no idea this would happen. Are you all right?" She moved to help him sit up and he brushed her away.

Jewell looked down at Oberon's hands, now showing signs of arthritis, slightly bulbous knuckles, thick veins pushing against thinning skin. Her breath caught in her throat.

"I guess I'm all right," he said. He swung his legs over the side of the bed and shuffled into the bathroom. Jewell followed him and stood behind him as he examined all the changes in the mirror. "How old would you say I look now?"

Jewell shook her head. What had she done?

"Well, how old?"

"Sixty? Sixty-five?" she said.

"How old would you have said I looked before Titania kissed me? Forty? Fifty?"

Jewell grimaced.

"Well?" She could see he was not going to let her remain mute. He turned from the mirror and stepped in close. The heat from his body radiated against her skin.

"Yes," she said more to herself than to him.

"I can't hear as well as I used to. What did you say?"

She looked at him, her mouth a hard straight line. "Yes. I would have thought before that kiss you looked closer to forty-five or fifty." She turned and stalked out of the bathroom. He followed her.

"What were you thinking?"

She ignored him and continued into the kitchen where she shoved two mugs full of water into the microwave.

"Answer me, Jewell. What were you thinking?"

"I was thinking that I was finally going to set you free."

"I didn't realize I was anyone's prisoner."

Jewell half-laughed as she slammed drawers and pulled out spoons and tea bags. "The truth is you were everyone's prisoner. It was either me or Titania—you had no choice in anything. I was trying to at least give you something."

Oberon ran his hands through his hair. He looked at Jewell with an expression she hadn't seen in a long, long time. Those eyes, so dark and soulful, rimmed in white. An expression that said: *love me.* She felt like someone was sitting on her chest.

"Jewell, why can't you understand? I did choose, all those years ago, when you first opened that crate and let me into your life. My love for you was never forced by anyone or any magic spell." He sat down at the table with a heavy sigh. "Is that why you released me, because you thought I didn't really love you?"

"I don't know what is real anymore, but I do know that when you were my dog, you were my property. I paid money for you, and you were my responsibility. Get it? Melody pointed out to me that as a man, you're no one's property. Certainly not mine."

"You'd better be making me some tea, too," he said. She set a bubbling mug of hot water in front of him. "I don't know why I'm so angry." He reached for a tea bag. "I told you I'd rather die than go to the Realm and that hasn't changed. I actually don't feel that different, except that my back hurts again." He poured some milk into the mug while Jewell sat down across from him. "So my hair's gray again. So what?"

Jewell reached for his hand. "I love you so much. I was afraid I'd lose you. No one knew what would happen, but they all encouraged me to release you. They said nothing would change, for better or for worse, unless I did." She stared down at her mug of tea, wishing there were magic leaves at its bottom telling her what to do next.

"Faeries are artful liars. What made you think you could trust them?"

"You trust Bobby, don't you?"

Oberon sighed.

"Well?"

"In most things, yes. I don't think he'd willingly work against us."

"Maybe we're just too naive."

"Maybe." Each of them stared into their respective mugs without saying anything for some time.

"I did what I thought was best." Jewell looked up. "Can you forgive me?"

Oberon squeezed her hand. "I don't suppose you can un-release me and my back will stop hurting?"

"I don't think so." She smiled at him, wondering if she looked as helpless as she felt.

"We'll figure this out, just like we have everything else."

Or we won't, she thought.

Jewell wanted to ask him about Titania, if he felt a shift in any of those compulsions, but she was too afraid. They sipped the rest of their tea in silence, not sure what was left to say.

## 2.

The next morning, they woke to Bobby pounding on their door. Jewell opened it, cinching her robe around her. "I'm surprised you didn't just shimmer into bed with us," she said as she flung the door open.

"I don't usually shimmer into people's bedrooms uninvited," he said. "Despite what you may have heard."

"What do you want?" Jewell's patience was threadbare.

"I felt a ripple last night about 3 AM."

Jewell shrugged. "And?"

"I'm assuming you released Oberon from your spell."

Jewell said nothing. "So," Bobby said. "What happened?"

"Nothing."

"Really?" Bobby pointed toward Oberon, who was shuffling toward them from the bedroom.

"I thought it was you out here making all this racket." Oberon's hair was now completely gray. He appeared to have aged even more overnight.

"He says he feels fine," Jewell said as Oberon lowered himself onto the couch.

"He doesn't look fine," Bobby said. "What the hell, Jewell?"

"Don't what the hell me, Bobby. I did what you and Thomas and everyone else said I should do. I released him. You didn't say that would make him old again. I think he's aging faster than he was before."

"What?" Oberon said. "I didn't quite catch that."

"See!" Jewell said.

Oberon laughed. "You're too easy. Could you two settle down please? I can hear just fine."

Jewell looked at Bobby and gestured for him to come in and have a seat. "I need some coffee. Does anyone else want anything?"

They both shook their heads and waved her toward the kitchen. She could hear them talking from the other room. Bobby asked Oberon if Titania had tried to contact him, and Oberon replied that she hadn't.

"Maybe that's a good sign," Bobby said as Jewell returned to the living room. She sat down next to Oberon on the couch.

"Hopefully she's been released now, too," Oberon said. "Maybe she's already gone back to the Realm, and I can finish out my days here in peace."

Jewell stared at Oberon. "Please don't say things like that." She squeezed his leg. He covered her hand with his and she did her best to relax. "I wish there was a rule book somewhere. You know, in case of inadvertent spell, do X. In case of ancient reincarnation, do Y." Jewell turned to Bobby. "Why isn't there a rule book?"

"Spoken like a true human. You're an engineer, right?"

Jewell snorted. "Most days."

"Well even though a spell may have if/then properties, it's not science. You can't engineer something that comes from chaos. Even under the most controlled circumstances magic is unpredictable."

"I know some pretty unpredictable humans."

"Yes, but even the seeming randomness of their unpredictability can be forecast and imagined within certain parameters. Isn't that the basis of psychology?"

Jewell sat back and exhaled low and slow. "What is with you? In one conversation, you act like a comedian, but then there are times when you sound like someone who's been alive for over 400 years. Who's the real Bobby Fellowes?"

Bobby laughed. "My name is Robin Goodfellow, and until about a hundred years ago, my nickname was Puck. Now I'm Bobby. I've always loved an excellent prank. But I'm not a complete ass. I know how to suck it up when things get serious."

Oberon yawned loudly and stretched his arms. "Do you mind if I go back to bed for a little while? I think the last couple of days have taken their toll."

Jewell shot Bobby a concerned glance and then smiled at Oberon. "Of course. Do you want me to help you get settled?"

"Good lord, woman," Oberon said brushing her aside. "I'm not an invalid yet." He winked at her. "Next week you can go out and buy me some adult diapers. It'll give you some practice for the baby."

Jewell wanted to play along and say something funny, but she felt appalled as she watched Oberon slowly push himself up from the couch and shamble toward the bedroom. Once the door closed, she turned to Bobby. "What the hell have I done?"

"We tried to explain to you that we didn't know what would happen."

"And yet you worked so hard to convince me."

"You did the right thing," Bobby said. He leaned back and crossed his legs. "He hasn't run off to be with Titania, and she wasn't the one here banging on your door this morning."

"So what? At this rate he'll be gone in a few days."

"You don't know that."

"Seems I don't know anything."

"Magic can make us all feel that way."

"I don't really care how it makes me feel. I want to know what we can do to save his life."

"There's really only one thing that I can think of, and you're not going to like it."

Jewell crossed her legs underneath her. "You'd better lay it on me."

Bobby stood up. "Why don't you get dressed and we'll go talk to Thomas. We'll need his help." With a sinking feeling in her gut, Jewell left to change into some street clothes.

# 3.

Iolanthe and Titania had both slept fitfully the rest of the night. In the morning they rose and dressed without much discussion. Iolanthe suggested they breakfast in the hotel brasserie and Titania agreed. After they'd filled up on chocolate croissants and full-fat café au laits, they strolled around Rittenhouse Square, each thinking the same thing, but neither of them speaking it aloud.

Finally, Iolanthe could stand it no longer. "All morning long, I've been wanting to ask you."

Titania linked her arm in her sister's as they brushed past the fountain and out of the park. "You want to ask me if I was released, too."

"Yes."

"The compulsion is gone. The feeling as if some giant hand were constantly trying to push me toward him, but something remains. Some residue of something." She pulled her sister's elbow close. "I believe I could leave now, but I don't want to."

"Shall we go this way?" Iolanthe asked as they turned onto Lombard Street.

"Why not? There is another lovely park down this way," Titania said. "I believe it's a favorite spot of Oberon and the woman."

"Why is that?" Iolanthe asked.

"I believe it's where they used to spend a lot of time before we arrived on the scene."

Iolanthe chuckled. "You mean when he was still a dog."

"Yes," Titania said, smiling.

They ambled silently down Lombard Street, past the stately Philadelphia brownstones and intimate BYOB restaurants. The breeze was cool and carried the portent of rain, the sky overcast but not dreary. As they reached the Schuylkill Banks Park, children and their parents or nannies scurried around the playground equipment, laughing and talking. Dogs yipped and chased each other around the dog run, while cyclists and joggers entered and exited the boardwalk.

"I can see why they liked it so much," Iolanthe said. "It is veritably bustling with activity."

Titania waved her hand dismissively. "It surely holds nothing to the grand meadow in the Glade on a festival day, does it? Where are the orcs, the goblins, the elves?" She stopped and faced Iolanthe. "I find this world so drab. Everyone looks the same. Where is all the color?"

A skateboarder whizzed by them on the sidewalk. "Yo! Love the locks, dude."

"Did that human creature just call me dude?" Titania raised her hand as if she were clutching a ball.

"Don't do it, sister," Iolanthe said.

Titania lowered her hand and linked her arm in Iolanthe's again. Together they walked past the dog park where they stopped briefly to observe the owners and their dogs. "This was Jewell's mistake," Titania said. "She should have been concentrating on the men, not the dogs."

Iolanthe smiled. "Yes. Look at that one there, the man with the largish sort of fluffy beast. He looks nice enough. Trim and nicely dressed."

"Yoo-hoo!" Titania waved at the man, who looked up and pointed at himself. Titania waved him over. "Excuse me, but we couldn't help but notice your beautiful and well-behaved creature. It is a dog, correct?"

The man smiled at her like she couldn't be serious. "Yes, he's a dog."

"What's your name?" Titania said. "You're handsome enough, and those glasses make you look smart."

"Thanks?" He held out his hand and Titania placed her fingertips against his, expecting him to kiss her hand, but instead he shook it up and down. She snatched it away quickly and he laughed. "My name's Steve. This," he said pointing toward his dog, "is Fang."

"Fang?" Iolanthe said. "What a dreadful name."

Steve bent down and scratched Fang's head. "She didn't mean that buddy." He stood up, still smiling. "He's named after a famous dog in literature. You know, White Fang? Jack London?"

Iolanthe and Titania exchanged glances. "You should meet our friend Jewell. She loves dogs named after literary characters."

"Jewell Jamieson?" They nodded, even though neither of them knew Jewell's surname. "I haven't seen her in quite some time," Steve said, his smile fading. "I saw her once after her dog died, but I guess she just doesn't have the heart to come back to the park. Can't say that I blame her."

"Oh, her dog didn't—" Iolanthe elbowed Titania, interrupting her.

"Yes," Iolanthe said. "It was very sad about Jewell's dog. He was sweet."

"It's too bad. She gave me some great advice about a trainer for Fang." He bent down and hooked the leash to the collar. "I've got to get this fellow home and then I'm off to work. Do me a favor, would you?"

"Anything for you, Steve," Titania said.

"Tell Jewell that Steve from the dog park said hello."

"We'll tell her," Iolanthe said.

After Steve had walked away, they linked arms again and headed for the boardwalk. "Are we going to tell Jewell?" Iolanthe asked.

"I'll leave it up to you," Titania said. "He seemed to remember her fondly."

Iolanthe waved her hand. "Some humans are like that. They like everyone. My son was like that."

"I suppose he was," Titania said. "He took after his beautiful mother."

Iolanthe squeezed her sister's arm as they entered the board-walk. "So, does all this calm good humor mean we can go home?"

Titania paused before answering. "Not quite yet—I don't know how to describe it exactly—I feel like there's something I've forgotten, a memory I can't quite reach. I can't go without saying goodbye."

"Do you think that's such a good idea?"

"When have I ever cared whether something was a good idea?"

# 4·

On the cab ride over to Thomas's shop, Bobby tried to explain as calmly as possible to Jewell that the only way to save Oberon was to let Titania take him. "The issue now is," he said as they stepped out of the cab, "she might not want him, and he defi-nitely doesn't want her."

"Which is why you brought me here," she said.

Thomas met them at the door and a wave of patchouli and incense swirled around them. "Thomas!" Bobby hugged Pease-blossom as if he hadn't seen him for months. Peaseblossom held up his hand as if to stop Bobby from starting in on some spiel.

"I know why you're here," he said. "Come inside." He ush-ered them across the main floor, through the jewelry cases and stacks of books, to a back stairway that led down to his office. He settled himself behind a modest desk and motioned for Jewell and Bobby to take their seats across from him.

Jewell wasn't sure what she expected. Velvet curtains and a crystal ball, maybe, but not a humdrum office, so like her own. Jewell leaned forward. "I don't know why, but I trust you, Thomas."

"He is the most trustworthy faerie I've ever known," Bobby said with a straight face.

"No punchline?" Jewell said.

He shook his head.

"You'll tell me the truth, right?"

Peaseblossom nodded that he would.

"All right. Is this the only thing we can do?" She felt the catch in her throat but shook it off. "We can't slow the aging down with some kind of potion or elixir?"

Peaseblossom sighed. "I don't think so. There are a few remedies that slow aging, but not by any real measure. How fast would you say he's aging now?"

"I don't know. It's all just a guess." Jewell tried not to sound panicky. "Maybe five years?"

"And how old would you estimate him to be when you saw him this morning?"

Jewell looked at Bobby. "Sixty-five. Maybe seventy," he said.

"Really?" Jewell said. "Did you think he looked that old?"

"I don't know," Bobby said. "Fairies are terrible at this sort of thing. He looked crazy old to me."

Jewell took a deep breath. "Okay. Yes. He looked about sixty-five. A young and vigorous sixty-five. I don't even think of sixty-five as being old."

"Who does?" Peaseblossom said. "But when you're aging approximately five years every day, even a young vigorous sixty-five is a problem."

"Yes. Yes, of course it is." Jewell twisted the tail of her shirt in her lap. "What if we convinced Titania to come kiss him every few months?" Bobby and Peaseblossom exchanged glances but said nothing. "Do you think that would work?"

Peaseblossom shook his head. "It takes a lot out of a faerie to travel through the veil. I can't imagine convincing Titania to come do that every few months, which to her might feel more like every few days. There's nothing in it for her, plus it might not even work again now that you've released him." He tapped his fingertips together. "The fact that she did not show up on your doorstep this morning, makes me think that she's been released, too. Why she and Iolanthe are still here, I don't know. But I think it's a good thing."

"You're saying once and for all, that for us to save Oberon's life, I'm going to have to convince him to leave me and go willingly with Titania."

"Yes. Once he's in the Realm, his aging will most certainly stop. I've never known a creature to continue to age in the Realm the same way they do here, especially after they've had something to eat or drink."

Jewell's voice was caught in her throat. "I don't know that I can convince him. He swore he'd rather die."

"You might not have to convince him," Bobby said. Jewell looked at Bobby and Peaseblossom in the dim light of the office. For a moment, she thought she could see their real countenances and they frightened her. Long sharp noses, quick eyes, and those ears.

"What do you mean?" she said, her voice tight.

Peaseblossom held a small vial of lilac liquid to the light. "There's always the potion of last resort."

"Is that?"

"Love-in-idleness," he said.

"I didn't think that stuff was real."

"It's very real and very powerful," Bobby said. "It doesn't work quite the same as it was described in Shakespeare."

"No, I suppose not," Jewell said.

"You know writers. Poetic license and all that," Bobby said.

"I've hardly ever known its effects to be reversed, even when used on faeries, although there is a first time for everything," Peaseblossom said. "Once you decide to do this, there will be no going back."

Jewell felt the bile rising in her throat. After all her talk of agency and letting Oberon make his own decisions, was she actually considering this? Either way, she would never see him again. He would never know their child, but wouldn't it be better for him to be alive, perhaps fulfilling his destiny, even if it wasn't with her?

"For this to work, we would need Titania's cooperation. She would need to be the first thing he sees upon awakening," Peaseblossom said.

"And she has to agree to take him with her," Bobby said. "She might not want a king."

Jewell shifted in her seat. She still couldn't imagine Oberon as a king. "So, is Titania also reincarnated?"

Bobby sighed. "I don't think so."

Peaseblossom shook his head. "Definitely not. The last time the Elf King was corporeal the elves and faeries were not unified. In fact, the Realm was very fractured and partisan. This was eons ago. And there are no stories about there ever being a Faerie Queen and an Elf King as co-rulers. At least not any stories that I ever heard."

"Isn't there anything written down?" Jewell said.

Peaseblossom shrugged. "We're not big readers."

"Good lord."

"Look," Bobby said, "we can't afford to worry about the possible ramifications of the return of the Elf King. We must think about Oberon. We are trying to save his life, aren't we?"

"Yes. If Titania won't take him, one of us could," Peaseblossom said. "But if he doesn't want to go, I don't know that we can force him. He's weak, but he also still has a powerful amount of magic in him."

"True. And if he tried to resist, it could use up what life force he has left," Bobby said.

"Could he heal himself?" Jewel was desperate.

"We can transform our looks, the way others perceive us, superficial things, but I've never known a faerie or an elf to be able to heal themselves or anyone else," Peaseblossom said. "There have always been those in our community, like me, who dabble in herbs and potions to enhance our magic or remedy temporary illnesses. But these things rarely affect our kind."

"Lucky you."

"Yes and no," Bobby said.

Jewell felt like her head was going to spontaneously combust. She couldn't just sit there and chit-chat anymore. They could talk and talk and talk, and nothing was going to change. Oberon was going to die. This was all her fault. Every decision she'd made had been wrong. Always, always wrong. Oberon wouldn't save himself. She couldn't make him unlove her, but she was human. If she could have waved a magic wand and saved her mother from that car crash or her father from cancer, even if it meant she could never see them again, she wouldn't have hesitated for a moment.

"Will he forget me?"

"Do you want him to?" Peaseblossom asked.

She blinked at him and the tears she'd worked so hard to tamp down began to flow. "I don't know. I just know I want him to live." She stood up, shoving the chair behind her. "I can't do this anymore. Just sit here and talk." She grabbed Bobby by the hand. "Let's go get Titania, shall we?"

# 5.

Bobby shimmered Jewell over to Titania's suite. Jewell couldn't say she was getting used to spreading her atoms across the city, but she didn't feel quite as queasy when she found herself reassembled inside the most luxurious hotel suite she'd ever been in. Titania sat lounging near the mini-bar. Iolanthe sat on a small divan under the window that looked out onto the Ben Franklin Parkway. "Look who's dropped by to say hello," Titania said.

Jewell marched across the room and knelt in front of Titania. Her shoulders shook, her mouth a hard knot.

"What in the world?" Titania said.

"You are a queen, are you not?" Jewell said. "I thought it was customary to kneel in the presence of royalty."

"Well, as much as I appreciate the gesture, I'm not your queen."

"That may be," Jewell said, not standing, "but I am begging you." She reached up and grasped Titania's wrist and immediately felt a jolt and then something strange shift in her abdomen. If she hadn't known it was much too early for such things, she would have sworn she'd felt her baby kick. Titania must have felt it, too, because she tried to jerk her arm away. She looked at Jewell as if she might get ill. Jewell also felt a wave of nausea and then a wave of euphoria.

"It's not customary to touch a sovereign without permission." Titania's voice was tight, but she'd stopped struggling.

Jewell stood and grabbed both Titania's wrists. As she did, she again felt a jolt, this time much stronger, and she definitely felt her child moving inside her. "As you said, you're not my queen."

"Let go of me," Titania said. Jewell enjoyed how frightened Titania looked.

Bobby and Iolanthe stepped closer. "Jewell," Bobby said, "what are you doing?"

Jewell smiled at Titania. "I'm not doing anything," she said. She looked at Titania. "Am I?"

"Please let me go," Titania said. Her voice was small and quiet. "What do you want?"

"You know what I want. Why are you playing these games with me? I know you want to see him, so let's go see him." Jewell let go of Titania's right wrist and the skin was marked with a bright pink handprint, as if Jewell had burned her. She kept hold of Titania's wrist and addressed everyone. "I think Titania and I will go together. We'll see you two at my place."

Seconds later all four appeared in Jewell's apartment. Jewell pulled Titania close. "I'm going to let go of you, but you're not going anywhere, correct?" Titania nodded and Jewell let go. Titania rubbed her raw wrist and took a few steps toward her sister. "I can't be here when you do this," Jewell said. "Thomas, I'm trusting you with his life. I'm going to go say goodbye and then you all, please just do what you need to do. I'm not sure I ever want to see any of you again." She didn't wait for a response but turned and walked into the bedroom.

The room was quiet and dark, the shades drawn. Slats of gray light filtered into the room. Oberon lay on his side, facing the bathroom and Jewell knelt on the floor next to the bed and brushed Oberon's cheek. His eyes fluttered open, and he smiled. She could not believe how frail he looked in the dim light. His skin felt smooth and cool, almost papery, like her father's had near the end. "Oberon," she whispered. "Tell me you want to live." She kissed his dry lips. "Tell me you love me."

He grabbed her hand and held it against his cheek. "I want to live," he whispered and then his eyes drooped shut and his breath came in soft gentle puffs. She kissed his eyes, his cheeks, his lips. She whispered, "I love you, too." She didn't want to go, but she knew if she stayed that would be the end. She'd be planning his funeral. Slowly she backed out of the bedroom, and then she ran from the apartment, unable to look at anyone.

After Jewell left, Bobby stepped forward and examined Titania's wrist. "What do you think this is all about?"

Titania snatched her arm away. "How should I know?"

Bobby turned to look at all of them. "We could just leave and let the magic take its course. It's not like all of us haven't done worse." Peaseblossom crossed his arms and frowned. "Well, okay, it's not like most of us haven't done worse."

"I thought you said you wanted to see him, sister. Why do you act so afraid now?" Iolanthe said.

"Because I don't know what will happen. Before I was acting under a compulsion outside my control. Now I have a choice. If I put those drops in his eyes, he'll be mine forever."

"Or not," Peaseblossom said. "It's almost always permanent, but nothing's a sure thing with faeries and elves, is it?"

"Give me the bottle," she said. Peaseblossom handed it over and she tucked it in her pocket. "I never imagined I'd ever do anything so selfless for a human."

"But he's not a human, is he sister?" Iolanthe said. "Is that why you're afraid? Are you afraid of what it will be like to have someone love and worship you?"

"Don't be ridiculous. Robin loved and worshipped me."

Iolanthe stared hard at Bobby. "He also tricked and fooled you."

"Shakespeare loved and worshipped me."

"But Shakespeare was just a man in the end, wasn't he? And he betrayed you, too. Oberon is surely the Elf King reborn and ready for redemption. Imagine the possibilities."

"I'm not sure I want to share my throne or be part of any kind of prophecy fulfillment."

"Whether or not you decide to take a king, your position as ruler of the Realm will never change, Titania," Bobby said.

Iolanthe knelt and kissed her sister's hand. "My queen," she said, then she stood and gestured for Bobby and Peaseblossom to do the same. Each one knelt before Titania, kissing her hand, and pledging their fealty.

"That was all very touching," Titania said. "Wish me luck." Before they could respond she shimmered into the bedroom and stood next to Oberon, who snored softly. Standing so close to him, she felt that familiar urge to touch him, but she knew she needed the drops first. There had been a time not so long ago, when she had tried and failed to do this very thing. Now she was filled with apprehension. She took a deep breath and removed the potion from her pocket. The vial felt warm to the touch, not just from being in her pocket, but as if it were spontaneously generating its own heat. She removed the stopper, and the lilac-colored liquid began to glow. Quickly she bent over the sleeping Oberon and let the liquid drip onto his eyelids. They fluttered, but he did not wake, and Titania could see the potion working its way under his lids. A lilac aura formed over his eyes, pulsing and shifting, cycling through all the elemental colors: green, blue, yellow, red. Then the aura covered the entirety of Oberon's sleeping body. His skin began to glow. Titania put the stopper back in the bottle and hid it in her pocket. Oberon's wizened appearance took Titania aback, but the urge to be with him persisted. Something was happening and not just to Oberon—Titania could feel it, too. She knelt near the edge of the bed. As the love-in-idleness worked its way through his system, the energy in the room began to stir. She could resist him no longer and she reached out and stroked his cheek. His eyes fluttered open, and they glowed lilac in the darkened room.

"My queen," he said, his voice somehow changed and yet the same. It was as if he were speaking from a deeper place. "You've come for me at last. I thought perhaps the time might not ever come." He raised himself up on his elbow and leaned in and kissed her. She rose up to meet him, throwing her arms around his neck. He pulled her onto the bed. They lay locked in an embrace, much like the one they had shared before, only this time the magic that swirled around them did not shake the room or cause the windows to rattle. Lavender, gold, and a brilliant white opalescent energy twined them in a cocoon, then slid out the door and through the rest of the apartment. Iolanthe grew concerned and tried to shimmer into the bedroom but was unable to do so. Bobby tried the door handle, but it was immovable. Peaseblossom shrugged and turned on the television.

# 6.

Jewell met up with Melody in the park. She felt oddly calm, but she knew this was denial. Melody linked her arm in hers and they walked down the boardwalk and up the trail toward the Art Museum in silence. When they reached the skate park, Melody finally spoke.

"Are you sure you don't want to go back and see what happened? Maybe things will be different than you think. Maybe he'll be healed and his old self again."

Melody's face was so full of hope it made Jewell even sadder. "I don't think there's much chance of that, although it's a very lovely thought."

Melody swung them back around toward Locust Street and Jewell followed her. "I'm here to support you no matter what, but I honestly think that you will regret not being there to say goodbye, if that's what it is."

Jewell shook her head. "I've got nothing but regrets anymore." She let her hand rest on her belly.

"I know it feels that way. But when that baby comes, he or she is going to be so beautiful."

"And will remind me every day of Oberon and what a foolish, foolish woman I am."

"No, Jewell. That baby is going to remind you of how much you loved him. Loving someone, even if it ends, is never a mistake. Come on." Melody tugged her close. "I'll go with you. It will be okay. Me, Bobby, Thomas, we'll all be there for you. I promise you won't be alone. You need to say a proper goodbye."

Jewell nodded and leaned against her friend as they walked back to her apartment.

# 7.

When Jewell and Melody pushed open her apartment door, they found Iolanthe, Peaseblossom, and Bobby all sitting in the living room, drinking her coffee and watching *Good Morning America*. The entire apartment was filled with swirling swaths of pulsating energy that seemed to have no effect on the three faeries as they watched George Stephanopoulos interview some new starlet Jewell had never heard of.

Bobby looked up. "Hey, you decided to come back."

Jewell nodded.

"So," Melody said still clutching Jewell's hand, "what's happening?"

Bobby sighed and shook his head. "Your guess is as good as mine. This," he waved his hand around indicating the pulsating light, "has been going on since you left."

"This kind of phenomena is usually an indication of strong transformative magic," Peaseblossom said. "I think we just need to wait it out."

Jewell glanced at Iolanthe who seemed, from her expression, to be doubting all of this as much as she was, but she took a seat next to Peaseblossom on the couch and tried to concentrate on the TV.

Eventually the light waned and receded, like the tide being sucked back out to sea. Everyone roused themselves a bit and turned to look at the bedroom door. Jewell hadn't let herself think about what kind of transformation was happening exactly. She'd been asleep through Oberon's first transformation, and she'd been watching an inane television show during this one. As the bedroom door opened, she grabbed Peaseblossom's hand. He squeezed it in return, and she swore she felt a little boost of magic come through him. She felt calmer, anyway.

Titania and Oberon emerged from the bedroom, changed and yet the same. Titania's hair was no longer lavender, but a violet so deep as to almost look black. Her skin was its natural pearlescent shade, but when she shifted in the light it looked green or even blue. She wore a glittering lilac gown, the skirt of which was decorated with beaded peacock feathers. Oberon's warm brown eyes now glowed with flecks of lilac and gold, his countenance returned to its youthfulness, his skin a burnished opalescent bronze. The tips of his ears yielded to delicate points, and his hair was a stark stiff white. He seemed taller somehow, stronger even than he had on that first night when Titania, Iolanthe, and Ondine brought him forward into the world. Jewell gasped at the sight of the two of them. She was not alone. Again, she felt her baby, which was too young to be felt, stir in her belly.

"Isn't he magnificent?" Titania said. "Just look at him."

"Wow," Bobby said. "Look at the two of you."

"Shall we go?" Iolanthe said.

"Robin and Peaseblossom, I do wish you would return with us to the Realm and witness our royal return. The prophecy is true. I can feel it," Titania said. "There will be peace and unity."

"Tell that to the orcs," Bobby said.

"Must you always quip?" Titania said.

"Yes, I'm afraid I must. Now that you've got a king, that doesn't mean I don't still know who you are, my liege." Bobby bowed.

"Are we to assume," Peaseblossom said, "that Robin is no longer banished?"

"That is correct," Titania said. "Now, really I cannot stay in this sad little dwelling one minute longer. I'm feeling quite anxious to return home. Who's coming?"

Bobby and Peaseblossom exchanged glances. "Well, now that I'm free to come and go," Bobby said, "I'll be staying, at least for now." He stole a glance at Melody, who came and stood beside him. "Perhaps we'll come for the coronation. Drop me a line, okay?"

"Suit yourself," Titania said. "How about you, Peaseblossom?"

"I think I will stay as well. Jewell may need some help in the days to come and I'd like to offer my services, if she'll let me." Jewell's hand reflexively went to her belly. "I'm sure I will return sometime in the next one thousand years." Peaseblossom smiled and bowed. "Your majesties."

"Come my lord, it is time to take you home," Titania said. "My sisters will prepare for us a royal reception and feast. All the inhabitants of the Realm will rejoice with festivities and offerings of gratitude."

"Yes," Oberon said. "That sounds delightful, and it has been a very, very long time since I have set foot in the Realm. But first, Jewell?"

Jewell stood and stepped forward. She thought her heart might crack in half and yet she was standing, speaking. "I'm here Oberon. I didn't think I could say good-bye, but I'm here."

Oberon looked down at her and tucked her chin toward him. His touch was as warm and gentle as it had always been. Jewell again felt something stir within her. Something that she knew was impossible. Oberon's head tilted, as if he felt it too, but he did not acknowledge it in any way. Instead, he cupped Jewell's face in his hands, and she blinked back tears, unaware of the flecks of gold churning in her own eyes.

"I am grateful to you, Jewell. You will always be my human." He bent down and kissed her lightly on the lips and a pulse of heat radiated through her core. Was it magic or a physical remembrance of things now past? She would never know.

Jewell looked up into Oberon's magical eyes swirling with flecks of gold, at his opalescent skin, and his delicately pointed ears. He was beautiful, but he was no longer her Oberon. She took his hand and held it against her cheek one last time. "I loved you very much," she said.

"And I you."

As Jewell stood and watched, Oberon and Titania, hand in hand, shimmered away and through the veil in a whorl of gold and lavender magic.

# THIRTEEN

## 1.

IGHTEEN MONTHS LATER.
"Come on girl, let's go for a walk!" Jewell bent over her dog, a runty black and brown Cairn terrier mix with crazy wiry hair, and fixed the leash to her collar. She stood and turned too quickly and almost crashed into Jackson, who sat strapped in his stroller. The baby pointed his chubby fingers at the dog, who jumped up and licked his face. The baby squealed, and Jewell sighed. Even a simple walk to the park took on the gravitas of a grand expedition. Water bottle. Check. Sippy cup. Check. Diaper bag. Check. Doggie treats. Check. Dog. Kid. Stroller. Phone. Keys. Check. Check. Check. Blastoff!

Now that she had everything that she needed, she was ready. Out the door they went, Maggie leading the way, her nubby little tail beating out an enthusiastic rhythm in the air. They piled onto the elevator, down to the lobby, and out into the fresh spring day. Jewell's company had a generous maternity leave policy and she had been determined to make each day home with Jackson count. Now that she was back at work, she was exhausted most days, but also finally felt as if she'd turned a corner. Finding Maggie had been the final step. Everyone thought she'd been crazy to get a dog so soon after having a baby, but she knew they were wrong. Melody understood, but she was the only one. The first time someone from work said she shouldn't get a dog, she started say, "Well I don't have a husband," but she stopped herself. Sometimes she still dreamed of Oberon, but the dreams came less frequently. She had Jackson, and now Maggie, to fill her days, and that was enough.

Once they were outside, Maggie ran ahead to sniff things, and then ran back to Jewell to make sure she was still there. Then she jumped up and licked the baby's face, which always made him laugh. As Jewell negotiated through the playground toward the dog run, Maggie pulled even harder on the leash. "Okay, girl, we're almost there," she said.

Finally, she pulled up behind the gate and parked the stroller. "Looks like you've got a lot going on there," a vaguely familiar voice said from behind her. "Let me grab the gate for you." She turned around and found Steve and Fang. "Jewell is that you?"

"Steve, right?" she said knowing full well what his name was.

He nodded. "Wow, it's so nice to see you. It's been forever." He moved around to the gate. "Here, I said I'd get this. Sorry!" He pushed the gate open, and Fang sprang ahead, as did Maggie, pulling Jewel behind her.

"Whoops!" Jewell said, "Can't leave the kid behind." She bent down to release Maggie into the park and then went back out and through the gate with the stroller.

"Who's this little guy?" Steve said wiggling his finger at Jackson.

"His name is Jackson Jamieson, just like his grandad."

"He yours?" Steve asked.

"All mine," she said.

"Well, I can see why we haven't seen you around here in so long. You've been busy."

Jewell pursed her lips. "If you had a few months, I could tell you all about it."

Steve crinkled his brow. "It's that long of a story?"

"You have no idea."

"But everything is okay?"

Jewell smiled. "Yes," she said. "Everything is great. Single motherhood suits me, I think. Plus, Maggie is the best. I never have to wash Jackson's face." Jewell laughed. "I've got this mom thing nailed."

Steve laughed, too. "Sounds like it."

"So, how are you doing? You look great by the way. And look at Fang. He's the champ of the park now."

Steve looked over the top of his glasses at her. "I'm fine. And Fang is great, too. That trainer you recommended was a miracle worker. Thanks again."

Jackson started to fuss, and Jewell bent down to unstrap him, pulling him up into her arms.

"Can I?" Steve asked.

"Sure," Jewell said. "But he's not always great with strangers."

"It's okay," Steve said taking the baby from Jewell. "I'm kind of known as the baby whisperer among my married friends."

"Is that so?"

"Absolutely." Steve rocked the baby up and down, gently patting his back. Jackson quieted down almost immediately and soon was asleep on Steve's shoulder.

"Uh-oh," Jewell said. "Now you're stuck with him for the next two hours."

Steve smiled and sat down on a nearby bench. Jewell followed him. "I can think of worse things," he said. He paused for a moment and Jewell couldn't read his expression. His gaze shifted back and forth between her and the dogs who were now chasing each other around the run.

They sat on the bench for a bit, watching the dogs. Jewell couldn't help but be impressed by how quiet Jackson was with Steve. He generally did not like strangers. The only other person he'd taken to that way was Thomas, who'd turned out to be an excellent nanny, or manny, as he preferred.

"Can I ask about Jackson's father?" Steve said after a bit.

"You can ask, but there's not much to tell. He left before Jackson was born." Steve nodded, and she looked up at him and smiled. "It's okay. It was very intense and then it was over. Just like that." She snapped her fingers. "Leaving was the best thing he could have done for all of us. No baby daddy drama. Just me and the boy. We're good."

Steve patted Jackson lightly. "I can see that."

"Here, I'll take him," she said reaching out for her baby. Steve handed the child back and Jewell strapped him in the stroller, still sound asleep.

"I can't believe we ran into each other again like this. Did your friends ever tell you that I said hi?"

"Which friends?"

Steve kind of laughed. "That's funny. I never got their names. I told them mine." He shook his head. "They were both tall and striking. One had lavender hair, and the other one had blueish hair, I think." Jewell covered her mouth to stifle her rising laughter. "Normally, I'm not a big fan of the crazy colored hair, but on them it looked pretty good, I have to say." Now Jewell was laughing so hard Jackson woke up and started kicking his legs. "What's so funny?" Steve said.

"It's just that of all the people in this city that you could have run into that knew me, it had to be those two."

"Are they friends of yours?"

"Not really," she said. "They were friends of Jackson's father, sort of."

"I guess they never passed along the message."

"No," she said. "It doesn't matter. I was a mess for a long time after he left. It really wasn't until Jackson was born that I started to pull myself together. First, I lost my dad, then Oberon." Her eyes welled up and she felt like an ass. "I'm sorry," she said. "Stupid hormones."

"It's okay," he said. "My sister cries all the time."

"Really? When did she have her baby?"

Steve smiled. "Twelve years ago."

"You're terrible."

"Yeah? You should meet my niece!"

"I'm sure she's adorable."

"She's something," he laughed. "Actually, she is adorable. Speaking of adorable, what's your dog's name?"

"Maggie. She's so sweet. I wasn't sure I could ever have another dog after Oberon, but my life felt kind of empty, even with the baby." Jewell sat back. "Wow, I hope the mom patrol isn't out here recording me."

Steve laughed. "Your secret's safe with me. Is she another rescue?"

Jewell nodded. "PAWS. I love them."

"They are great," Steve said. He paused and crossed his legs. "Maggie. *Cat on a Hot Tin Roof*?"

"I hadn't really thought of that, but sure, why not? I just thought she looked like a Maggie."

They sat for bit, watching the dogs run and sniff and chase and play. Jackson gurgled and cooed in his stroller and dropped his rattle on the ground. Steve bent over and picked the rattle up, held it in front of the baby to get his attention. Jackson smiled and grabbed for the rattle. Jewell looked out over the park, like she had so many times before and sighed. It just never got old. "So," Steve said. "Are you interested in doing something Saturday?"

"Yes," she said without any hesitation.

"Great. It's a date then." He stood. "I wish I could sit here with you all afternoon, but I need to get Fang home. I've got some errands to run. Can I give you my number?"

"Of course," she said. They exchanged numbers. Steve collected Fang, gave Maggie a little ear rub and said his goodbyes. Jewell sat on the bench for quite a while, watching the dogs play in the late afternoon sun. Finally, an exhausted Maggie plopped down at her feet, signaling that it was time to go home. Jewell bent down and gave her a good scratch and then attached her leash. Together the three of them made their way home as the sun sank low behind the Schuylkill River.

## 2.

Later that night, as she was tucking Jackson into his crib, she noticed, not for the first time, swirling flecks of gold in his dark brown eyes. Thomas had told her that this was perfectly normal, and she'd finally decided to give up worrying about it. After everything they'd been through, worry seemed pointless. So, instead of tucking him all the way in, she pulled him out of the crib and cradled him on her lap. As she rocked him to sleep, she began to tell him the story of Oberon the Elf King and his beautiful wife, Titania, Queen of the Faeries.

# THE END

# Acknowledgements

There are many people to thank, so many who've helped and encouraged me. Undoubtedly, I will leave someone out, so please, to all of you who've ever offered a kindly piece of constructive criticism or cheered me on when the whole business felt pointless, thank you.

I've been so lucky over the years to have so many wonderful teachers, as a musician and as a writer, particularly, Dan Kovats, Jeffrey Foote, and Meredith Zara. Also, Dan Driscoll, Bob Finnegan, Kevin McIlvoy, and most especially, Charles Holdefer whose generosity over the years has been astounding.

I'd like to thank my parents, Martha Bottomley and Carlo Spataro for never telling me no when it came to artistic pursuits. It never occurred to me that I couldn't become a professional musician or writer until I actually tried to do it!

I've come to depend on the women in my writer's group for more than just their outstanding advice and feedback on my work—but for their companionship and encouragement. So, thank you to Trish Rodriguez, Chelsea Covington Maass, Tori Bond, Teresa FitzPatrick, Marleen Hustead, and Nicole Contosta. Thanks also to Kelly Simmons, Gregory Frost, Christine Weiser, Mitchell Sommers, Marguerite McGlinn, and Jillian Sullivan; to Julie Odell and Jennifer Steil for additional feedback on the manuscript. To my sister, Angela Cook, who it turns out is an amazing beta reader, and to Liz Abrams-Morley and Courtney Bambrick for their friendship and support.

Thank you to my students who inspire me every day with their enthusiasm, energy, and bigheartedness. You have given me the courage to push beyond traditional narratives and to not be afraid if my work doesn't quite fit into a neat little box. I am also deeply grateful to Jacob Smullyan and the entire team at Sagging Meniscus for making this all possible.

Finally, I am profoundly indebted to Vincent Natale Martinez for his love and support and for always believing in me, even when I do not believe in myself.

C.J. Spataro is an award-winning short fiction writer whose work has appeared in many literary magazines and anthologies, including *Taboos & Transgressions*, *Iron Horse Literary Review*, *december*, *Phantom Drift*, and *Exacting Clam*. She lives in Philadelphia, where she directs the MFA in Creative Writing and the MA in Publishing programs at Rosemont College and is a founding partner of *Philadelphia Stories*. More at www.cjspataro.com.